Erotic Spirituality

Erotic
Spirituality
The Integrative Tradition
from Leone Ebreo to John Donne

T. ANTHONY PERRY

The University of Alabama Press
University, Alabama

P N
5 6
. L 6
P 4 4

Library of Congress Cataloging in Publication Data

Perry, Theodore Anthony.
  Erotic spirituality.

  Bibliography: p.
  Includes index.
  1. Love in literature.   2. European literature—
Renaissance, 1450–1600—History and criticism.
I. Title.
PN56.L6P44   809'.933'54   79-16768
ISBN 0-8173-0024-4

Contents

For Sydney

mon plus possible

Acknowledgments

I wish to thank the editorial boards of the *Publications of the Modern Language Association of America*, the *Bibliothèque d'Humanisme et Renaissance*, and the *French Forum* for permission to reprint materials previously published in their journals, and the University of North Carolina Studies in Comparative Literature for allowing me to reprint a substantial portion of my introduction to Pontus de Tyard's translation of the *Dialoghi d'amore*. I am particularly grateful to Mortimer Guiney, Compton Rees, and Nelson Orringer, all of the University of Connecticut, and to Baruch Hochman of Hebrew University, for their helpful criticisms; to Hugh Clark and the University of Connecticut Research Foundation for financial support; and especially to Sydney, Rachel, Sarah, Michael, Danya, and Joshua for their patience and loving encouragement.

Publication of this book was made possible, in part, by financial assistance from the Andrew W. Mellon Foundation and the American Council of Learned Societies.

Erotic Spirituality

Introduction

Our nature is meteoric, we respect (because we partake so)
both earth and heaven; for as our bodies glorified shall be
capable of spiritual joy, so our souls demerged into those
bodies are allowed to take earthly pleasure. Our soul is not sent
hither, only to go back again: we have some errand to do here.

JOHN DONNE

This study attempts to document a philosophy of love that found its major
philosophical expression in Leone Ebreo's *Dialoghi d'amore* (1535) and its
most impressive poetic statement in John Donne's "The Ecstasy." It may
thus be viewed as an analysis either of the proximate European background
of what Herbert Grierson called Donne's "new philosophy of love" or of the
development of Leone's erotic philosophy among selected Renaissance authors. Each chapter offers a critical reaction to an important author or work
of literature and, as such, may be read in isolation from the rest of the book.
The roughly chronological ordering of the essays is a convenience of presentation and need imply neither a continuous argument nor a chain of historical
influence from one work to another. Yet the cumulative effect of these essays
will reveal the recurrence of major themes and preoccupations that become
expressive, each in its own mode and context, of a new idea of love. Con-
versely, awareness of the larger tradition should, in every case, advance the
understanding of the individual works.

The existence of such a tradition has hardly been acknowledged by literary
studies. The most notable essay linking Donne to Leone Ebreo, Helen
Gardner's study of "The Ecstasy,"[1] has been largely ignored by historical
scholars, who continue to deal with Platonic sources that preceded Leone,
with little interest in either Leone himself or that crucial period between the
Dialoghi and "The Ecstasy." As a result, there has been no major modifica-
tion of A. J. Smith's view that in "The Ecstasy" Donne has the distinction of
putting forward "these apparently incompatible attitudes [physical and
spiritual love] together for the first time in poetry."[2] Some reasons for this
critical neglect are real and must be met. On the one hand, the *Dialoghi*
themselves may be blamed: for their enormous learning and subtle dialectic,
their protean but difficult synthesis of traditional philosophies into what may
be called a Judaeo-Platonism. But a deeper reason lies in the distrust gener-

ated by the argument itself. We may take Donne as representative of the tradition when he characterizes his erotic philosophy as follows:

> You (I think) and I am much of one sect in the Philosophy of love; which though it be directed upon the mind, doth inherit in the body, and find pretty entertainment there.[3]

It is the very combination of erotic and reflective interests that has seemed suspect to critics—not surprisingly, Montaigne leads the band of skeptics with the supposition that "my Page makes love and understands it feelingly; Read Leon Hebroeus or Ficinus unto him; you speak of him, of his thoughts and of his actions, yet understands he nothing what you meane."[4] From here the passage to cynicism is short indeed, for it seems less repugnant to view such elaborate philosophies as malicious than to believe that they are simply useless, and such poems as "The Ecstasy" thus come to be thought of as poems of courtship wherein indecent proposals are advanced under the guise of respectable philosophizing.[5]

Skepticism in such matters—openmindedness but not cynicism—is not only the reader's privilege, it is also the attitude recommended by the tradition that probably inspired "The Ecstasy." Sofia remains hesitant but inquiring throughout the *Dialoghi d'amore,* and there is no clue whatever as to the outcome of Filone's amorous attempts. How could it be otherwise for a philosophy that, while recognizing a hierarchy of love's Doctors and Saints, insists on personal experience as the only real test of the sincerity of its claims? As critics we note that the phrase "philosophy of love" has a dual emphasis. To take seriously Donne's (and his predecessors') claim to such a philosophy would allow us to view him both as an apostle of mutual love and sane sexual relations, and also as an accomplished philosopher of erotic ecstasy—meaning, of course, not the delight of physical union but rather the opposite, the contentment arising from detachment. Unless such a precarious dual perspective is maintained, Donne may appear merely as a forerunner of sexual libertarianism (which he is in several of his poems) and thus deserve C. S. Lewis's stricture: "nasty."[6]

A more helpful characterization of Donne's erotic writings was advanced by Herbert Grierson:

> There emerged in his poetry the suggestion of a new philosophy of love which, if less transcendental than that of Dante, rests on a juster, because a less dualistic and ascetic, conception of the nature of the love of man and woman.[7]

In order to make Donne's but also Scève's and a number of other poets' witty images comprehensible, we need merely extend "man and woman" beyond their social and especially sexual meanings and allow analogical extensions that were readily recognized as legitimate in the sixteenth century. Specifically, these would include psychological, cosmological, and theological levels,

and the metaphors "male and female" would indicate the following entities: spirit and body, heaven and earth, and God and the creation. It is
essential to realize that such parallelisms were not regarded as mere poetic
conventions; they were felt to express the analogous nature of things, thus
requiring that any given feature on one level be mirrored at all other levels.
As a result, a "philosophy of love" could not possibly be restricted to a single
sphere, whether social or psychological or sexual; it necessarily implied
different relations between man and his body and between God and man.
There is no better example of this approach than the seminal work out of
which the new philosophy of love developed, Leone Ebreo's *The Dialogues
of Love (Dialoghi d'amore)*, a modest title for what was in fact a vast treatise
on precisely the multiple levels of the entire universe, the analogical relationships among the various levels, and the unification of the whole by the
idea of love.

Chapter 1 of this study is an analytic summary of the philosophical content
of the *Dialoghi d'amore*. Readers familiar with the work may skip this chapter, but others may wish to be reminded of Leone's main themes and of their
development. Chapter 2 discusses the literary aspects of the *Dialoghi* and
their relation to the work's philosophical and religious thought. The unifying
concept is that of dialogue, an organ of thought that invites synthesis, while
maintaining opposition, of the work's main antitheses: love and desire, action
and contemplation, service and ecstasy; or, viewed more metaphysically, the
antitheses that strive for reconciliation are body and soul, male and female,
heaven and earth, God and the creation.

The two essays on Maurice Scève's *Délie* (chapters 3 and 4), the first
Petrarchan *canzoniere* in French, are to be read as companion pieces because together they state the two essential terms of the Scèvian dialectic of
the soul's death and rebirth into the world. The first movement of the
dialectic develops the stated subject of the *Délie*, which is not love but
rather "the deaths that you renew in me" ("les mortz, qu'en moy tu renovel-
les"). According to a philosophical tradition at least as old as Plato's *Phaedo*,
man's mortal life is described as the linking of soul to body, and his death as
the dissolution of this link or bond. It was commonplace for Renaissance
authors to view the body-soul relation in this way, and the preferred term for
the bond was *lien* ("link"), which at death became untied or *délié*. However, Platonic writers were familiar with another kind of death as well: that of
the philosopher, whereby the soul voluntarily unties itself from the mortal
self, again as in the *Phaedo*. Indeed, the essential striving of the philosopher
may be characterized by this single imperative: "Délie," unloose the soul
from the body! Délie's beauty, and especially her grace and virtue, inspired
this stringent ideal in Scève, and it was a felicitous poetic discovery to have
suggested this idea in the very name of his mistress.

To view the *Délie* as part of the ascetic tradition of the *Phaedo* is to insist on Scève's "Platonic love," as the term has usually been understood both by modern critics and in such a famous poem as DuBellay's "L'Idée." Is not "Délie" in fact the anagram of "L'Idée," as older critics have insisted? The answer is affirmative, but here the second movement of the dialectic comes into play, for Délie is not only a Platonic Idea but also its concrete manifestation. In addition to being a call to the purification of desire, she is also—in a movement of higher to lower—an "*object* de plus haulte vertu," an objectification of a higher power and, as such, a descent into the body and the world of material reality.

Our next two authors, Pernette du Guillet and Antoine Héroët, have neither Scève's poetic grandeur nor his tantalizing hermeticism, yet both are important examples of Platonic sensibilities in France on the eve of the Pléiade. They share both a common-sense distinction between love and lovers and also the opinion that love cannot exist without lovers. In other words, our emotions signify concrete relations between two real persons. The point seems trivial except when viewed against its two extreme opposites: on the one hand, the Epicureanism of an early Ronsard, which dissolves personality into sensual delights; on the other, the absolutism that deifies love and absorbs personality into the infinite.

Pernette avoids the taint of *littérature*. Her poetic notebooks, collected and published posthumously, seem addressed only to Scève, who was both her teacher and beloved. The poems record thoughts, fantasies, astonishing expressions of mutual love such as "Je suis la Journée, Vous, Ami, le Jour." Some bear the mark of poetic essays submitted to her teacher for criticism. The constant characteristic is a love that strives for authenticity and self-clarification, that tries to achieve what was called, in a well-worn but adequate phrase, "la perfection d'amour" (love's perfection). Her poetry, formulated in terms of the relation of love to desire, is perhaps the best poetic statement we have of Leone Ebreo's idea of integration at the first level: that microcosmic union of soul and body that both preconditions and, by way of analogy, prefigures all others.

Antoine Héroët took up Pernette's feminist voice and became the daring advocate of erotic experimentation as a major aspect of the full life, or, as Héroët would have preferred to view it, as a main path to spiritual liberation and psychic integration. Héroët discusses various "exercises"—ranging from erotic temptation to directed meditation—as means of knowing and coping with the pleasures as well as the pains of normal, concrete experience. His model of humanity is the "amie," the person who has learned to love "lovingly" and, through an active use of the passions, to experience that slow maturation of the heart that prefigures its total reintegration. Both forms of integration, the psychological as well as the amorous, are represented by the image of the androgyne, the symbol of an old harmony between body and spirit and between the sexes. Héroët's dominant interest, however, is in microcosmic integration at the second level, the union of persons, which he regards as the true meaning of the androgyne myths. His *Parfaicte Amye* and *Androgyne* can be considered as signs of a new understanding of human marriage, the marriage of both true minds and true bodies.

Paradoxically, the most appropriate literary vehicle for Leone's integralism is perhaps the pastoral—paradoxically because it is common to view the pastoral as merely poetic, not *engagé* or true to real life. Montemayor's unabashed use of entire pages of the *Dialoghi* argues differently, as does his systematic blending of history with poetic elements. If myth and allegory dominate, nevertheless, perhaps our objections are based on different habits of thought and expression. Montemayor's readers knew very well what the Temple of Diana meant; or at least they knew that it signified "chastity," and they probably realized, too, that the veil of mystery would be lifted to the degree that they perceived the meaning in their lives as well as their critical minds. The mystery of Montemayor's pastoralism may be not so much a literary ploy as a realistic representation of mysterious processes. And if we feel discomfort with the vanity and equivocality of the mode, or with the alliance at the end of the novel between human happiness and Fortune (as, incidentally, in Shakespeare's mature romances), it is possible that we are reacting not to a literary mode so much as to the inadequacy of our imagination, the paltriness of our desires.

The argument of "The Ecstasy," briefly, may be summarized by the pun that for Donne loving is knotty but not naughty. Rather than an indecent proposal, his call to return to the body is an act of integration, a binding of our opposite tendencies into a unified and living being through that subtle knot that defines our humanity and that is delicately alluded to as a "naked thinking heart" ("The Blossom").

The chapter on *King Lear* proposes, on the basis of Leone's new philosophy of love, both an emblematic theory of Cordelia's name and a different perspective for defining the play's tragic quality. Viewed in terms of emblematic kinds of thinking that were habitual in Shakespeare's time, Cordelia is quite simply the best incarnation of the Delian figure that we have. By virtue of her "heart unbound" she is the perfect mediator—through her ideal of service—between spiritual and worldly concerns.

As to the basis of tragedy in *King Lear*, one must here refer to the central concern of the *Dialoghi d'amore* and of all its descendants: the refutation of dualisms and the justification of universal unity. To appreciate the point one should be aware that there is little in common between Leone's concept of duality and the usual Manichean belief in the existence of an irreducible Evil in the world. Leone begins with different perceptions: that the creation is good (Genesis 1) and that Satan himself is a servant of the Almighty (Job 1). The problem, rather, is the conflict between two *desirable* goals, which Leone formulates in the most general way as contemplation versus action.

As an heir to Maimonidean intellectualism, Leone identified man's highest goal as intellectual contemplation, withdrawal from the world, and delight in God's eternal Ideas. From this perspective Leone's eroticism could have only one possible association: with the Song of Songs, allegorically read as the drunken bliss of the soul in union with God, as exemplified in the supreme instance by Moses, who "dies by the kiss of God." There is no philosophical problem in such a view of love, defined in Socratic terms as the desire to fill a need, the highest form of which is ecstasy. But this theory does not explain why God, who is totally without need, should love in return and yet He does. As Cordelia says, while shedding tears of forgiveness upon her repentant father: "No cause, no cause." The point is thus neutralized at the philosophical level, for if there is no reason why love should be returned, there is also no reason why it should not.

Of course, both Shakespeare and Leone offer reasons, remarkably similar in substance, as to why we love. Cordelia describes it in terms of natural bonds; Leone prefers the metaphor of the universe as a single organism. The important point is that in both cases our love and care of the world, our bodies, one another, are viewed as superior rather than inferior forms of conduct, even when our "higher" and more intrinsic activities—contemplation for Leone, union with Cordelia for Lear—are curtailed as a result. Working from dualistic premises, so eminent a critic as A. C. Bradley can only arrive at the view that nothing becomes Lear's life so much as his withdrawal from it. I do not reply, of course, that we can go so far as to condemn Lear's abdication by the play's end; but how much more admirably human was his manly pride, his kingly show of authority, his tenacious love of life, his tragically unfulfilled desire to "shake the superflux" of his riches to the less fortunate. Lear's tragedy, I suggest, is best explained not by a wrong choice between bad and good but rather by his wrong choice between two goods, or, more precisely, by his failure to reconcile man's opposite needs of ecstasy and goodness, which are none other than the dialectical processes of life and death that, in Leone Ebreo's view, define our human condition.

These brief summaries may suffice to suggest my themes as well as the parameters of my title. L'érotisme des corps—desire that seems both to originate and expire in the nerve endings—is of no concern here, though both Héroët and Donne gave approving theoretical accounts of the phenomenon.[8] Similarly, while our authors regarded a Platonic érotisme des esprits as the usual origin of physical desires, they showed little interest in its pure, disincarnate possibility. The attachment of true hearts—l'érotisme des coeurs—held a greater fascination, one that is partially explained by what we may call the dominant emotion theory. Briefly, the heart was thought to "house" the passions, and love was, of all the passions, by far the strongest and most tyrannical:

Nostre terre est subjette aux passions,
A ung millier de perturbations,

Dont y en a de maulvaises et bonnes.
Quand ceste là d'amour vient aux personnes,
Elle est si forte et a telle efficace
Qu'affections toutes aultres efface.
Aultres pourroient estre en extremité,
Toutes ensemble, et d'une infinité
Troubler les sens de l'homme et jugement;
Mais si l'amour y passe seulement,
Il veult regner seul et sans compaignie.
O bon tyrant! o doulce tyrannie.[9]

Our earth is subject to the passions,
To a thousand disturbances,
Some of which are good and some bad.
When the passion of love comes upon people,
It is so strong and efficacious
That it obliterates all other affections.
Other [affections] may be intensified to the extreme
And, all together and in infinite number,
May trouble man's senses and judgment.
But if Love merely passes in their midst,
He wishes to reign alone and unchallenged.
O good tyrant! O sweet tyranny!

A union of hearts under such conditions, however, was achieved only through a radical concentration or reduction of all other passions and dimensions of the psychic life.

The authors studied here were, as a rule, critical of such an approach. In reacting to a lady's excessive grief, Héroët wonders whether *any* passion should be allowed to become dominant:

Elle [the mourner] dira, je t'en puis asseurer,
Que corps ne peult en terre demeurer
Sans passion, que toutes les avez,
Et que dompter nulles d'elles scavez,
Si l'on ne faict que la plus vehemente
Sur vostre chair seigneurise et regente.[10]

She will claim, I can assure you,
That a body cannot reside on earth
Without passions, that all of you have them,
And that you never succeed in mastering a single one of them
Unless the most vehement of them is made
To rule and lord it over your flesh.

For Donne the imbalance of the times is shown in the fact that "every modern god will now extend / His vast prerogative as far as Jove" ("Love's

Deity"), and the greatest tyrant by far is Cupid. In France the complaint was often expressed by a similar contrast with earlier times: "In the past Love tickled his lovers with pleasure; / nowadays he strikes them down with lightning" (*Délie* 374). The dangers of *l'érotisme des coeurs* were exposed by Pernette's distinction between contented love and a totalizing heart-desire that consumes our lives' sweetness or *douceur* while creating the illusion that it is somehow all beyond our control:

> Point ne se fault sur Amour excuser,
> Comme croyant qu'il ait forme, et substance
> Pour nous pouvoir contraindre et amuser,
> Voire forcer à son obeissance:
>   Mais accuser nostre folle plaisance
> Pouvons nous bien. . . [11]

> We must not excuse ourselves on Love,
> Acting as if he had force and substance
> To restrict and fool us,
> Indeed force us to obey him.
>   We must rather accuse our foolish pleasures. . .

But Leone and his followers had more serious misgivings about purely sentimental attachments, indeed about all horizontal and unidimensional eroticisms, whether Platonic or "sublunary." This has to do with their view of the function of *eros*, which is the vertical integration of the multiple levels of man and the cosmos:

> Love is not only a *mixture* of man and beast but of an infinitude of contraries that are *united* in him alone—but they would take too long to relate. [12]

Correspondingly, the heart is viewed as the center of human personality, a new creation termed a substantial unity because it integrates and unifies the polar opposites of our human nature into a distinct substance.

While this study is to my knowledge the first to examine in an extensive way the implications of Leone Ebreo's erotic philosophy for literature, its theme of integration has drawn inspiration from several quarters. Among historical critics Peter Dronke's research on the origins of the European love-lyric is a distinguished demonstration of the nondualist thesis, as is Richard Cody's suggestive exploration of pastoral ideology. [13] But the approach may be traced back to Plato himself, for students have long realized that the detachment of the *Phaedo* is not contradicted by the exuberant *Symposium*, that each is an essential phase of a recurrent dialectic. As the modern Platonist Ananda Coomaraswamy has put it:

> Life has *at all times* a twofold direction,
> Pursuit and Return, Outward and Inward,
> Affirmation and Denial. [14]

Or, as one of Plato's greatest sixteenth-century students expressed it, in a statement that has the spirit of our theme:

> Aristippus defended but the body, as if we had no soule: Zeno embraced but the soule, as if we had no body. Both viciously. Pythagoras (say they) hath followed a Philosophie all in contemplation; Socrates altogether in manners and in action. Plato hath found a mediocrity between both. But they say so by way of discourse. For, the true temperature is found in Socrates; and Plato is more Socratical than Pythagorical, and it becomes him best. When I dance, I dance; and when I sleepe, I sleepe.[15]

It is hoped that this study will suggest new directions for the discussion of erotic philosophy. On the process of psychic and sexual integration, for example, a chapter could be devoted to the mediative role of temperament[16] or to the formation of personality theory. More could be said about the pastoral, both as an ideal mode of synthetic thinking and as a model for God's relation with the soul; Fray Luis de León's commentaries on the Song of Songs would be major texts here. There is always the temptation to linger on English turf, with Spenser's debt to Leone, with Shakespeare's "The Phoenix and Turtle." But, again, my aim is analytic and not exhaustive, with the expectation that the major concepts, once clarified and examined in representative contexts, may then be applied to yet other instances—*che troppo è lungo il contare.*

In the difficult endeavor to reconcile the requirements of readability and scholarly demonstration, I have relegated many parallel and supporting materials to the notes. Secondly, while poetic works must be cited in the original, I have assisted the English reader by supplying literal translations in text. Prose works are consistently given in translation, though, of course, references will enable careful scholars to check the originals if they wish. *All translations and italics are mine unless otherwise indicated.* Although capitalization of nouns was somewhat arbitrary in sixteenth-century texts, my translations retain or add capitalization only where a clearly allegorical sense was intended. Likewise, because sixteenth-century punctuation was less precise than ours, my translations are guided by modern usage, but editorial re-punctuation of an original text occurs only when the meaning would otherwise be obstructed for the modern reader. Original spellings have been retained except that in the French texts grave accents have been added to words like *pres* and *tres,* and acute accents to feminine endings in *-ee;* consonantal *i* and *u* have been changed to *j* and *v.*

Chapter 1
Leone Ebreo's *Dialoghi d'amore:*
The Argument

[Leone Ebreo's aesthetics is] the most notable monument of
Platonic philosophy in the 16th century and, indeed, the most
beautiful that this philosophy has produced since Plotinus.
                    MARCELINO MENÉNDEZ Y PELAYO[1]

Under the guise of a polite courtship between a lover and his beloved (Filone
and Sofia), the *Dialoghi d'amore* is a loosely structured series of discourses
on an encyclopedic variety of questions unified by the idea of love.[2] There
are three parts or *dialoghi*. The first is ontological, attempting to define the
essence of love and desire by examining the various kinds of good or lovable
objects available to man. The second dialogue expands the scope of the
discussion by considering the "broad community" of love, which is seen no
longer solely in its human and psychological dimension but also as a cosmological fact. The third dialogue—by far the most lengthy and important—
is an essentially theological discourse on the origins of love in the universe,
wherein love is viewed as the principle that defines the relationship between
God and His creation. At the end of this third part Leone announces a
dialogue on the effects of love, but this section is either lost or unwritten.

The opening statement places the entire work under the sign of a Platonic
and rationalistic theory of love: "My knowledge of you, Sofia, engenders in
me love and desire." Love (and desire) is always based on knowledge. There
is, to be sure, an inferior kind of loving in which passion precedes knowledge
of the beloved, as Filone later recognizes. But in its true sense love can arise
only from a knowledge of the beloved, of what Corneille calls her *mérite*.
Thus, one cannot simply "love," for love always expresses a relationship
between lover and beloved, subject and desirable object. In view of this, for
example, it would be improper to describe one's affection toward his yet
unborn child as love. For if love is based on knowledge, the latter in turn can
only be of what *is*, the beloved object must have real existence; at most one
can *desire* the child's existence but can love him only after knowing him as a
real being. Further, since evil and ugliness cannot be loved in any meaningful sense of the term, the knowledge that produces love is always of an object
judged to be good or beautiful.

The proposition that love expresses a relationship between a subject and an object both real and lovable rigorously follows Socrates' own conclusions in the *Symposium* (200e–201b). Socrates' further observation that one can love or desire only what one does not have, however, seems unacceptable or at least requires clarification. The objection is raised by the quick-witted Sofia, apparently to divert the ardor of her suitor's bold opening declaration: How can Filone claim to feel *both* love and desire, she asks. Health or children, for instance, are desired but not loved by a sick or childless man; when these are possessed, however, he then loves but no longer desires them. Love and desire thus seem to be mutually exclusive. Filone counters with the example of a man's affection for his wife, which may be described as both love and desire. Further discussion reveals that desire always implies a lack, either because the desired object is not possessed or because it does not exist. Thus one can desire a diamond ring which he does not possess, or a child as yet unborn. But, no less than love, desire also presupposes the being of its object—if not its actual being, at least its possible being. Otherwise, since desire is also based on knowledge, there can be no knowledge of a nonentity and hence no desire for it.

Having progressed to the point of distinguishing three categories of objects—loved and desired, loved but not desired, desired but not loved— Filone perceives that the impasse in the argument over love and desire can best be resolved by a systematic study of these objects. In agreement with Aristotle, they are said to be of three kinds: useful, delectable, and honest or noble.[3] The useful is subordinate to the delectable (e.g., one seeks external goods such as money or a house in order to promote bodily well-being in the form of health), and both are considered virtuous when pursued with moderation. Thus, on the order of useful objects already possessed (there are different terms for the acquisition of such objects), the good man avoids the vicious extremes of avarice and prodigality and pursues the middle course of liberality. On the order of the delectable, virtue consists in being moderate and avoiding both overindulgence and excessive abstinence. While following Aristotle, Leone is quick to relate these categories to his own subject matter: avarice and overindulgence are similar in that each shows an excessive love or desire to possess, while excessive abstinence (Leone emphasizes that this opinion is his own), like prodigality, is deficient in love for those necessities through which life is preserved. By contrast, on the order of the noble, which consists of the intellectual virtues of Prudence and Wisdom, Sofia argues that moderation is to be avoided and that virtue is found only in the total, impassioned pursuit of the extreme. For, contrary to the active man, the contemplative man or lover of Wisdom nelgects the useful, abstains from the delectable, and sets his mind entirely on the noble. Filone admits this difference between the active and contemplative ideals and tries to reconcile these opposing views by observing that useful and delectable objects are not good in themselves but derive their goodness from moderation, which is a rational principle and hence of the order of the noble. However, Filone's characteristic syncretism is only partially convincing here. For if a man busies himself with acquiring material goods, albeit in order to sustain his own life or to be generous to others (both rational and reasonable goals), then he is turning his mind to noncontemplative pursuits that are intellectual only by participation. This opposition between action and contemplation traverses Leone's entire thought and is a persistent point of difference between Filone and Sofia.[4]

The introductory section of Dialogue One, whose purpose is to offer preliminary elucidation of the terms of discourse, concludes with concrete illustrations. Filone applies the hierarchical categories of useful, delectable, and noble to the following human goods: health, children, conjugal love, power, lordship, honor, fame, and friendship. This naturally leads to the noblest object of man's desire, which will also give him the greatest happiness.

The central and most important section of Dialogue One discusses the highest goal of man, the love of God. God is the noblest of lovable objects because He is the beginning, middle, and end of all activity, or, as Leone later puts it, the efficient, formal, and final cause. Leone examines and rejects utilitarianism and hedonism and postulates that God can be reached only by man's highest or intellectual faculties, which are five: artistic intellect, practical intellect, science, understanding, and wisdom.[5] Like many of the Scholastics, Leone restricts art to the mechanical trades and quickly dismisses it. Prudence, the second intellectual virtue, provides the necessary purgation before the soul can effectively acquire the three highest or purely intellectual virtues: science, which grasps self-evident moral and intellectual truths (e.g., the law of noncontradiction); understanding, which leads these principles to their necessary conclusions; wisdom, identified with *prima philosophia*, theology, and metaphysics, which consists of the union of the preceding two and which alone can lead to a knowledge of all things and of God.

Like Maimonides, Leone Ebreo asserts that a rigorously intellectual preparation is necessary to reach man's highest beatitude. As a prelude to theology the student must have studied logic, natural philosophy, and the sciences.[6] But even the most exhaustive empirical study cannot yield a knowledge of all things. Leone replies that the adequately prepared intellect that receives divine illumination will thereby see all things not in their particularity but as they exist essentially, in eternal unity in the mind of God. At the moment of illumination by the agent intellect, man enjoys his highest felicity, which is an intellectual vision of God. But since knowledge produces love, the question arises as to which of these is the true source of beatitude. After examining various opinions, Leone says that highest beatitude consists of neither love nor knowledge alone but rather—and this is extremely important for his entire thought—of a union of the two, in the "copulation" of the human with the divine intellect.[7]

Dialogue One concludes by returning to the point of departure: human love, and especially Filone's love for Sofia. Filone renews his plea, but the clever Sofia first wants to know, on the basis of all that has been said about the various human goals, how Filone's love for her is to be classified. After considerable confusion, Filone confesses that his desire "aspires to delectation," which, as Sofia snaps back, depends on the sensation of touch and is therefore most likely to lead to satiety and hatred. Filone tries to justify his desire by observing that physical love increases spiritual love; further, since love is a desire for union, this should apply to every aspect of one's being, including the physical.[8] More plausibly, he then reflects that his love is based not on passion but rather on a true knowledge of his beloved's almost divine perfection—which furnishes an occasion for considerable hyperbole. Sofia interrupts with an interesting question: If love is born of knowledge or reason, how can it be so passionate or *un*reasonable? Filone's allegorical interpretation of the god Cupid merely restates the problem, however, and Sofia asks again: How can excessive love for another person be considered virtuous? Filone's reply, the celebrated theory of extraordinary reason, argues that extravagance characterizes *every* great love, be it carnal or the generous love for a friend or God. Further, one must distinguish three senses of reason: (1) knowledge, the basis of all love; (2) ordinary reason or reasonableness, also called self-love or the beginning of charity, which moderates between extremes and whose goal is the conservation of life; (3) extraordinary reason, which disregards the normal rules of prudence and often leads to self-alienation and self-sacrifice.[9] However, Sofia senses the ambivalence of the notion, which can denote both disinterested love as well as a desire to "acquire" the beloved. Be this as it may, one will have little difficulty in recognizing in the distinction between normal and extraordinary reason the paradox already mentioned between action and contemplation, wherein the world of normal reasonableness is challenged by a radical intransigence and an exaltation of love and desire. Nor will one fail to admire in these closing pages the noble artistic expression of Filone's paradoxical desire both to live and die, composed of dramatically contrasting rhythms and Petrarchan antitheses, an exemplary prose presentation of the joys and especially the pains of human passion.

At the end of Dialogue One it is clear that no solution has been reached, either to Filone's courtship of Sofia or to the intellectual positions that the courtship somehow reflects. Through a dialectical give and take, the dialogue has merely clarified rather than reconciled the opposing views of the two parties. For Sofia, desire and love remain exclusive notions: Desire reigns while its object is lacking, and is replaced by love at the moment of possession. Love is thus a *gaudium*, an actual enjoyment of a real object. While Filone verbally agrees that this is the definition of true love, he nevertheless insists on another kind of "love," based on an object whose existence is not real but rather imaginary. For example, whereas Sofia would speak of love between man and woman as arising out of their actual union, for Filone the very anticipation of this union is also a kind of love. Since love is thus a *desire* for union, the two cannot be mutually exclusive. Further, even after union or acquisition of the beloved object, desire does not cease but even intensifies because it is located mainly—at least for Filone, who returns to the point with unusual persistence—in the bottomless imagination of man.

Dialogue Two expands the discussion to cosmological proportions by showing that love is a principle that governs the entire created universe. Again the point of departure is, albeit briefly, dramatic and psychological rather than abstract, arising out of Filone's hope that an awareness of love's ubiquity will perchance incline his mistress' heart in his favor. Filone describes in turn how love characterizes all three areas of the universe: the lower world below the heavens, the heavens, and the separate intellects or angels. In the final section—by far the most crucial—he shows how love is the force or principle of interaction and unification among these three levels. In short, on the basis of a traditional geocentric view of the universe's structure, Leone nevertheless counteracts both the medieval theological opposition between a "this world" and an "other world," as well as a mechanistic physics—both traditionally allied with Ptolemaic theories—by a single principle which traverses and unifies the entire universe, the "idea of love" or, in more modern terms, life.[10]

Proceeding as usual from the familiar to the more abstruse, Leone begins by discussing the omnipresence of love on this sublunar earth, first among sentient creatures and then in the lower beings. Among the animals, which are those beings that have life and are subject to propagation and death, Leone distinguishes five causes of reciprocal friendship: sexual pleasure, love of one's own offspring, gratitude, the natural love of one's species, and the friendship produced by prolonged association. Among humans these causes are supplemented by two others: elective affinity due to astrological coincidences, and noble love of Virtue and Wisdom. In addition to sensitive and rational love, there is a third level, the natural love that holds sway in the realms of inanimate matter and vegetation. Here the terms become metaphorical, since stones and trees cannot be said to know, and hence to desire and love, in the senses just described. Yet even inanimate bodies pursue their natural good. Just as animals instinctively seek food and pleasure and avoid pain, fire naturally rises toward its place of origin, the sky, and flees from the cold earth. The latter, in turn, avoids the heat that would dissolve it and is naturally attracted by gravity.

By clever analysis Leone shows that the same five causes of love among sentient creatures are also applicable to the various combinations of the four elements. The most important of these is that described first in the case of sentient beings: the desire for sexual union and propagation. At this point one begins to perceive a central and persistent feature of Leone's philosophy, perhaps influenced by his readings in Kabbalah: the radical polarization of the entire universe in terms of male and female symbols. At the lowest extremity of things the author posits the Aristotelian *Prima Materia,* identified with chaos or pure potentiality, which, because of its passivity and disposition to receive forms from the higher world, is termed the "wife of the heavens." Indeed, it is precisely because of matter's desire for forms that the lower world exists, for through their sexual union the four simple elements are generated. These in turn, through their mutual friendship and unity, become capable of the various composite forms which occupy the entire range of lower beings: mixed inanimate (metals, stones), vegetative, sensitive, and intellectual, the latter being due to the "unified, equal and perfect love among its elements." This being so, Leone can conclude that no body below the heavens is without love, be it rational, sensitive, or simply natural. It need only be added that man, the epitome of the lower creation, is capable of all three varieties.

Love among the celestial bodies is the subject of the long middle section of Dialogue Two, first as the sky's paternal or marital affection for earth and then as the principle that governs the heavens in their own inner workings. The description of the sky's love for his spouse earth is based on the traditional notion of man as a microcosm or miniature replica of the universe. According to this theory, physical creation is a single living "animal" or organism made up of a union of upper and lower, active and passive, or male and female elements, just as "Adam" or man, generically speaking, denotes both sexes. In the first of an elaborate series of "correspondences," the exuberant and ingenious detail of which need not detain us here, Leone states that the principle kind of love in both man and the physical universe is generative, and then he examines the physiological and cosmological causes of generation. Just as the male's sperm can be introduced into the female only through the cooperation of seven principle organs, in the same way the sky inseminates the sublunar world through the influence of the seven planets.[11] In addition, man's generative organs correspond to his perceptual organs, the seven apertures of the head, while the seven planets have both generative and cognitive functions. This latter observation, incidentally, is said to follow from the view that the universe is a living being.

The loves that govern the heavenly bodies in themselves cannot be ascribed to the five causes operative in the lower world; they may be compared, however, to the two higher loves found in man. For since the heavens are superior to earth and, indeed, are a perfect organism in themselves, is it not conceivable that their steady regularity and magnificent harmony may be due to an innate tendency to unity and intellectual virtue? The question furnishes Leone with the occasion for a long treatise on Greek and Roman mythology. To Sofia's objection that the lascivious pagan gods are unfit to be compared to the majesty of the heavens, Filone explains that the so-called lies of the poets contain important truths, but these are concealed under the cover of allegory for six reasons: (1) to withhold truth from the unworthy; (2) to facilitate memorization through poetic brevity and rhythm; (3) to attract and encourage the weak by beauty; (4) to preserve truth from temporal change through fixed versification; (5) to provide something for everyone through the various levels of meaning; (6) to increase the chances of passing on truth to succeeding generations, since more people can assimilate literature than abstruse discourse. In short, allegory is a necessary vehicle for the conservation of truth or doctrine. The idea that underlies the subsequent discussion of the pagan gods is that they are allegories that represent poetically the various levels of truth: literal or historical, moral, psychological, celestial, and metaphysical. After a long poetical exegesis, the author returns to purely astrological matters and concludes his discussion of the various friendships and enmities among heavenly bodies, but in a dry and technical manner and without the pleasant shell of allegory.

In the closing section of Dialogue Two, which discusses love among the heavenly intelligences, Leone introduces what is perhaps the crucial problem of his entire thought. It is readily granted: (1) that spiritual beings love one another, and (2) that inferior beings love more perfect beings, desiring to be joined with them so as to share in their perfection. But how does one explain a superior's love for an inferior? Why should the intelligences desire to activate the lower spheres, or why should a perfect God love a sinful world?

Leone begins by explaining that generous love is better than selfish love. A father loves his son in order to improve the latter and not for any personal benefit. More provocatively, Leone states that in the universe a defect in the lower creation implies a defect in the Creator, just as "the imperfection of the effect denotes the imperfection of the cause." The inference would be that God loves and blesses His creation for the sake of His own self-perfection. The notion that man's sin may adversely affect God Himself is a bold one, however,[12] and Leone prefers to emphasize the argument that such mutual love between superior and inferior will lead to the principle end of God's creation of the world: a universe having the "ordered diversity and unified plurality" of a single organism or "animal."[13] Such unitive love between higher and lower is imitated in lower organisms as well, so that without generous love the universe could not even exist. Just as God is united with His creation, in the same way the angels join with the celestial bodies, the world soul with the lower globe of physical generation, and the intellectual soul with the human body. The principal descriptive terms of these syzygies are by now familiar: upper and lower, spiritual and physical, active and passive, light and dark, and—especially meaningful in a discourse on love—male and female. We are now prepared for the insight that "all creation is female with respect to God the Creator"[14] and for the next dialogue, which elaborates the grand reunion between God and His creation.

The stated intention of Dialogue Three is to examine five questions concerning love: whether it was born, and if so, when, where, from what, and why. Again, the discussion is made to arise from the courtship between the two characters. Filone fails to greet his beloved in a chance encounter, and the proud Sofia demands an explanation. This furnishes the occasion for a long digression on the nature of the soul. Filone explains that his neglect is due to his profound inner contemplation of the image of his beloved, and that during such a state, as during sleep, man undergoes radical alienation both from himself and from the external world. Filone goes on to show how the soul is constantly drawn by these opposing forces. During sleep the soul is absent from its normal affairs and involved in restorative operations of the physical body. By contrast, during contemplation the soul almost entirely neglects bodily functions and is turned to spiritual things. The mean between these extremes is normal waking activity, during which the soul succeeds in balancing these two opposing "loves." Filone thus defines the soul as an intermediary principle between the physical body and the understanding, a notion that he develops through the analogy that exists between spirit and soul, on the one hand, and the sun and moon on the other.

The sun is a visible image of the divine mind. Corresponding to these two levels of reality (physical and spiritual or intellectual), there are two kinds of knowledge: sensible and intelligible. The latter is higher, but since incorporeal things are known through the corporeal, man begins his spiritual ascent through sensible knowledge, the noblest of which is visual. In physical sight three things may be distinguished: the organ of perception, the perceived object, and the space intervening. But perception cannot occur without the sun, which illuminates both the eye and the object, as well as the medium. Similarly, on the parallel order of intellect, understanding occurs only when the divine intellect illuminates the human mind, the forms, and the Ideas. Moreover, while true light is intellectual, the light of the sun in the lower world is not a mere accident or quality resident in a subject but rather—recalling that in the Genesis account light was created on the first day and extended to the luminaries only on the fourth—a true image of divine light. Thus visible light is a spiritual act that conjoins with a diaphanous body but can never mix with it or suffer thereby any alteration in its purity.[15]

These parallels are elaborated in great detail. Just as the sun is an image of the divine intellect, the eye is an image of the human mind. Further, just as the divine and human minds both see and produce light, in the same way it is shown that: (1) the eye illuminates the object perceived, and (2) the sun is the "eye" of the heavenly body and has its own peculiar powers of perception. Thus, in their respective domains of physical, psychological, and celestial reality, the eye, the human mind, and the sun are images of divine intellect, especially insofar as they perceive and illuminate or, to put it differently, insofar as they avoid the passiveness of brute matter and reflect the pure activity of divine intellect.

The moon is an image of the world soul and hence of the latter's progeny, human souls. Like the soul, the moon is a varying combination of light and darkness, as befits its intermediate position between the earth and the sun. Leone discusses systematically the spiritual meaning of the various phases of the moon. The full moon, for example, whose light is turned toward the dark earth, is an image of the soul turned toward bodily concerns, while the new moon, turned toward the sun, signifies divine contemplation. The highest kind of spiritual experience, union with God, is portrayed by the lunar eclipse, in which the earth is completely overshadowed and the lighted half of the moon is turned entirely toward the sun. In this state of utter abandonment by the soul's light, the body dies and the soul is joined with the divine intellect, this being the death reserved for "our ancient and beatific Saints Moses and Aaron," who are said by Scripture to have died by the "kiss of God."

As the long introductory section draws to a close, it is apparent that, far from introducing extraneous materials, Leone has returned to the crucial problem of contemplation versus the active life, of total involvement in divine union versus legitimate ethical activity and concern with the body. For, in both sublunar and celestial reality, it is the nature of the soul to act as an intermediary between spirit and matter and thus to be drawn constantly in both directions by these contradictory "loves." What is new is the grand perspective of reconciliation of these opposites by means of the notion of cyclical activity. Just as the moon regularly spans the entire range of possible opposition and harmony between sun and earth, the human soul "moves from itself to itself, that is to say, from its intellectual to its corporeal nature, and then returns from the corporeal to the spiritual, and so on in a continual and circular motion" (p. 179). What follows in the dialogues will further prepare, at yet deeper levels and with fuller orchestration, the final vision which crowns the entire *Dialoghi:* the presence of such a cycle as the most valid metaphorical description of the entire created universe in its relation to the Creator.[16]

Leone concludes his introduction only to engage in another. After permitting considerable "idle" love talk from her suitor, Sofia wishes to review their previous findings concerning love and desire. Typically, what follows is more a new departure than a dry summary. Filone now holds that, despite their superficial and verbal difference, love and desire are "essentially" the same, that although not all desires should be dignified by the high name of love, all human love is desire. Leone does not abandon the notion of love as based on deficiency but rather, following the *Symposium* (206–208e), observes that all human love is deficient because of the mutations of time. Love "desires to enjoy the beloved object in union" not only in the present but forever.

The view that love implies a deficiency in the lover reintroduces an acute problem. If God loves the world, is He then deficient? Leone first cautions that human language cannot be applied to God, whose love is not mere passion but pure act. The best image of God's love remains that of a father for his son or that of a master for his disciple, a love of pure beneficence that seeks to remedy a deficiency in the beloved only. Further, one must distinguish between God's unknowable essence and His operation or creative action *ad extra*, only the latter of which is affected by the conditions of His creatures.[17]

Filone explains that Plato was not wrong to emphasize the lover's inferiority to the beloved, since he was concerned only with the most usual kind of *human* love, defined as a desire for beauty. Speaking in the most general terms, however, Aristotle defined love as a desire for the *good*, a definition that also includes beneficent love. Now all beauty is good, but not all good is beautiful (e.g., health, clean air). Goodness is thus more general than beauty and is, in fact, identical with being, according to the traditional formula that "ens et bonum convertuntur." As a rule, however, humans are drawn to the good under its aspect of the beautiful, which Leone describes as a "gracious spirituality" removed from the three lower or material senses and restricted to sight and hearing.

The first of the five questions—whether love was born from some cause or whether it is eternal and self-produced—discusses more fully the problem of God's love for man. The important point is repeated that love is an intermediary force or daemon that causes a lover to aspire to a more perfect object. This being so, the beloved or more perfect of the two is the true father of love, engendering it in the soul of the lover "just as the child is engendered in the womb of the mother." This notion, by the way, is an interesting gloss on the Provençal poetic habit of calling the beloved lady the masculine epithet "my lord" (*midons*), she being the true active cause of love in the lover. Upon learning this, Sofia returns to her most persistent difficulty, that of justifying philosophically or "with reasons" God's love for man. Filone retorts with arguments by now familiar: that God desires the perfection of the whole universe, and that love in God is not a defect or passion but pure beneficence.

Worthy of note throughout this discussion is Leone's critical treatment of revered source materials. Sofia bases her argument of the lover's superiority to the beloved on the *Symposium* (180b), where the point is made that a lover is possessed of divine fury and hence is himself almost divine. Filone observes that these arguments are advanced by the gallant young Phaedrus (*Dialoghi*, p. 232) and are indeed later refuted by Socrates himself. In accord with Leone, recent criticism regards such apparent contradictions among the various interlocutors of the *Symposium* as serving a literary and philosophical purpose. By contrast, one thinks of Ficino's famous commentary, which tries to justify and reconcile the most divergent views, or even of Heinz Pflaum (*Die Idee der Liebe*, p. 120), who seems to ascribe Phaedrus' doctrines to Plato himself.

The question as to when love was born is related by Filone to the problem of the world's origins. In a long and somewhat parenthetical discussion Leone explains the three leading views: Aristotle's theory of the eternity of this world; the Hebraic or Mosaic belief in a creation *ex nihilo*; and Plato's vision of an eternal succession of transitory worlds. Leone is especially interested in Plato's theory of the cyclical generation and destruction of successive worlds that arise from and revert to prime form and matter, the father and mother of all things. Moreover, these regular cycles are said to be based on the number seven: destruction of the sublunar world after six thousand years and its regeneration after a rest of one thousand years; destruction of the heavens themselves after seven times seven or forty-nine thousand years, and their rebirth after a fallow period of one thousand years. Here Leone indulges his tendency to Hebraicize Plato by recalling the importance of the number seven in Scripture.

Returning to his subject, Leone states that the first love is God's love for Himself and is therefore eternal. Though God is perfectly one and simple, there occurs a mysterious multiplication within Him: just as Eve is mythologically said to have sprung from the body of Adam, in an analogous way the original active entity (God's beauty or simple essence) produces a feminine entity. Thus we may distinguish: (1) God's beloved beauty or goodness; (2) His wisdom or intellect that loves; (3) the love that arises from the two. Since the beloved is always superior to its lover, Leone concludes that God as beloved is superior to God as lover of Himself, in contradiction to the Christian view that Father and Son are equal. Since God is pure act, however, beloved, lover, and love are identical in Him—an interesting extension of the traditional notion of the identity of knower, known, and knowledge during the act of knowing.[18]

Beyond this original, intrinsic love, God also loves extrinsically. In loving Himself, God also desires to reproduce His beauty. Thus, God has two loves: the first toward Himself, the second toward His images or creatures. The crucial role here is played by the divine intellect, which, in addition to loving God in perfect contemplation, also contains all the Ideas or patterns of creation. Now whereas the Intellect in its first love is female, in its love toward the creatures it is active or male. The same process is now repeated at this lower level. The divine Intellect no longer contemplates God but rather its own self, and from this contemplation a female entity is produced, again on the pattern of Adam and Eve. This female element is Chaos or Prime Matter. These two, alternately conceived as male and female, Prime Form and Prime Matter, or Intellect and Chaos, are the original parents of creation, and from their mutual love all generation occurs.

The question as to where love was born provides the occasion for a treatise on the angels and the hierarchical ordering of all beings from God to Prime Matter. Leone emphasizes that whereas divine Wisdom and Prime Matter are *produced* from a single entity (as Eve from Adam), all the children of these two "parents of all creation" are said to be *born*, that is, from two parents. The question, then, directs itself to the engendered worlds of angelic, celestial, and sublunar or corruptible reality.[19] Filone advances the view that love is first born among the angels and from there descends to the other levels of beings. Sofia objects that, while angels have greater knowledge of God, it seems true that men, who are lower in the order of beings, suffer a greater deficiency and hence a greater desire for God; and, since love is based on desire and since desire (chronologically) precedes knowledge, it would seem that love originates among men rather than among the angels. Leone replies with Cusanus' theory of the equality of all finite beings with regard to the infinite,[20] there being no possible common measure between created beings and God, although there are real differences between, say, men and angels. Further, the angels feel greater desire than men, since desire is based on knowledge. A king has greater knowledge of precious jewels than a peasant, and he therefore desires them more keenly.

Following the intellectualistic tradition of Maimonides, Leone holds that only the intellect in man is eternal and capable of approaching the divine. He describes five levels of intellect, each of which reflects the divine beauty according to its own nature or capacity: human intellect *in potentia*, human *in actu*, human in "copulation" with pure or angelic intellect, angelic, and divine. The discussion centers largely on man's union with the agent intellect, which is defined according to two traditions: (1) the philosophers, who regard the agent intellect as the lowest of the angelic intellects; and (2) the true believers, who identify the agent intellect with God Himself.[21] These views are seen to be complementary rather than contradictory; the first describes the limits of man's natural reason, and the second, the glory conferred by divine grace, which is the angelic vision of God.

Corresponding to the ascending order of intellectual love is the birth of lower beings from higher ones through the two kinds of contemplation and love proper to each. The highest angel or first intelligence, for example, which moves the first heaven and enjoys the vision of God without intermediary, contemplates *"the beauty of its cause* [i.e., God] and out of love for Him produces the second intelligence; the other contemplation is of *its own beauty,* for the love of which it produces the first heaven, composed of an incorruptible, circular body and an intellectual soul" (*Dialoghi,* p. 282). In turn, the second intelligence produces both the third intelligence and the second heaven, and so on down to the lowest of the upper intelligences, that of the sphere of the moon, which, through its two contemplations, produces the lower agent intellect containing all the forms of the sublunar world, as well as the lowest or human intellect.

Among the five questions which make up the argument of Dialogue Three, a definite structure now seems to emerge from the abundant and various materials. The first question focused sharply on God's love; the second, on the first parents of love, Prime Form and Matter; the third, on angelic love. Continuing the hierarchical ordering of the argument, the fourth question first considers human love, the highest in the lower world and the lowest among intellectual beings. Then, in a second section, the argument comes full circle by returning to the nature of God, the origin of all beauty and hence of all lovable things.

The fourth question, then, which sets out to identify the parents of human love, begins with an allegorical reading of the fables of poets and philosophers. Two traditions would have love spring from either Mars and Venus or Jupiter and Venus. This is not a contradiction but rather an accurate view of man's two loves. From the first union comes Cupid, symbol of carnal love, while Jupiter and "magna Venus" generate noble or honest love. This familiar notion of the soul's two directions is now developed by a long exegesis of the Genesis account of Adam and Eve. Originally, man's nature was androgynous, a harmonious mixture of male understanding and female matter. But with the Fall, man became too concerned with his own body and with the useful and delectable, to the neglect of the intellectual virtues. Plato's fable of the Androgyne in the *Symposium* is seen as confirming these views: all human love and desire is a peculiar combination of intellect and matter, the father and mother of love, and thus a reflection of man's dual nature. When loved with moderation, matter contributes to the true well-being of the whole person, as when the knowledge of eternal truths first reaches the mind through sensual knowledge.

The discourse is next expanded to include "the common father and mother of all love" and is marked by a change in manner: Sofia now wants plain talk, without the cover of fable. Although mind and matter, knowledge and lack, characterize all love, these cannot properly be called the "parents" of love. For the true father of love, which generates love in the lover, is beauty itself, while the mother of love is the very knowledge of that beauty in the soul of the lover "combined with a lack of it." The central problem, then, is that of the nature of beauty, Leone's compact discussion of which is a veritable treatise of Neoplatonic aesthetics and has been the most influential part of his whole work.[22]

Engendered in the soul by that beauty that the soul knows and desires, love is the lover's desire to reproduce the image of beauty and also the desire to be joined with that beauty. These desires are complementary but distinct: the reproduction of beauty is the first end of the soul's love, while the final end is to be reduced to or united with the desired object. Though Leone is not intent on drawing out the distinction at this stage, it should be clear that the aesthetic treatise under discussion concerns itself with the idea of love as a *production* of that beauty engendered in the soul of the lover.

Like the light of the sun, beauty is in the world but not of it. Essentially spiritual and formal, beauty is inaccessible to the three material senses and perceived only by hearing and sight, especially the latter. Further, physical beauty does not consist of proportion, for this would exclude simple bodies such as light and color. Leone's intent is to demonstrate that the beauty resident in physical bodies is not essential but derivative from the world of forms. To show this Leone recalls the traditional analogy between natural and artificial forms. Any product of human art derives its beauty from the idea in the mind of the artist, and this intellectual model is both prior and superior to its realization in matter. Similarly, all of nature's forms have prior and more unified existence in the World Soul, the common reservoir and producer of all the patterns which undergo change, diversity, and corruption. Contrary to Aristotle's notion of ideas as generalizations of empirical fact, Leone views Ideas in the Platonic manner, as those primary and incorporeal substances from which physical bodies originate. Physical beauty is thus a mere shadow or image of the intellectual "splendor" of its forms or Ideas. Such shadows are necessary, however, since Ideas are first known as images of sensible objects, just as the artistic concept in the mind of the artist is known through the work of art.

If Ideas are the original patterns of all created things, must they not also share the enormous diversity and even, to some extent, the multiplicity of these things? Leone answers by recalling two Plotinian assumptions: that an effect is always inferior to its cause, and that corporeal substance is caused by incorporeal substance. Ideas need not, therefore, suffer the same defects as the bodies they produce. Further, Leone returns to the idea of the Universe as an organic whole, whose many different parts are nevertheless unified in a single body. Thus, in the mind of the divine artist, the multitude and diversity of His creation is also "pure unity and true identity." This unity-in-multiplicity of Ideas is appropriate to their intermediate position between the artist and his works, or, theologically speaking, between the One God and His multiple creation.

In the universe Leone distinguishes three degrees of beauty: the Author or fountain of beauty; Beauty itself, also known as Sapientia, which is God's Idea of Himself; the Universe produced by this Idea in the mind of God. Properly speaking, the Author is beyond beauty, just as the adjective "beautiful" is applied to the artifact rather than to the artist who produced it. The first Beauty is God's first hypostasis, the divine Logos, which is also the Idea of the Universe from which all other Ideas originate.

This does not mean that God's Idea of Himself is identical with the Idea of the Universe but rather affirms that the Idea of the Universe is produced directly in the mind of God. None would think of equating an artist with the idea of an artifact to be produced, and yet, during the act of knowing, the mind and its idea are identical.

The relationship between the Logos and God is more problematic.[23] Just as the visible universe is an image of its Idea, in a similar way the Logos is the perfect image of the Father. Leone again has recourse to the analogy of the sun, whose body is inaccessible to human vision and which yet beautifies the world, and especially lucid bodies, with its light. This light is of the same nature as its source, which it extends, by way of emanation, and communicates to the universe. Leone concludes with a mystical reading of certain verses of Genesis (which he regards as the historical source of Plato), the Song of Songs, and the Sapiential books of the Bible. It is noteworthy that Sofia, the heroine of philosophical reasoning, is virtually silent in these inspired pages, the author obviously feeling that in such high matters philosophy must give way to theology and even secret wisdom. Finally, Leone returns to themes especially dear to him: the presence of a female element within God Himself, and the doctrine that the beautiful Universe—and hence love—is engendered from the union of God with His Wisdom, as from father and mother.

The fifth and final question seeks to determine why love was born. Having established that the first end of love is God's desire to reproduce His own Beauty by creating the Universe, Leone is now prepared to consider the *final* end of love in the created Universe. The distinction between these two loves is drawn with great care. In the first instance, God's love for His Universe is that of a superior for an inferior, analogous to that of a father for an offspring, a teacher for a disciple, or a cause for an effect. At the outset, a father desires to produce offspring not out of love for it (which is impossible until it has actual existence) but rather out of self-love, or the desire to reproduce his own beauty. Once the offspring has independent being, paternal love is now extrinsically directed toward it in a beneficent desire to show its own goodness or beauty. By contrast, the love of an inferior for a superior beauty is defined as a desire to enjoy union with it. This re-ductive love is the necessary complement of pro-ductive love and is the subject of the remainder of the work, which is a grand summary of the various arguments depicting love as the universal desire of all things to return to the Godhead whence they came.

The argument, mainly metaphorical, is based on the image of a great circle of beings proceeding from God to Prime Matter and then back to God, love being God's desire first to produce the Universe and then to reduce it back to Himself. Although each level of being also desires both to reproduce its own image in its inferiors and also to be joined with superior beauty, God Himself is the true final, as well as the effective, cause of the Universe and fountain of universal love, desiring to perfect what He has already produced. In the return to its true source, the intellect "lovingly knows and knowingly loves" and thereby accedes to man's highest felicity: union with God, which is beyond knowledge and love—the daemons that led man to his goal—and is the delectation of the lover in the Beloved.

Chapter 2
The *Dialoghi d'amore* as Literature: The Uses of Dialogue

On its literary level Leone Ebreo's *Dialoghi d'amore* is presented as a long courtship between an ardent lover, Filone, and his reluctant mistress, Sofia. At one point the clever lady summarizes their respective attitudes by the casual observation that she is more interested in the theory of love, while Filone is more bent on the practice thereof.[1] This wry comment is a capsule of the entire work, for it explains not only the constant narrative shift between amorous language and philosophical investigation, but also the basic paradox that pervades the entire *Dialoghi*, that of speculation versus action, which appears as the tension between Filone's amorous involvement and Sofia's aloofness but especially as the opposition between the contemplative life and the active life.[2] In this chapter I shall suggest that Leone Ebreo's work may be defined as a dialogue between two philosophies of life or two kinds of people, the contemplative man and the active man, and that these two human types are represented by the two interlocutors, Filone and Sofia. This view will require revision of the usual critical approaches to the *Dialoghi*. For one thing, if we take Leone's title seriously and consider the work as a true dialogue, as a confrontation of two substantially divergent points of view, then it is difficult to describe it as essentially a monologue in which only one of the characters—Filone—expresses the author's ideas. Moreover, in addition to the purely philosophical argument, we shall have to pay close attention both to the psychological nature of the characters and to the precise levels of their allegorization. In short, we shall no longer be able to neglect the work's literary nature.[3]

Master and Disciple

The commonly held view that in the *Dialoghi d'amore* "Filone is the author himself" (Caramella, in *Dialoghi*, p. 427) denies any substantive meaning to the concept of dialogue as either a philosophical or a literary device. The pattern for such a view is Ibn Gabirol's *Fons Vitae*, "a dialogue that nothing interrupts or diverts and that, far from all human contingencies, pursues its central subject unswervingly," which is a more or less systematic development of certain philosophical ideas.[4] Similar to the *Fons Vitae*, which had a direct influence on Leone,[5] the *Dialoghi* have long stretches of straight philosophical exposition, and especially the third dialogue surpasses in length the normal human endurance of a single session. Further, like the disciple in the *Fons Vitae*, Sofia's role seems limited to summarizing her tutor's discourses and introducing these by convenient questions; it is the learned Filone who does a large bulk of the talking and who has the authority to provide answers. Sofia approaches Filone with the confidence that he can solve her doubts, whereas, by contrast, she herself is several times chided— by means of a pun on her name (pp. 24, 260)—for her lack of wisdom. It would thus seem true that Filone is indeed the author's mouthpiece and, consequently, that the dialogical form used by master and disciple is an artifice of mainly expository importance.

Some aspects of Filone's character and opinions cast doubt on this view. First, why would Leone's only spokesman be named Filone (meaning love) rather than Sofia or wisdom, since, as we shall see, the latter represents the higher principle in man? No less puzzling is the discrepancy between the hero's fine ideas on the intellectual love for God as the source of man's happiness and his own immediate desire, which "pursues sensual delight" (p. 47). Also, it must be granted that, as a master, Filone is curiously lethargic. At the beginning and end of each section, it is always Sofia who demands a continuation, whereas Filone would rather pursue more urgent matters. Indeed, the initial impetus for the philosophical dialogue is provided by Sofia, who successfully turns her suitor's bold statement of affection (p. 5) into a terminological problem. In the ensuing discussion Filone is often content to transmit the opinions of other thinkers (pp. 236–39), and it is Sofia's criticism that compels him to distinguish and give his own view (e.g., p. 5). In such instances Sofia appears to be the master—a Socrates who arouses and requires the personal discovery of truth through criticism— whereas Filone, to a certain degree, is the student who has consumed large bodies of information without having digested them sufficiently.

Even more telling than the master's reluctance and evasion is the active role of the disciple. In their long discussion over the proper object of love and desire, for example, Sofia succeeds not only in presenting a serious objection to Filone's arguments but also in establishing an independent position of her own. In a thoroughly Aristotelian analysis (p. 13), Filone categorizes the objects of human love and desire as useful, delectable, and noble, and then he shows how human virtue may be defined as an excessive love and pursuit of noble or intellectual objects, and as a moderate love and pursuit of useful and delectable objects. Sofia challenges this doctrine of the golden mean by arguing that, since man's highest virtue and happiness consist in the love and pursuit of intellectual objects, then whatever distracts him from this goal is rather a vice than a virtue. Thus, useful and delectable objects such as money or health may not be loved even moderately but rather as little as possible. Filone concedes the truth of her point "in a certain kind of man" (p. 23), but with respect to the moral life he asserts that earthly goods are necessary (pp. 23–24); for example, one cannot clothe or feed the poor without having acquired the means to do so. At this stage of the dialogue Filone succeeds in establishing two rather modest points: (1) Sofia's radical rejection of all useful and delectable pursuits cannot be universally acceptable (p. 23), perhaps because all men cannot be contemplatives; (2) moderation is also an intellectual virtue (p. 25), albeit of a lower order than contemplation. It must be emphasized, however, that Filone does not refute Sofia's claim but merely clarifies it. Indeed, Filone agrees that contemplation requires an utter rejection of all earthly things and that this activity alone is the source of man's highest felicity (p. 15).

A second point of difference between the two protagonists constitutes the central topic of Dialogue One, the nature of love and desire. From the start, Sofia argues that love and desire can never coexist, for desire implies deficiency or absence of the desired object, whereas love is a *gaudium*, the actual possession and enjoyment of this object: "whatever is loved is first desired; and, when the desired object has been acquired, love begins and desire ceases" (p. 5). Further discussion brings mutual acceptance of the classical view that love is based on knowledge[6] and that knowledge is based on being, since one cannot love what one does not know, nor can one love nonbeing. While accepting these propositions as valid statements concerning true love, Filone at this point introduces two crucial distinctions: (1) things have not only real or objective being but also a certain kind of being in man's imagination; (2) this duality of being corresponds to two levels of knowing, one that precedes love, and the true knowledge of the beloved object which comes only from union with it. For example, "the first kind of knowledge of bread causes a hungry man to love it and desire it. . . . And it is through this love and desire that we come to the real unitive knowledge of bread, which occurs when we actually eat it. For the true knowledge of bread is in the tasting" (p. 44). With this in mind we can now understand Filone's admirable summary of the two positions:

> Although we may say, speaking imprecisely, that all objects that are desired are also loved (because they are judged to be good)—speaking more correctly, we may not call those objects loved that have no particular existence. I am referring to *real* love; for imagined love may be extended to all desired objects, due to the existence that these have in the imagination. And from their being imagined there arises a kind of love, whose subject is not the real, particular object of desire (for that object does not yet have real existence) but rather the mere concept of that object, which is derived from its common being. [Pp. 11–12]

Here Filone concedes Sofia's central view that real love arises only from the possession or enjoyment of a real object. Yet, since things can in a lesser sense exist and be possessed in the imagination, Filone argues that the term love can also be applied here: "Although health or wealth—when lacking—can't be loved because we don't have them, yet we would love to have them" (p. 5). Sofia observes that the expression "would love to have them" can only mean to desire them (p. 6), which implies that for Filone there is no essential difference between love and desire. Indeed, he later defines love precisely as a *desire* for union (pp. 45, 56). Such arguments provide the theoretical basis for Filone's constant emphasis on the roles of both imagination and desire in human love. For Filone, love is desire because the human condition is experienced as one of want or deficiency. Even at the moment of fulfillment, the lover anticipates future absence and thus desires to be united with the beloved object not merely in the present but forever (p. 211). Man's desire is boundless, Filone continues, not merely in his higher senses, but even more so in his spiritual faculties of imagination and especially mind (*mente*, p. 48). As one proceeds up the ladder of human faculties and the corresponding gradations of desirable objects, moreover, desire itself (rather than fulfillment) defines the true nature not only of love but even of happiness or delight. Thus, "in the pure appetite for delectable things there is a fantastic delight, even though there is not yet real enjoyment" (p. 19). Yet even more desirable is the "delight of the mind and intellect in acts of virtue and cognition, the enjoyment of which is excellent and honest *to the degree that it is insatiable*" (p. 48). In short, from Sofia's elevated perspective, love indicates the joy of fulfillment; from Filone's more human viewpoint, love is essentially absence and craving desire.[7]

A third point of controversy between Filone and Sofia concerns the justification of God's love for man. According to Filone's view, love implies desire and desire implies deficiency (p. 155); love is thus always of an inferior being for a more perfect being, the former's love being nothing but a desire to supply his want by sharing in the latter's greater perfection. But if this definition is correct, Sofia asks, why then should God love His creation: can He be thought to suffer any need whatever, or could He possibly derive any benefit from such a relationship? Stated differently, does a defect in the creation imply a defect in the Maker? Does God's love imply deficiency? Sofia's insistence in solving these doubts leads Filone to speculate as follows: "Imperfection in the effect implies imperfection in the cause. In loving its lower effect, therefore, the higher cause desires the perfection of the lower being, desires to unite with it in order to save it from defect. For by freeing the latter the higher being saves itself from defect and imperfection. Wherefore the ancients say that the sinner stains and offends the divinity, whereas the just man exalts it" (p. 157). The notion that God Himself is affected by human imperfection is a daring one, and Filone's later remark that this applies only to God's activity and not to His essence (p. 223) does not remove the difficulty entirely. It should be noted that in both instances Filone takes care to ascribe this doctrine to the "ancients" (probably the Kabbalists)[8] and that he prefers to approach Sofia's question with very different kinds of arguments, as we shall see.

In the three instances just examined, Sofia goes far beyond the task of mere interrogation and summary. In matters that are at the very center of the *Dialoghi*'s meaning, the disciple has advanced an independent position which, far from being refuted, seems closer to what we would imagine the author's true opinions to be: Sofia argues that the contemplative man must not love or even bother with earthly things; she defends the traditional objectivistic definition of pure love, which is always of an existent object; and she persistently raises the central problem of Leone's thought, the mystery of God's love for the world or, more generally speaking, the love of superior beings for inferior beings. If Leone Ebreo has presented a master and disciple situation, then we may wonder who is the master and who the disciple, and which in fact voices the author's true opinions and concerns.

Until Filone's point of view is more fully understood, we cannot speculate as to what extent his ideas may coincide with those of the author. However, in his presentation of philosophical problems as emerging from a complex dialogical exchange, Leone Ebreo seems to be suggesting either that his own views are not the privilege of either party alone, or, at the very least, that the dialogical form is not of mere expository importance: it is a method of philosophical discovery, of the transformation of learning into understanding. Whether Sofia is thought of as a real person or as the master's own critical sense, it is through her serious and persistent questioning that Filone's own philosophy becomes explicit.[9] Moreover, such critical activity is central because it reveals—whether in the outer world or within the psyche—the presence of those antagonistic elements that give dialectic its necessity. This occurs to Filone with his acknowledgment that there are different kinds of men and with his growing awareness that his beloved Sofia is precisely another kind of person. Leone Ebreo made the artistic choice to unify these forces that oppose Filone: the disciple-master whose brilliant questions challenge and clarify Filone's ideas is also the lovely lady whose beauty torments and eventually purifies his affections.

Sofia and Filone as Courtly Lovers

The fact that Sofia and Filone are in some sense obvious allegorizations of philosophical notions does not require that they be lifeless as characters, as certain conceptions of allegory seem to imply.[10] Quite the contrary, an unprejudiced reading of the *Dialoghi* reveals the presence of lively characters in real situations, based on both observation and literary tradition. As psychological creations, Leone's protagonists are representations of well-known literary types. As a "belle dame sans merci" of almost divine perfection—at least in the eyes of her lover[11]—Sofia recalls the lady (*Midons*) of Provençal poetic tradition, while her grand manner of directing the discussion bears some resemblance to such strong female personalities as Castiglione's Duchessa Elisabetta Gonzaga. Her dominant trait is lofty independence, both in love and in intellectual matters. She seems to show displeasure at being neglected (*Dialoghi*, p. 171) and a good-natured patience with Filone's extravagant flattery (p. 172); yet she remains aloof from any avowal of mutual affection. In discussion she is fond of invoking reason against authority (p. 241) and personal experience against reasoned argument (pp. 50, 279). In brief, she is one of those proud spirits for whom matters of both love and belief must be preceded and sustained by good reasons.

Sofia is important for her suitor not as an independent thinker, however, but rather as an object of devotion. Despite his clear reverence for religion, Leone as an artist did not shrink from portraying the most controversial aspects of that religion of love that is vaguely termed "Provençal" and that forms a tradition from *Tristan e Iseult*, Chrétien's *Lancelot*, *Flamenca*, and down to Petrarch. Filone's affiliation with this tradition is intimated by the detail, otherwise gratuitous, that the love relationship in question is potentially adulterous (*Dialoghi*, p. 122). Another aspect of this courtly tradition is the divinization of the beloved, either as a beauty almost divine (Petrarch) or even as a substitute for the divinity (*Flamenca; Dialoghi*, pp. 232, 389). For Filone, Sofia is a "divine beauty" (*Dialoghi*, p. 198) and, as such, becomes a total preoccupation, a "goddess of my desire" (p. 174). To this literary habit of viewing the lord-lady as the superior and masculine element in the love relationship, Leone adds interesting theoretical clarification (*Dialoghi*, pp. 230–31). It is the lady who, by inspiring the lover by her divine beauty, is said to *act* in the real sense, while the receptive lover is merely acted upon. Thus, it is the lady who engenders love in the feminine soul of the lover, whereas the lover remains essentially passive—not meaning, of course, that he shows no outward activity in the pursuit of his mistress, but rather that his soul suffers passion.

As a counterpart to such an aloof mistress, a well-known type existed in literary tradition: the humble and devoted courtier of not always chaste intention. Because he has studied a great deal, Filone naturally performs his love service (*Dialoghi*, pp. 201, 391) not by daring deeds but rather by learned discourse; but his high ideas on the intellectual love for God are unable to disguise his more urgent needs, to which he often returns. His center of gravity is desire, especially desire to be joined with his lady. This explains his highly lyrical outbursts, his reluctance to discuss anything except his love, and even, to some extent, his indifference to contradiction. For example, he states that men whose desire is for delectable objects such as physical love are usually "happy and jocund" (pp. 19–20). However, Filone is too acutely aware of the suffering and dangers of his own passion to hold this view for very long. In his extreme preoccupation with the thought of his lady, Filone becomes insensitive to the outer world—even to the physical presence of his beloved! (pp. 61, 171)—and alienated from himself (p. 199). His "stinging and insatiable desire" has become a "pernicious and very raging poison" (pp. 198–99), which leads to death (p. 53) or a state of living death: "love continuously causes the lover's life to die and his death to live on" (p. 55). He is without free will and without rest: "my spirits burn, my heart is consumed and my being is all aflame" (p. 55). Such passages— complete with Petrarchan metaphors of Cupids and gazes that wound the heart like arrows and culminating in Filone's long description of his passion (pp. 51–56)—are fine poetic achievements, all the more remarkable in that they highlight the presence of a rich literary and psychological tradition within a work that is usually regarded as philosophical.

Filo-Sofia

These characters are also allegories. A clue to their general identity may be seen in Sofia's warning that she is moved more by "gentle and sincere mental dexterity" than by "amorous intentions," and that Filone would therefore be better advised to "quiet my intellect rather than arouse my passions" (*Dialoghi*, p. 7). Typologically, Sofia represents those philosophical temperaments that thirst for intellectual enlightenment and are content to live in a world of abstract thought.[12] Since she does not feel the pull of lower, physical reality, she has no need for Filone's love, and her reluctance to requite his love is perhaps related to her intellectual perplexity as to why God should love the world. Sofia's name evokes a more practical sense of wisdom as well, a distrust of a passion that can only lead to alienation (*Dialoghi*, p. 206) and suffering. By contrast, Filone's name—love—invites us to identify him with *l'amorosa volontà* ("the will-to-love") and to view him, in Platonic terms, as a daemon or intermediary between physical and spiritual reality and as being constantly drawn in these opposite directions. Such a position is uncomfortably ambivalent, for, if Filone can complain that his lady is too far removed from normal human desire and mercy, Sofia in turn can suspect him of using the high name of love to dignify his lower appetites. From a more sympathetic viewpoint, however, it seems possible to regard Filone as an example of those paradoxical Platonic temperaments (Héroët, Scève, Donne, and others), neither mere sensualists nor pure contemplatives, who seek ideal beauty without wishing to renounce the earth that is man's birthright.[13]

Leone Ebreo seems also to have intended more abstract senses of allegory, especially connected with epistemological problems. Filone (or love) is "the first passion of the soul" (*Dialoghi*, p. 281), and man's passions and appetites are located in the will. Further, since we have identified Sofia with the cognitive faculties, we may say that her superiority to Filone reflects an important psychological commonplace, as it were, the intellect being "the most noble and spiritual of the soul's powers" (*Dialoghi*, p. 44). However, the essential relation between these two faculties is by dialectical progression rather than by opposition: love and desire are based on knowledge, and these emotions in turn serve as mediative forces between this imperfect knowledge and perfect unitive knowledge, the true end of love and desire. Moreover, man's final knowledge is an *"amor* intellectualis,"" and it is affirmed that in pure separate intellect there is no real distinction between love and knowledge (*Dialoghi*, p. 373).

In the *Dialoghi d'amore* prominence is given to yet another pair of dialectical opposites, that of desire or want (*mancanza*) and knowledge, since love can arise only from a combination of both (*Dialoghi*, p. 259–73; the identification of desire with Filone is a simple one, since for him love is essentially desire). It is argued that in the causation of love, knowledge is superior to desire, just as Sofia is superior to Filone or (masculine) beauty is superior to the (female) soul. But with equal emphasis Leone maintains that there can be no love without a feeling of absence or want, a requirement poignantly expressed by Gaston Bachelard in his daily prayer: "give us this day our daily hunger" (*pain: faim*). The point of all this seems to be that true wisdom is not only learning or only love (piety or enthusiasm or desire) but rather a union of the two, which arises dialectically in the soul which both knows and loves. The goal of this progressive dialectic between Filone and Sofia is of course Filo-Sofia or true wisdom, *scientia con amore*, which is identical with theology and *prima filosofia* (*Dialoghi*, p. 35).

With these central dualisms in mind we may now return to Filone's views. We have seen how, in the discussion over contemplation and praxis, Filone accepted Sofia's position that contemplation is prior to action and is the true source of man's highest felicity. In the third dialogue, Filone reintroduces the discussion as part of an attempt to explain God's love for the world, and the love of superior beings for inferior beings. He argues that mutual love between superior and inferior will lead to unity, which is "the principal end of the highest Maker and sovereign God in the production of the world" (p. 158). Leone then gives his own elaboration of the ancient Stoic idea of the universe as a single animated organism:

> The entire universe is like an individual or person, and each of these corporeal and spiritual or eternal and corruptible parts is a member and part of this great individual, the whole and each of its parts having been produced by God for the common end of the whole, together with an end proper to each of its parts.... The end of the whole is the unity [and] perfection of the entire universe, in accord with the design of the divine architect; and the end of each of the parts is not only the perfection of that part in itself, but also that it may thereby properly contribute to the perfection of the whole; and this universal end is the prime intention of the divinity. [Pp. 162–63]

The importance of this argument cannot be overrated, since it is intended to legitimize a suspension of the intellect's essential act of contemplation. Thus, although "the proper and essential act of the intellect is to know itself and all things within itself, just as the divine essence, like the sun in a mirror, shines in a clear vision," yet it must consent to "move a material heavenly body, an act extrinsic to its own true essence" (*Dialoghi,* p. 162). The same injunction is pointedly applied to man, along with the remark that the joys of contemplation may best be enjoyed after death: although man's highest or intellectual souls would be far better off in the exercise of pure and intrinsic contemplation,

> yet they attach themselves to our body solely out of love and service of the sovereign Creator of the world, bringing life and intellectual understanding and divine light from the eternal upper world to the corruptible lower world, so that even this lowest part of the world might not be deprived of divine grace and eternal life, and so that every part of this great living Universe may share in that life and intelligence which He is entirely. [P. 164]

Here Filone goes far beyond the usual notion that ethical activity is a necessary preparation for contemplation. While agreeing that contemplation is indeed man's highest felicity, he raises the profound question as to whether *in this life* (*Dialoghi,* pp. 46, 164) man should pursue such happiness to the detriment of his own body and of his fellow man. This is perhaps the reason for Leone's repeated emphasis that only Moses, the greatest of the Prophets, saw God while still in the flesh. The implication is that such total detachment or ecstasy is not only unrecommended to the rest of mankind, but impossible as well.[14]

Filone's language of "love and service" toward the Creator suggests that an important aspect of man's activity in the world is based not on philosophical discovery but on religious precept: rather than seek happiness, man acts as a divine agent in the lower world because he is commanded to do so. Such a religious orientation may be seen in other aspects of the book as well. For example, while constantly striving to syncretize Aristotle and Plato, Filone nevertheless admits his preference for Plato because of the latter's strong affiliation with the Mosaic theological tradition (e.g., p. 251). The same attitude may be seen in Filone's usual manner of argumentation: the procedure is to clarify problems through dialogical exchange and to proceed to conclusions that do not exceed the bounds of philosophy, at which point Sofia, the voice of purely human reasoning, becomes silent and Filone summarizes and extends these conclusions by scriptural exegesis.

In the final analysis, the *Dialoghi d'amore* is a debate between two kinds of people: on the one hand, those philosophical temperaments who seek to withdraw from the world and to pursue the joys of contemplation already in this life; on the other, those who respond to the demands of normative religion to live in the world and to regard doing as a necessary coordinate to thinking.[15] It would be a mistake, however, to regard Sofia's notion of contemplation as Leone's own. Just as Leone's opposition to total contemplation is religiously motivated, his concept of man's relation with God also has a peculiarly religious quality. His preferred term to describe the most intimate contact between God and man is *coppulazione*, the meaning of which may be seen in the description of final beatitude that crowns the first dialogue:

> And, in conclusion, I say that ultimate felicity . . . consists solely in that copulative act that joins us with God through the intimate and unitive cognition of His divinity, which is the highest perfection of the created intellect. . . . It is for this reason that Holy Scripture—having exhorted us to know God's perfect and pure unity and, after knowing it, to love it more than profit or the delectation of our sense or all honest objects of the soul and rational will [Deut. 6:4–5]—concludes by saying: "Wherefore you shall join yourselves with this God [*Pertanto con esso Dio vi coppulate*]." And, in another passage, Scripture promises ultimate felicity by saying simply: "And you will join yourselves with this God [*Et con esso Dio vi coppularete*]," without promising any other good such as life or eternal glory . . . , for this "copulation" is the most proper and precise term that can be used to signify Beatitude, which contains all the good and perfection of the intellective soul. [P. 46]

The accompanying exegesis of these passages is philosophical and is thus in harmony with the *intellectual* love of God described in other sections of the book. It must be stressed, however, that Leone prefers to derive his central concept of union from Scriptural rather than philosophical sources. Moreover, as a pious Jew, Leone the Hebrew used these verses not only as aids to philosophical reflection but also as integral parts of his daily devotions, which he performed as religious duties.[16] Such liturgical elements are deliberately subdued in the *Dialoghi*, which purports to be a philosophical and literary work addressed to a non-Jewish public, and yet they are essential to understanding Leone's real thinking. Such hints allow for a different interpretation of Leone's religious philosophy, which is usually termed intellectualistic. Although humans only rarely attain the distant intellectual vision, yet they may cleave to God with their will, by daily service and performance of their duties, since "the enjoyment of union may be effected by the will and may apply to things we lack as well as to things we have" (*Dialoghi*, p. 13).

Chapter 3
Délie! An Old Way of Dying
(The Meaning of Scève's Title)

The relations between body and soul—this is the main theme
of all "metaphysical" poetry.

JEAN-PIERRE ATTAL

Death is twofold, one known by all when the body is loosed
from soul, and the other that of the philosophers where the
soul is loosed from body.

PORPHYRY[1]

Plato's Phaedo

The above epigraphs are intended to provide the proper perspective for
what is to follow. The point in citing the first is not to discuss the definition of
metaphysical poetry but rather to assert that Scève's *Délie* is metaphysical
in Attal's sense because it places a primary focus on the relationships between soul and body. The Porphyry passage is a succinct reminder of two
traditional ideas: (1) that death may be described metaphorically as an "untying" or "loosening" of bonds; and (2) that philosophers may engage in such
untying already in this life, indeed that this is their chief preoccupation. The
usual philosophical source of these ideas of Porphyry, Plato's *Phaedo*, provides a suggestive discussion of death and, therefore, may be regarded as an
excellent introduction to the *Délie*.[2] The single concern of philosophers, we
are told, is "nothing other than dying and being dead" (*Phaedo*, 64a), but
people fail to realize what kind of death this implies (64b). Now all agree that
death is "nothing but the separation of the soul from the body" (64c), and this
is in fact the constant preoccupation of the philosopher: "releasing his soul,
as far as possible, from its communion with the body" (65a).[3] This is the
catharsis alluded to by the ancient Orphic tradition: "the parting of the soul
from the body as far as possible, and the habituating of it to assemble and
gather itself together . . . released from the body as from fetters." This is, in
fact, the precise meaning of death: "a release and parting of soul from body"
(67c–d).

Délie: Source of "Deaths"

In dealing with a poet whose hermeticism has been the despair of excellent critics, we had best strive for simplicity. In an eight-line verse dedication "A sa Délie" Scève states the poetic argument of this first French *canzoniere* as follows:

> Non de Venus les ardentz estincelles,
> Et moins les traictz, desquelz Cupido tire:
> Mais bien les mortz, qu'en moy tu renovelles
> Ie t'ay voulu en cest Oeuvre descrire.[4]

> Not Venus' burning sparks,
> And even less the arrows that Cupid shoots:
> It is rather the deaths that you renew in me
> That I have tried to describe for you in this work.

The key verse (3) has four central notions. First, the subject of the poem is not love but death. Second, death is in the plural and thus cannot allude to death in the usual sense. Third, these multiple deaths are renewed *en moy*, at a certain locus within the poet. Fourth, the source of these repeated deaths is *tu*, explicitly named at the outset as "Délie."

It is generally agreed that the meaning of the title *Délie* is far from exhausted by its possible allusion to one or more of the poet's mistresses. Saulnier senses that "the name itself takes on an existence of its own: it comes mysteriously alive... , sustained by a capricious inspiration."[5] The current theories that seem worthy of note are the following: (1) "Délie" is a fictitious name for Pernette du Guillet; (2) "Délie" is the anagram of *l'Idée* and thus at least in part of Platonic inspiration; (3) "Délie" is Diana, with many of the poetic associations traditionally related to the Delian goddess: moon goddess, virgin, huntress, sister of the poet Apollo, and Hecate. While accepting these biographical, anagrammatic, and mythological suggestions, I wish to offer a semantic hypothesis based on the usual meaning of *délier*, to untie or unbind. Accordingly, the title *Délie* is much more than a capricious inspiration; it is rather a veiled anticipation of the central theme of the cycle, since I propose to show that *délier* is synonymous with dying, both in Scève and in authors closest to him in time and in spirit.

I have chosen to focus on three such authors: Antoine Héroët, Marguerite de Navarre, and Leone Ebreo. Praised by Dolet for his "felicitous and luminous interpretations of Plato's lofty conceptions,"[6] Héroët was in close contact with Marguerite de Navarre from at least as early as 1524. He was probably friendly with Scève, and his major poetical works, *L'Androgyne* and *La Parfaicte Amye*, both appeared only two years before *Délie*. Marguerite de Navarre, patroness of Platonic studies in France, was addressed by Rabelais in 1546 in the following way:

Esprit abstraict, ravy, et ecstatic,
Qui frequentant les cieulx, ton origine,
As delaissé ton hoste et domestic,
Ton corps... [7]

Withdrawn, enraptured and ecstatic spirit,
Who, frequenting the heavens (your original home),
Have abandoned your host and servant,
Your body...

We must also mention the totally exceptional honor granted to Scève in 1547, when Marguerite allowed two of his poems to appear in the first edition of her collected poetical works.[8] Leone Ebreo's *Dialoghi d'amore* have long been recognized as the "breviary of Lyonese Platonism,"[9] and while the French translation by Pontus de Tyard (Scève's famous disciple) did not appear until 1551,[10] the Italian princeps had been published in 1535 and was followed by the excellent Aldine edition of 1541. We need only add that Sofia, the heroine of the *Dialoghi*, may be regarded as the literary prototype of the female *esprit abstraict*.[11]

Knots, Ties, Bonds (*Lien, Lier*)

Lien-soul, *Lien*-love, *Lien*-obligation

In their view of creation as a series of hypostases extending from the One all the way to prime matter, Neoplatonists considered the soul as the crucial link in the chain of being because it mediates between two very disparate realities: spirit or intellect and matter.[12] Leone's description is perfectly traditional when he alludes to the soul as an "intermediary between the physical and intellectual worlds (an intermediary and link [*milieu et lien*] through which the one is joined to the other)" (Léon, *Dialogues*, p. 162; Leone, *Dialoghi*, p. 178). In other passages it is love which performs the essential linking function: "the [parts of the] universe are successively joined and bound together by the bond of love [*se lie avec le lien d'amour*], which unifies the physical world with the spiritual world" (Léon, p. 144; Leone, p. 158); "love is a spirit that pervades and gives life to the whole world, it is a bond [*lien*] through which the entire universe is unified and bound up [*lié*]" (Léon, pp. 149–50; Leone, p. 165). This is viewed as the highest kind of love because it fulfills a divine obligation: "Men's spiritual intellective souls attach themselves [*se lient et couplent*] to so fragile a thing as a human body out of obedience to the divine command to attach themselves to and unify the entire universe" (Léon, p. 148; Leone, p. 164). Héroët's rendering of this central notion of *lien*-obligation stresses the common etymon:

Jusques à tant que l'ame soit purgée
De ceste terre, où elle est *obligée*... [13]

Until the soul may be purged
Of this earth, to which it is ob-ligated...

L'ame..
Faict que la chair, qui luy est *obligée*... [14]

The soul...
Causes the flesh, which is ob-ligated to it...

Lien-prison, *Lien*-body, *Lien*-desire

In keeping with the ambivalence of Platonists with regard to physical
reality, the soul's meritorious obligations to or with the body are also considered as liabilities: "In this life our Understanding is bound [*lié*] to the matter
of this fragile body," but after death the soul becomes "separated from this
bodily bond [*lien corporel*]" (Léon, p. 66); and Héroët complains: "Our
souls, having forgotten [heavenly] beauty because of its attachment to the
body [*estant au corps liée*], fears that it also will be forgotten."[15] The *Phaedo*
distinguishes two basic types of bonds. The primal one is with the body,
which can be dissolved only at death.[16] The second, added to the first and
sponsored by it, are the affections of the heart, usually designated as pleasure and pain, hope and fear.[17] Thus Leone can speak of a *lien* of sensual
enjoyment, and Marguerite, of the *liens* produced by "ennuy."[18] It was
commonplace, moreover, to locate such bonds in the heart:

Et puys desir d'estre et valoir beaucoup
Suyvoit cuyder, et plaisir tout à coup
Après les deux venoit le cueur lyer... [*Prisons*][19]

And then the desire to be someone important
Followed upon pride, and pleasure, quickly
After these two, came to bind my heart...

Once again, the main bond is love, but at this level we must speak of a *lien* of
desire, to be distinguished from the *lien* of love already studied: "It is Love's
bondage [i.e., desire] that first binds [*lie*] lovers' wills."[20] It is in such
passages that *lien* takes on its most recurrent meaning: without freedom or
power.[21] It is highly significant that the richest development of the *lien*-
prison theme in the French language was written within four years of the
Délie, that it was authored by Marguerite de Navarre herself, and that it was
named the *Prisons*. Considered by Jourda as Marguerite's masterpiece,[22]
this long autobiography written shortly before her death describes her progressive liberation from various kinds of bondage:

Las! mon amy, qui sont ces troys lyens
De la prison où vous trouvez tous biens?
L'un qui vous tient le cueur charnel captif:
C'est ung lyen qui est faict d'argent vif... [*Prisons*, p. 174]

Alas! my friend, what are these three shackles
of the prison where you [think you] find all good things?
The first, which holds your carnal heart in captivity,
is a shackle made of quicksilver...

The three *liens* are pleasure, avarice, and worldly honor. Elsewhere in the *Prisons* she refers to the *liens* of ambition (p. 162 ff.), of *cuider* or pride (p. 199), of the body (p. 262), of the prison of love (pp. 121–22), and of affection (p. 145).

Délier, Deslie-soucy, Deslie!-meurs!

When *lien* has the sense of a necessary link between two orders of reality or between male and female, the opposite concept, *délier* (to unbind), has negative overtones. Thus the *Heptaméron* alludes to the Franciscans as "those who bind us to women in marriage and who [then] through their wickedness try to unbind us"; again: "the bond of marriage can last only as long as life itself, whereupon we are released from the bond."[23] In a related sense Héroët describes the reunion of the Androgyne as retying an untied knot ("le vray neud deslié se relie," *Androgyne* v. 268). Such uses of *délier* are exceptional, however, for if *liens* and *lier* usually signify a painful loss of freedom, *délier* performs the opposite, liberating operation. The following examples show how *délier* can take on the connotations of openness and lightness while retaining its clear sense of unbinding:

Me fut descloz, ouvert et délié
Le sens qui trop m'avoit esté lyé,
Couvert, caché...
Par ignorance. [*Prisons*, p. 238]

I experienced an uncovering, an opening, an unbinding
Of my common sense, which had been too shackled,
Covered over, obscured...
By ignorance.

Or, in the *Heptaméron*, p. 224: "a vicious kind of love destroys itself and cannot abide in a good heart. But virtuous love has bonds so subtle [*a les lyens de soy si deliez*] that one is caught up before becoming aware of it." This general sense of release from all kinds of pain has been well rendered by

Ronsard, who refers to Nicolas Denizot as "desli-soucy, donne-vie, oste-soin" (reliever of anxiety, giver of life, remover of care).[24]

The most important sense of *délier* for Platonic authors in the 1540s, however, is not mere removal of pain but a release from more radical bondages of the spirit. For example, Marguerite speaks in a theological sense of a properly cleansed soul as "de tout péché deslyée" (*Le Malade*, v. 112), and the continuous liberation or imprisonment of the soul is termed a succession of bindings and unbindings: "In removing the shackles [*delyant*] of one evil, honor has bound you to a greater one, which is ambition" (*Prisons*, p. 166). The appropriate concept for such purification is death, and Marguerite can therefore describe the goal of evangelical death as "to separate the Soul from the body."[25] This simple definition of death, which goes back to the *Phaedo*, was used repeatedly: "if death is but the separation / Of soul and body" (Héroët, "Epitaphe de Marguerite de Navarre," p. 120); "since death is the separation / Of soul and body" (*Parfaicte Amye*, vv. 818-19). It must be stressed that *délier* was a usual term for all these levels of dying:

> Au corps duquel mon ame est alliée;
> Mais si par mort est toute desliée... [*Amye*, vv. 1017-18]

> My soul is bound to my body;
> But if by death it is totally unbound...

> Mais vous aurez repos alors
> Quant à vous mesmes serez mort...
> Pour ce que l'âme humiliée
> En congnoissance de son riens,
> Estant de son corps deslyée...
> [Marguerite de Navarre, *Le Malade*, vv. 261-67]

> But you will have peace
> When you are dead to yourselves...
> For the humbled soul,
> Recognizing its nothingness
> And being unbound from the body...

Tyard's translation of Leone gives a rich orchestration of this usage, which he probably learned from Scève. Having described the heart's vital force as the *lien* between the upper and lower parts of man, Leone states that "if it were not for the *lien* of this force, our soul would fly from us and would untie itself from the body [*se deslieroit du corps*]" (Léon, *Dialogues*, p. 161; Leone, *Dialoghi*, p. 177). This is in fact what occurs during contemplation:

> ... when the soul is placed between the body and the intellect, that is to say, when it is joined and united with the intellect, the soul receives in its upper part all the intellectual light and its lower, bodily part remains dark; where-

upon the body, deprived of the soul's light, loses its essence and the soul is dissolved from the body [*e lei si dissolve da lui;* Tyard: "l'ame se deslie du corps"]. . . . And it is just and reasonable that such a perfect union of the soul with the divine intellect should result in the dissolution of its bond with the body. . . . Therefore, since the human soul has two loves (the one towards the beauty of the intellect and the other towards beauty reproduced in bodies), it can happen that the soul is so drawn to the intellect's beauty that it completely abandons its love for the body and dissolves itself totally from the body [*elle est desliée d'avec luy*], which results in death . . . [Leone, *Dialoghi,* pp. 194–96; Tyard, p. 174]

I have quoted this passage at length because it is an excellent transition to Scève's *Délie* in its description of man's two loves—and hence deaths.[26] For it is clear that the poet's first death is caused by his love for "beauty reproduced in bodies": "Ingenious in planning my deaths, Délie / From the first day slew me with her beautiful eyes" (*Délie* 16). The opening *dizains* or stanzas of *Délie* are a classic description of aesthetic ecstasis inspired by the sight of a beautiful woman, especially her eyes: "My Basilisk with her withering gaze" (*D*1). Her body is perfect (*D*2) and her image divine (*D*3). Her beauty (*D*6, 7, 9, 10) enters the eye and quickly performs that death that is now familiar to us, the separation of body and spirit: "Great was the stroke that, with no sharp blade, / Caused my Spirit to depart while the body lives on" (*D*1: "vivant le Corps, l'Esprit desvie"). In *D*2 death is evoked by Pandora;[27] in *D*3 the poet "sacrificed with his Soul his life." Rather than a true unbinding of spirit from body, however, such aesthetic ecstasis is a deviation (*D*1, v. 8) leading to idolatry (*D*1, v. 10, *D*3, v. 2). Indeed, such a death is actually a further binding: "She holds me in bondage [*lyé*] through this hair of hers" (*D*14). The theme of the *lien d'or,* of Petrarchan provenance,[28] is a sharp antithesis dramatizing the dangers of aestheticism for its own sake.

In stanza 4, however, the poet's admiration extends to Délie's grace and the beauty of her actions, whereupon "I am dissolved in joyful tears." Different from that death provoked by physical beauty, dissolution (*dissoudre*) suggests in other contexts a dissolving of the heart-ego, and we are not surprised to learn that *dissoudre* is synonymous with *délier,*[29] as we can see in the following passage.

Rien, ou bien peu, faudroit pour me dissoudre
D'avec son vif ce caducque mortel:
A quoy l'Esprit se veult tresbien resouldre,
Jà prevoyant son corps par la Mort tel,
Qu'avecques luy se fera immortel,
Et qu'il ne peult que pour vn temps perir. [*D*446]

It would require nothing (or very little) to dissolve
My mortal frame from its vital principle.

> The Spirit is quite willing,
> And its body is already preparing for Death in such a way
> As to become immortal with it
> (For it can perish only for a brief time).

It is this untying of the self that is the poet's goal. Such detachment had been foreshadowed only imperfectly in the aesthetic contemplation of Délie's physical beauty, for, in addition to the poet's death or alienation of spirit from body, there occurred the simultaneous birth of erotic desire (D7).[30] The true meaning of "Délie," therefore, is precisely the death of the self through the dissolution of these "gloomy desires" (D7, v. 8), resulting in a victory over death. This is in fact the simple meaning of "Délie," as the rhyming pun of D22 emphasizes:

> Mais comme Lune infuse dans mes veines
> Celle tu fus, es, & seras DELIE,
> Qu'Amour a joinct à mes pensées vaines
> Si fort, que Mort jamais ne l'en deslie. [Vv. 7–10]

> But as the Moon instilled into my veins,
> You were, are and will be DELIE,
> Whom Love has joined to my vain thoughts
> So strongly that Death may never unbind her.

First of all, this passage proves Scève's awareness of the linguistic tradition documented above: that death's action is a *délier*. Secondly, taken by themselves these four verses seem to show that "Délie" is to be associated with a binding rather than an unbinding. The important point, however, is that Délie's binding is stronger than physical death; furthermore, Délie is in fact true to her semantic associations, as we see in D278:

> Qui veult scavoir par commune evidence
> Comme lon peult soymesmes oblyer,
> Et, sans mourir, prouver l'esperience,
> Comment du Corps l'Ame on peult deslyer,
> Vienne ouyr ceste, & ses dictz desplier. [Vv. 1–5]

> Who wishes to know with clear evidence
> How one can forget himself
> And, without dying, experience
> How to unbind the Soul from the body:
> Let him come and hear her and explain her words.

It is clear, then, that Délie inspires a true *délier*, the death of self-forgetting that is not the common untying of body from soul ("mourir," v. 3) but rather that ascetic untying of soul from body (v. 4) that has been the goal of philosophers from the *Phaedo* and from Porphyry.

Despite Scève's hermeticism, a Platonist in the 1540s would immediately have penetrated the enigma of Délie's name: through its contiguity with the stated theme of the entire poem, through recurrent allusions both to death and its vocabulary of unbinding and dissolution, and especially through the texts we have analyzed. To have been more explicit would have destroyed its value as an enigma and perhaps also tended to exclude the other legitimate poetic extensions of the name. Finally, there is perhaps one further hermetic refinement of "Délie." The two following texts go a step farther than the one just quoted in that the death-inflicting power of Délie is transferred to the magic of her name itself. "At the sweet remembrance of her name I feel / My spirit pierced through entirely . . . " (*D267*). The same theme is magnificently developed in *D168*:

> Toutes les fois qu'en mon entendement
> Ton nom divin par la memoire passe,
> L'esprit ravy d'vn si doulx sentement,
> En aultre vie, & plus doulce trespasse:
> Alors le Coeur, qui vn tel bien compasse,
> Laisse le Corps prest à estre enchassé:
> Et si bien a vers l'Ame pourchassé,
> Que de soymesme, & du corps il s'estrange.

> Whenever in my mind
> Your divine name passes through my memory,
> My Spirit, ravished with such sweet feeling,
> Crosses over and enters a different and sweeter life.
> Then the Heart, aiming at a similar good,
> Leaves the Body (ready to be placed in a coffin)
> And pursues the Soul so well
> That it foresakes both its self and its body.

Such estrangements of soul from body are by now familiar and may be provoked by Délie's beauty and goodness, as we have seen, or by her image in the poet's mind (*D141*), as may be the case here. It seems more likely, however, that the lady's name (not her image) can produce such an effect because of its meaning: *Délie!* the imperative form of the verb *délier*. Délie would thus be, in a precise, literal, and perfectly traditional sense, a *memento mori*.

Chapter 4
Return and Reincarnation
in Scève's *Délie*

My theory that *Délie* is part of the ascetic tradition of the *Phaedo*[1] will surely upset some critics because, being concerned with asceticism and so-called Platonic love, it fails to account for the sensual side of man's nature. Yet it will be clear that Platonic authors such as Antoine Héroët, Pernette du Guillet, and John Donne were rarely puritanical about sexuality; that, while firmly insisting that the meaning of human life exceeds the normal cycles of pleasure and pain, hope and fear, they were supremely able to accommodate concrete sensual experience as necessary for any truly human development. The two moments of the dialectic were clearly grasped by Ronsard, for example, in a poem that accompanied a gift of Leone's *Dialoghi d'amore* to Charles IX:

> L'un pousse les âmes guidées
> Aux belles contemplations,
> A l'intellect et aux idées,
> Purgeant l'esprit de passions.
> L'autre à Nature est serviable,
> Nous fait aimer et desirer,
> Fait engendrer nostre semblable
> Et l'estre des hommes durer.[2]

> One [kind of love] leads souls
> To contemplations of beauty,
> To the intellect and the Ideas,
> While purging the spirit of the passions.
> The other serves nature,
> Causes us to love and desire,
> To procreate our fellow man
> And to sustain our lives.

Referring to Scève, Dorothy Coleman has correctly detected that Délie's "unsubdued virginity has an element of wildness: her rule over the world of nature and the favours she has accorded to Pan and Endymion seem to place her *on the borderline of chastity and sensuality*."[3] Such a state of grace is a sign not of moral indecision but rather of a conscious ideal that may be studied in a number of texts and in a formulation that becomes typical of all of Leone Ebreo's descendants: the question as to the proper relationship of spirit to soul, of soul to body, or of spirit to body through the mediation of the heart-soul. In this descent of spirit to body Scève distinguishes two motivations and states each of these in a *dizain* of unusual beauty and complexity. *Délie* 247, with its abstract statement of moral law followed by a mythical proof-text, is paradigmatic of all unions that higher beings perform with lower ones in the name of a moral or religious imperative. In *Délie* 367 the approach is rather experiential, the echoing rhythms express the longing for such unions from the perspective of the lower entity.

D247: Love as Faithfulness

Here is the text of *D247*:

Nature en tous se rendit imparfaicte
Pour te parfaire, & en toy se priser.
Et toutesfois Amour, forme parfaicte,
Tasche à la foy plus, qu'à beaulté viser.
   Et pour mon dire au vray authoriser,
Voy seulement les Papegaulx tant beaulx,
Qui d'Orient, de là les Rouges eaux,
Passent la Mer en ceste Europe froide,
Pour s'accointer des noirs, & laidz Corbeaux,
Dessoubz la Bise impetueuse, & roide.[4]

Nature became imperfect in all [of her creatures]
In order to perfect you and be praised for you.
And yet Love, a perfect form,
Strives for faithfulness rather than beauty.
   And as confirmation of what I say,
Consider those so beautiful Parrots
That, from the east and beyond the Red Sea,
Cross the sea to this cold Europe
In order to couple with black and ugly ravens,
Through the stiff and violent north wind.

The correct context of the poem, I suggest, is the theological problem of God's love for His creatures or, more generally, the love of more perfect beings for less perfect ones. Leone Ebreo's formulation and solution of the question may have influenced Scève and, at any rate, provide an especially lucid exposition.[5] If, as Socrates would have it in the *Symposium*, love is the desire to possess or become united with a beautiful object, then the lover *qua* lover is deficient with respect to the beloved, since desire implies want or deficiency. It follows that a beautiful being could not love another being having the same kind and degree of beauty, since it is absurd to desire what one already has. This is especially true of God, who has no deficiency whatever and hence no desire. God's love, therefore, remains unexplained.

Leone's solution, as well as the different ontological levels to which it is applicable, may be studied against the background of *Délie* 247. In keeping with the poem's pedagogical tone, the poet-professor delivers a lesson in a crisp philosophical style (vv. 1–4) and then cites authority to drive home his point (v. 5). The idea is that all of Nature's creatures have been rendered imperfect by comparison with Délie's perfect beauty; yet love, as a perfecting form, strives for "foi" more than for beauty. One should note that the poem does not set up an absolute dichotomy between physical beauty and moral beauty or goodness.[6] Rather, it asserts that *perfected* love has faithfulness as its goal, while allowing its less perfect form to aim at beauty. The opening quatrain says more than this, however, for the poet has learned the professorial technique of Leone's hero Filone, the habit of combining abstract philosophical discourse and amorous assault. Thus the opening statement is also a typically Petrarchan exaggeration (Délie is the most beautiful of Nature's creations). Yet the standard compliment is quickly neutralized by the didactic language and especially by the teaching that *perfect* love aspires to moral rather than aesthetic perfection. To the urgent question as to whose love is being discussed, two answers may be given. First, in addition to striving for the perfection of beauty in the creation of her creatures, Nature (undoubtedly God, *Deus sive Natura*) also works out of an ideal of "foi" toward her creatures. Second, once this paradigm is perceived, it may be applied to other contexts, such as the relationship between Délie and the poet. It seems impossible to claim that this poem is *merely* another plea for the lady's pity,[7] that the poet deserves a reward because of *his* faithfulness. Rather, as the didactic tone suggests ("Voy," v. 6), Scève is reminding her of a higher form of perfection; he is urging *her* to become or remain faithful. If the poet deserves pity, it is because of *her* faithfulness, not his.

The proof-text of verses 5–10 is intended to explain what "foi" means both in its general sense and in the amorous context of the poem. According to the analogy, Délie's act of faith would be comparable to the departure of those beautiful parrots from their native land and their journey to a cold European climate in order to befriend and mate with ugly crows. Love's perfect form, in other words, involves displacement and intimate union with ugliness. We have already stressed that love's pursuit of a kind of beauty is not disallowed, but such beauty is superficial; its ambivalent nature is best rendered by a magnificent pun on *corbeaux*. From Nature's point of view, the lady's beauty is Nature's very perfection and praise; from the perspective of the so beautiful parrots, such bodies or *corps beaux* are likened to black and ugly crows. Such ambiguity illustrates that, as we saw in the first quatrain, physical beauty is surpassed but not negated by moral faithfulness. Moreover, the extravagance of the pun should cause no surprise. As a disciple of the *Rhétoriqueurs*, Scève was unusually sensitive to possible combinations of sounds, especially in rhymed position. In this case the pun seems simply borrowed from the acknowledged "source" of Scève's poem, Jean Lemaire de Belges's *Epîtres de l'amant vert:* "Or pleust aux dieux que mon *corpz* assez *beau* / Fust transformé, pour ceste heure, en *corbeau.*"[8]

Scève's lifting of an entire verse (v. 10) from the same poem (*Amant vert*, v. 236, p. 12) may be more than a gesture of respect to a revered poet; it may also be Scève's peculiar way of pointing to divergent meanings. For, if both passages are read primarily as amorous situations between lover and lady, then Frappier's perplexity must be shared: "Scève has enriched the anecdotal theme borrowed from Jean Lemaire by adding a new and very personal meaning; this *dizain* is, like many of his, a further example of his hermeticism, which often resorts to mysterious allusions."[9] In other words, the critic has no idea as to what the poem is about. As for Lemaire's poem, the Green Lover is a mock rendering of the courtly ideal in which the humble lover, impelled by his lady's sublime beauty and renown, undertakes a long and perilous journey reminiscent of Rudel's legendary homage to the countess of Tripoli. The first abrupt change that one notices in Scève's version is that the roles are reversed. It is Délie who is the beautiful parrot and it is she who takes upon herself the difficult service of love. The goal of her journey is not a beautiful creature, moreover, but an ugly bird, the poet himself.[10] Finally, when the Green Lover wryly states that an additional motivation of his voyage is "pour avoir l'amoureuse *accointance* de son désir" (*Amant vert*, vv. 239–40), he is exploiting an ambivalence somewhat similar to the acquaintance or "knowledge" of Genesis 4:1, which may evoke the entire range of human intimacies while at the same time specifying sexual relations.[11] The lover's argument would then run as follows: Délie should grant her favors not because of the poet's merit but rather because of her own "foi," which may mean either her constancy or her sense of doing good to the less fortunate. Scève has thus skillfully exploited the *courtois* setting of Lemaire's poem but transmuted the argument into one of *noblesse oblige:* Délie should quit being stuffy about her own beauty and allow herself to be moved by her own goodness.

Finally, the rich poetic context of *D247* seems to allow a further level of interpretation, along the lines of a deeper reading of the *Amant vert*. Scève may indeed have been a better reader of Jean Lemaire than we, he may have sensed profundities beneath the master's light naiveté and have felt called upon to develop them hermetically. The mythic aspects of the *Amant vert* are crucial in this respect, although we shall not belabor the well-known traditional symbolisms of the soul as a bird, of the soul's perilous migration into the body, of the direction of this journey as being from "east" to "west"—a significant gloss on Lemaire's "Ethiope" and "Egypte." At any rate, these central themes—especially that of transmigration—were available to Scève as possibilities for poetic elaboration, and it is a fact that the theme of the soul's love for the body did become one of the distinguishing features of Leone Ebreo's followers, as we shall see in the next poem.

D367

The form of D247 is that of a conundrum where one must figure out the relationships between sagacious pronouncement (vv. 1–4) and its poetic illustration (vv. 5–10). D367 deals with similar notions of absence and return, but it differs from D247 as an academic treatise on ornithology might differ from a flight of birds. Here is the full text:

> Asses plus long, qu'vn Siecle Platonique,
> Me fut le moys, que sans toy suis esté:
> Mais quand ton front je revy pacifique,
> Sejour treshault de toute honnesteté,
> Où l'empire est du conseil arresté
> Mes songes lors je creus estre devins.
>   Car en mon corps: mon Ame, tu revins,
> Sentant ses mains, mains celestement blanches,
> Avec leurs bras mortellement divins
> L'vn coronner mon col, l'aultre mes hanches.

> Much longer than a Platonic Year
> Has been the month that I have been without you.
> But when I again saw your calm brow,
> High abode of all chastity,
> Where the rule of wisdom is decreed:
> Then my dreams seemed prophetic.
> For into my body, my Soul, you returned,
> And I felt her hands (hands heavenly white)
> With their mortally divine arms,
> One encircling my neck, the other my hips.

Beyond the primary level of meaning—the return of Délie to the poet after a month's absence—Staub sensed a complexity of allusion, an intensity of experience, that led him to see the poem's connection with D247: "one can speak of reincarnation with regard to this embrace."[12] One can go much further, for here Scève has succeeded in integrating, within the dimensions of a single event and the space of one *dizain*, all the levels of incarnation recognized by the Neoplatonists. More than any poetic text to my knowledge, D367 summarizes the major movements of Leone's *Dialoghi d'amore*, but poetically rather than discursively, so that Leone's grand theme—the unity of the universe—is projected aesthetically, resulting in the experience of one of those *moments parfaits* that Weber detects in some of Scève's best poems, or, more ambitiously, inducing an imaginative vision whereby we are able to "effect a momentary attainment of the final aim of our life" or reintegration.[13]

One major achievement of the poem is that the plain meaning of the personal event is not in the least obstructed by the multiplicity of allusion, with the result that excellent appreciations of the poem have dealt mainly with this level. As it happens, however, Délie's absence and return are orchestrated at four additional levels. First, the separation is said to be longer than a Platonic Year, a strong hyperbole when we recall that this was variously reckoned at from 27,000 to 49,000 years.[14] The problem is put into its proper historico-cosmological perspective by Leone Ebreo, who explains that our universe is composed of the union of form and matter, of God's eternally luminous Ideas and Chaos, which go through successive combinations until the natural age of the universe is reached, whereupon complete dissolution occurs.[15] This marks not the final end of things but rather a universal sabbatical of one thousand years, whereupon chaotic matter is again impregnated. If we invoke the idea of man as a microcosm,[16] then the poetic idea is of great strength and beauty: in the absence of Délie—the anagram *l'Idée* is appropriate here, since it is with His Ideas that God impregnates matter—the poet has been formless and void.

A third level of reference is suggested by the fact that Délie's absence lasted for one month (v. 2), the period of the lunar cycle. The allusion is slight, yet adequate to conjure up the image of the white goddess. This dimension is hinted at in the subtitle to the *canzoniere:* "Délie, object de plus haulte vertu," meaning that the lady is a reflection or manifestation of a higher power,[17] and this is the relation of the moon to the sun (as well as that of the soul to the intellect, as we shall see). The identification of Délie as the lunar goddess Diana is central to the poem (*D*22), but the pervasiveness of the identity is usually not noticed because of the perfect ambivalence of Scève's metaphors for describing Délie, especially her face. A case in point is Emblem 2, showing a full moon with facial features, surrounded by lesser stars and two quarter-moons ("entre toutes une parfaite"). The following *dizain* interprets this motif by explaining the unique influence of this moon on the world's betterment, described as its "honneste estrangement" (*D*15). In *D*367 it is Délie's "front pacifique" that is the "high abode of all honesty." In referring to Délie's forehead could the poet have had in mind a more technical meaning as well? Indeed, "front pacifique" may be ambivalent in the same way as Délie's "face seraine" in *D*193:

Quand de ton *rond* le pur cler se macule,
Ta foi tachée alors je me présage:
Quand, palissant, du *blanc* il se recule,
Je me fais lors de pleurs prochaines sage. . . .
Mais je m'asseure à l'heure de ma paix,
Quand je te vois en ta *face seraine*.

When the pure clarity of your round [face] becomes dim,
Then I suspect a tarnish on your faithfulness.
When, growing pale, it declines from its white [fullness],
I anticipate imminent tears. . . .
But I am assured of my peace from the moment
That I see you with your serene face.

Is he addressing the lady or the moon? "Blanc" is her color but also that of
the moon; "rond" is the shape of the full moon but also of her face:

Puis sa rondeur elle [Diane] accomplit luisante:
Et toy [Délie] ta face elegamment haulsant.[18] [D176]

Then she completes her shining roundness,
And you elegantly lift your face again.

As these examples suggest, Délie's return and her presence are to be compared not to the new moon but rather to the full moon, as described by
Leone Ebreo:

Once a month the entire lower half of the moon [i.e., the entire side turned
toward the earth] is illuminated by the sun and we see it full of light—this
happens on the moon's fifteenth day—because it is in a position opposite the
sun and facing it.[19]

The point is that the full moon is that moment of the lunar cycle when the
moon has the role of perfect intermediary, when it fully receives the light of
the sun and reflects that light most beneficently on the earth.

To the devotee of Leone Ebreo the lunar presence is strengthened, even
made necessary, by the two further levels of meaning introduced by the
homophony *mois / moi*, "month" and "me," and the ambivalence of "mon
Ame." For the "returns" described in the poem occur not only cosmologi-
cally and celestially, after the Platonic Year or in the lunar sphere; they
happen also in the poet (*moi*), and they happen by the return of the soul to
the body—for it is clear that "mon Ame" can be taken literally and not only
as a gallant epithet referring to the beloved. We are back, then, to the theme
of reincarnation of soul into body, but for the complex connection with the
lunar cycle we must refer once again to the *Dialoghi*. There are instances in
our lives, Leone observes, when we may be said to "die" in the sense that
our soul takes leave from the body. Familiar examples are sleep and contemplation, this latter term meaning either religious rapture or the ecstatic loss
of self in the thought of the beloved. The soul is enabled to perform such
operations because of its mixed nature:

The soul, which is inferior to the intellect (for it depends on the intellect) is not
uniform. Rather, since it is an intermediary between the intellectual world and

the physical world (I mean an intermediary and bond whereby the one is linked to the other), it must have a mixed nature (mixed of spiritual intelligence and physical mutation); otherwise the soul would be unable to animate bodies. For this reason it often happens that the soul turns away from its intelligence and toward bodily things in order to engage in the sustentation of the body through its nutritive powers, and also to take cognizance, through its sensitive powers and operations, of those external things necessary to life and cogitation. And then the soul occasionally withdraws into itself and turns toward its intelligence, joining and uniting with abstract intellect, its superior. . . . Moreover, the soul's motion is circular and continual. I do not mean that it moves physically from place to place, rather that spiritually and in its operations it moves from itself to itself, that is to say, from its spiritual nature to its physical nature and then back again, in a perpetual circular manner.[20]

The most appropriate similitude for such experiences, Leone finds, is that of the two luminaries: "the sun is an image of the divine intellect, the source of every other intellect; and the moon is an image of the world-soul, from which all souls proceed."[21] The aspects of the question that interest Leone most are the "great and peculiar similarities between the moon and the soul" (Leone, *Dialoghi*, p. 188). The passage is worth quoting at length:

Just as the moon is composed of solar light and dark mutability, the soul also is composed of intellectual light and corporeal darkness. Moreover, the soul's light moves, as does the moon's, from the upper part to the lower, toward us, and then in the opposite direction. Thus the soul occasionally directs all the intellect's light toward the service of bodily things, during which time the soul remains totally darkened on its superior intellectual side, without contemplation, entirely turned toward matter, deprived of true wisdom, entirely filled with prudence and bodily knowledge. . . . [Thus], lest the physical part be entirely ruined [by contemplation], the soul must desist from its copulation with the intellect, very gradually sharing its intellectual light with the lower bodily part. This is similar to the [new] moon after union [of its upper part with the sun]—although the superior part loses light in direct proportion to the reception of light by the lower part (for perfect copulative union entirely removes any attention to bodily needs). Then the soul (like the moon) begins to direct its light and knowledge to the body, removing it gradually from God and turning all its providential care toward the body until it has totally abandoned its contemplation. Then it is similar to the moon in its fifteenth day, full of light toward us and in darkness on its heavenly side.[22]

The complex parallels are now fully drawn. Délie's return to her lover can be compared to: (1) reunion of the Ideas with prime matter, resulting in cosmic renewal; (2) the monthly return of the moon's full light to the earth; (3) the reawakening of the body to physical action and sensual life through the soul's beneficence, which may occur after sleep ("songes," v. 6) or (4) after contemplation.

*D*144

The thematic similarities of *D*247 and *D*367 should not prevent us from perceiving a deep tension at the psychological level. Granted that the soul's return to the body shows the workings of a higher power rather than the machinations of an evil spirit, as the dualists have maintained, still the motivations of duty and ecstasy stand in need of reconciliation. Leone's solution relies heavily on the inherent circularity of such processes: the soul shifts from intellectual delight to bodily duties like the moon from sun to earth. Scève's solution is suggested in *D*144:

> En toy je vis, où que tu sois absente:
> En moy je meurs, où que soye present.
> Tant loing sois tu, toujours tu es presente:
> Pour prés que soye, encores suis je absent.
>   Et si nature oultragée se sent
> De me veoir vivre en toy trop plus, qu'en moy:
> Le hault povoir, qui ouvrant sans esmoy,
> Infuse l'ame en ce mien corps passible,
> La prevoyant sans son essence en soy,
> En toy l'estend, comme en son plus possible.

> In you I live, however absent you may be;
> In me I die, however present I may be.
> However far, you are always present;
> However close, I am still absent.
>   And if nature feels wronged
> To see me live in you more than in me:
> The high power which, operating without passion,
> Places this soul into my passive body,
> Seeing my soul to be without its essence if left to itself,
> Extends it toward you as toward its highest potentiality.

The last phrase recalls a common Aristotelian notion: Délie activates the poet's *potentiality* toward its fullest development or perfection, but this extension into ideal selfhood involves a step beyond the descent of soul into body (v. 8). Or rather, the descent into body is but a preliminary step to full, essential perfection, described only as an extension "in you." Scève's solution differs only in its philosophical crispness—not in its content—from those magnificent metaphors of reintegration that form part of the same cultural tradition: Héroët's Androgyne, Donne's subtle knot, and Shakespeare's Phoenix and Turtle.

Chapter 5
Pernette du Guillet's Poetry of Love and Desire

Do I teach you to slay your desires? I teach you the chastity of
desires.

               F. NIETZSCHE, *Thus Spake Zarathustra*

Desire itself is movement
Not in itself desirable;
Love is itself unmoving,
Only the cause and end of movement.

               T. S. ELIOT, *Four Quartets*

Pernette du Guillet's small poetic legacy—amounting to less than 1,600
verses at the time of her death at the supposed age of twenty-five—was
posthumously collected, arranged, and published in Lyon in 1545 by the
poet-editor Antoine du Moulin.[1] This thin volume of *épigrammes, chansons,*
épîtres, and *élégies*[2] is a poetic *journal intime* of Pernette's nine-year love
relationship with the famous poet of *La Délie,* Maurice Scève. From both
the *Délie* and Pernette's verse we discover that, like Filone in Leone Ebreo's *Dialoghi d'amore,* the learned Scève was condemned to temper his
sexual impulses with elevated philosophical discourse. In turn, in her study
of Leone Ebreo, Pernette may have recognized a literary counterpart in the
beleaguered but serene Sofia. It may be that, like Sofia, Pernette was attracted as much by her teacher's "eloquent learning" (epig. 6) as by the
teacher himself, and such an attraction would have been intensified by her
own youthful search for knowledge (e.g., epig. 3). In her identification of her
teacher through the anagram "CE VICE MUERAS" (epig. 5), she says that
Scève will help her overcome the vice of ignorance. However, we shall see
that the new knowledge acquired from Scève (and from Leone Ebreo) is,
more than general humanistic learning, a deeper understanding about the
nature of her love experience. In fact, Pernette's poetic diary records her
grasp of that high doctrine of love that Scève was perhaps able to teach
but not to master.

    The central issue quite properly concerns the true nature of love, an issue
which is approached through Leone Ebreo's distinction between love and

desire. In the opening lines of the *Dialoghi d'amore* Filone declares his love to Sofia in a strange mixture of passion and philosophical precision: "My knowledge of you, Sofia, engenders in me love and desire."[3] This statement is not fully elucidated until near the end of the first dialogue, when Filone explains that his knowledge of Sofia causes love and desire *in that order:*

> I did not say "desire and love" because my love does not proceed from desire; rather, it preceded desire and from it desire is produced.[4]

Perfect love depends only on *knowledge* of the beloved; it is the emotional counterpart of that knowledge and, as such, derives its contentment only from the perfection of the beloved. Strictly speaking, love is indifferent to pursuit and possession, since it has already ideally united with the beloved (on the principle that only similar beings can love one another, the presence of love indicates that the spiritual identity of the two lovers has been perceived). By contrast, desire is based on a feeling of lack[5] and of the need to fill the lack by pursuit and possession. Whereas love is immobile, desire is the principle of movement toward the beloved, as Staub has shown in the case of Scève.[6] Sofia seems justified in witholding the gift of *mercy*, in view of Filone's disregard for his own definitions and his contradictory view that love and desire are essentially the same: " ... perfect desire, which is to enjoy union with the beloved, can never cease because desire is always united with love and of its very essence."[7] Whereas Filone in this context is trying to persuade Sofia that his passion is an essential part of love and is based on the latter, Pernette rarely doubts that their mutual love is well founded. Her question is more general: Is desire an essential aspect of love, or can there be such a thing as human love without the desire of possession?

Like Scève, Pernette is very careful in the use of technical terms, since precise distinction is one of the main intents of her poetic journal.[8] Desire has the same meaning as in Leone Ebreo, that of pursuit based on a feeling of absence. However, since *Amour* is the cognomen of Cupid, god of sexual love, the term *amour* is, rather than the opposite of *désir*, nearly its synonym. Pernette therefore renders Leone's concept of *amore* by the term *affection:*

> Soit que par esgalle puissance
> L'affection, et le desir
> Debattent de la jouyssance
> Du bien, dont se veulent saisir:
>   Si vous voulez leur droict choisir,
> Vous trouverez sans fiction,
> Que le desir en tout plaisir
> Suyvra tousjours l'affection. [Epig. 27]

> Although with equal claims
> Affection and desire

Argue the enjoyment
Of the good they pursue:
　If you wish to adjudicate the matter
Without hypocrisy, you will rule
That in every pleasure desire
Always follows affection.

With regard to enjoyment, then, desire is based on love; moreover, the pleasures of desire are precarious and must be maintained by effort:

Si le servir merite recompense,
Et recompense est la fin du desir,
Tousjours vouldrois servir plus qu'on ne pense,
Pour non venir au bout de mon plaisir. [Epig. 21]

If service merits reward
And reward is the goal of desire,
I would always wish to serve beyond what is expected,
So as not to exhaust my pleasure.

Beyond the arduous pleasures of love service, however, for Pernette a principle enjoyment of desire is sexual, as the following text seems to suggest:

Le Corps ravy, l'Ame s'en esmerveille
Du grand plaisir, qui me vient entamer,
Me ravissant d'Amour, qui tout esveille
Par ce seul bien, qui le faict Dieu nommer. [Epig. 12]

My body ravished, my soul is astonished
By the great pleasure that seeps through me,
Ravishing me with Love, who awakens all
To the happiness that alone earns him the title of god.

The ravishment, at first identified as belonging to the body alone, causes such pleasure as to astonish even the spiritual faculties or soul. In addition to its vertical penetration, the pleasure horizontally extends to the whole psychic unity ("ravishing *me* with Love") and even beyond, since the vague "all" of verse 3 could very well refer to all of Nature. Typically, Pernette chooses her terms with care: *plaisir* comes from the body, which is the domain of *Amour* or Cupid. What is more interesting is Pernette's ecstatic discovery that *Amour* can be divine.

The second half of epigram 12 holds the key to understanding Pernette's conception of love:

Mais si tu veulx son pouvoir consommer:
Fault que par tout tu perdes celle envie:
Tu le verras de ses traictz se assommer,
Et aux Amantz accroissement de vie.[9] [Vv. 5–8]

But if you wish to perfect Love's power,
You must totally lay aside that desire.
Then you will see him struck by his own arrows,
And an increase of life for lovers.

Here is the secret of perfecting love's power: the lover must completely lose
envie. This idea is of such importance that Pernette glosses it with another
text:

Le grand desir du plaisir admirable
Se doit nourrir par un contentement
De souhaicter chose tant agreable,
Que tout esprit peult ravir doulcement.
    O que le faict doit estre grandement
Remply de bien, quand pour la grand envie
On veult mourir, s'on ne l'a promptement:
Mais ce mourir engendre une autre vie. [Epig. 14]

The great desire for that astonishing pleasure
Must be fed by the contentment
Of aspiring toward a thing so delectable
As sweetly to ravish all spirits.
    Oh, how must the thing be abundantly
Full of enjoyment when the great longing for it
Makes one wish to die from not having it promptly!
But this dying engenders another life.

In conjunction with the *plaisir* arising from desire, Pernette's preferred term
for the serene joys of affection or love is *contentement*,[10] here described as
that delight that softly ravishes our highest or spiritual selves. The main
point, however, is that physical desires are not destroyed or "transcended";
rather, they must be nourished. Furthermore, *envie* is here based on a lack
(v. 7) that the lover strives to remedy through possession; it is therefore
synonymous with desire. Finally, the new life (v. 8) has been interpreted as
"the ecstasy experienced in the consumation of love" (*Rymes*, ed. Graham,
p. 22, n. 3), a view based on equating *mourir* with sexual consumation, a
metaphor common to both Scève and Shakespeare. It is clear from verse 7,
however, that "death" is caused not by fulfillment of desires but rather by
their nonfulfillment. As in epigram 12, it is the death of *envie* that confers
more life or new life.

What does all this mean? In part, Pernette seems to echo Sofia's worry
that her lover's love may be based on desire rather than vice versa—a fear
best illustrated by the subtle differences between her epigram 13 and
Scève's *Délie* 136:[11]

L'heur de mon mal, enflammant le desir,
Feit distiller deux cueurs en un debvoir:

Dont l'un est vif pour le doulx desplaisir,
Qui faict que Mort tient l'autre en son pouvoir.
  Dieu aveuglé, tu nous as faict avoir
Du bien le mal en effect honnorable:
Fais donc aussi, que nous puissions avoir
En noz espritz contentement durable! [Epig. 13]

The happiness of my pain, kindling desire,
Has melted two hearts into a single bond,
So that one lives for the sweet displeasure
That causes Death to hold the other in its power.
  Blind god, you have brought
Our painful joy to honorable result:
Grant also that we may have,
In our spirits, lasting contentment.

Scève hopes that the fragile happiness of their perfect moment can be prolonged. Although their physical union, the consummation of their flaming desire, entails no regret (*D*136, v. 7), Pernette is sad. She twice alters a phrase (vv. 1, 6) so as to view their experience as a *mal*, a source of suffering. Her concern is further clarified in the final verse, in her wish that Scève's impetuousness may be nourished by solid affection.

This quite human worry is not the main issue, however, for it merely explains the proper relation of (physical) desire to love; it leaves untouched the more radical demand that *envie* or desire must die completely. In this respect, one may be perplexed to find Pernette call upon Cupid in the verses just cited; (Scève's reasons for doing so are clear, since he hopes for a continuation of physical ecstasy). Why should the blind god have any connection with durable, spiritual contentment (note that "aussi" in verse 7 stresses his power over both kinds of pleasure)? Pernette's ambivalent attitude toward *Amour* can be seen in the remarkable *chanson* 6:

  O bien heureuse envie,
Qui pour un si hault bien m'a hors de moy ravie.
  Ne pleures plus, Amour: car à toy suis tenue,
Veu que par ton moyen Vertu chassa la nue,
Qui me garda long temps de me congnoistre nue,
  Et frustrée du bien,
Lequel, en le goustant, j'ayme, Dieu sçait combien.
Ainsi toute aveuglée en tes lyens je vins,
Et tu me mis ès mains, où heureuse devins,
D'un qui est haultement en ses escriptz divins,
  Comme de nom, severe,
Et chaste tellement que chascun l'en revere. [Vv. 24–35]

  O blessed desire,
That toward such a high good has ravished me beyond myself.
  Weep no more, Love, for I am beholden to you,

Since through you Virtue searched the skies
(Virtue that for a long time kept me from knowing myself naked,
    Kept me frustrated of the good
That, tasting, I love—God knows how much!).
Thus, blinded, I came into your bonds
And you placed me into the hands where I became happy:
Into the hands of one who is mightily—in his divine writings
    As in name—severe [Scève],
And so chaste that all revere him for it.

Again we find an enthusiastic praise of sensual pleasure, not only because it
brought her into contact with Scève, but also for itself (vv. 28–30). But since
contact was physical as well as spiritual, how can the author go on to praise
Scève for his chastity (v. 35)? The answer must be that chastity is an attitude
of mind that may, paradoxically, be present even during sexual contact. The
important point is not physical desire but rather desire itself. When desire is
rooted out, "you will see him struck by his own arrows" (epig. 12, v. 7).
Cupid does not die, he merely loses his arrows. The *trait* or arrow is the
perfect symbol of desire in its dual motion of conquest, since the arrow, after
being shot in pursuit, draws the wounded beloved back to the lover (Scève is
expert in the verbal intricacies of *traire/attraire*, as in *Délie* 5; 36). Once
defused of his pungent desires, *Amour* becomes *Eros*. This is what is called
perfecting love's power (epig. 12, v. 5), nourishing it by contentment (epig.
14, v. 2), and this is what allows the poetess to invoke *Amour* for both
physical and especially spiritual pleasures—but not for desire!

We must now ask ourselves why desire is to be subdued. Pernette discusses the problem in the form of a rather abstract debate:

A qui est plus un Amant obligé:
Ou à Amour, ou vrayement à sa Dame?
Car son service est par eulx redigé
Au ranc de ceulx qui ayment los et fame.
    A luy il doibt le cueur, à elle l'Ame:
Qui est autant comme à tous deux la vie:
L'un à l'honneur, l'autre à bien le convie.
Et toutesfois voicy un tresgrand poinct,
Lequel me rend ma pensée assouvie:
C'est que sans Dame Amour ne seroit point. [Epig. 24]

To whom is a lover more bound:
To Love or to his Lady? (For his service is proof to them
That he is of those who love honor and fame.)
    To Love he owes his heart, to his Lady his soul:
Which amounts to saying "the life of each."
The one leads him to honor, the other to well-being.
And yet here is a very strong argument
That satisfies my mind:
Without the Lady there could be no Love.

This may be a restatement of epig. 27, emphasizing that desire and love are based on prior knowledge. Here there seems to be the further awareness that one loves a person and not love itself—a sign of emotional maturity. But Pernette is especially intent on delineating the realm within which *Amour* or desire operates. The heart is the center of the self, the very life of the lover (v. 6). Its highest virtue is to pursue its own good, a pursuit called honor (v. 7). From the careful hesitations of epigram 24 it is obvious that Pernette is reluctant to condemn the egoism of desire, and for good reason. Leone Ebreo had shown that he who loves another to the point of hating himself commits an act "contrary to all reason and duty; for love is charity and must begin with itself" (Leone, *Dialoghi*, p. 53). Self-love is reasonable, for without it there would be no self. But with the conclusion that "without the Lady there would be no Love," the focus has subtly shifted from emotions to the human beings in which they reside. Pernette is well aware that love is a fiction, whether poetic or psychic:

> Point ne se fault sur Amour excuser,
> Comme croyant qu'il ait forme, et substance
> Pour nous pouvoir contraindre et amuser,
> Voire forcer à son obeissance.
>   Mais accuser nostre folle plaisance
> Pouvons nous bien, et à la vérité,
> Par qui un cueur plein de legereté
> Se laisse vaincre, ou à gaing, ou à perte... [Epig. 49]

> We must not excuse ourselves on Love,
> Acting as if he had form and substance
> To restrict and fool us,
> Indeed force us to obey him.
>   We must rather, in all honesty,
> Accuse our foolish pleasures,
> By which light hearts
> Are easily subdued, for gain or loss.

When the heart is weak, love becomes an instrument of deception and self-indulgence.

With this change of perspective we can now study what is certainly Pernette's most remarkable poem, the *élégie* 2. An extended examination of this text is in order, since it has so far not received adequate attention and especially since it is Pernette's most profound study of desire. In a poetic fantasy of unusual force and suggestiveness, she imagines herself with her philosopher "... in the heat of summer / Right near the clear fountain" (vv. 2–3). The two elements essential to the traditional pastoral landscape are present, along with their perpetual ambivalence: the cool waters protect the lovers from the heat, but without the latter the waters would lose their freshness. On the psychological level, the cooling pursuits practiced near the fountain, whether of music, poetry, or amorous contemplation, are maintained in delicious tension by the ever-threatening passionate desires of the lovers. She draws as close to the fountain as possible (v. 3), signifying her wish to be

> . . . accompaignée
> D'honnesteté, que Vertu a gaignée
> A Apollo, Muses, et Nymphes maintes,
> Ne s'adonnantz qu'à toutes oeuvres sainctes. [Vv. 9–12]

> . . . in the company
> Of Chastity, which Virtue has won
> From Apollo, the Muses, and many Nymphs,
> All occupied solely with holy works.

The clarity and purity of the waters suggest a second motif: the mirror. To draw close to a clear fountain is to wish to admire one's own beauty, and how better to perform this act than nude. After a long bout with the Muses, the lady slips away from her teacher and from his chastening occupations:

> Là quand j'aurois bien au long veu son cours,
> Je le lairrois faire appart ses discours:
> Puis peu à peu de luy m'escarterois,
> Et toute nue en l'eau me gecterois. [Vv. 13–16]

> Then, when I had thoroughly followed the drift of his discourse
> I would let him carry on alone;
> And, slowly, I would withdraw
> And throw myself into the water all naked.

Her self-concern can be seen in a seemingly total lack of interest in her lover, beyond her curiosity as to how he will react to her nudity.[12] Pernette receives confirmation of her own beauty to the degree that she can subjugate the lover, first through the *regard* and then the touch:

> Mais si vers moy il s'en venoit tout droict,
> Je le lairrois hardyment approcher:
> Et s'il vouloit, tant soit peu, me toucher,
> Lui gecterois (pour le moins) ma main pleine
> De la pure eau de la clere fontaine,
> Lui gectant droict aux yeulx, ou à la face.
>   O qu'alors eust l'onde telle efficace
> De le pouvoir en Acteon muer,
> Non toutefois pour le faire tuer,
> Et devorer à ses chiens, comme Cerf:

Mais que de moy se sensist estre serf,
Et serviteur transformé tellement
Qu'ainsi cuydast en son entendement,
Tant que Diane en eust sur moy envie,
De luy avoir sa puissance ravie.
  Combien heureuse et grande me dirois!
Certes Deesse estre me cuyderois. [Vv. 22–38]

But if he came straight for me,
I would let him boldly approach.
And if he wished to touch me ever so lightly,
I would, at the very least, throw a handful
Of the clear fountain's pure water
Right into his eyes or face.
  Oh, if the water only had the power
To change him into Acteon:
Not to the extent of having him killed
And devoured by his dogs like a stag,
But so that he could feel himself into my slave
And servant transformed to such a degree
That Diana herself would envy
My having ravished his strength.
How great and happy I would be!
Indeed, I would think myself a goddess.

The whole purpose of the temptation scene is to render the lady "contente à mon desir" (v. 39), paradoxically contented with her very desire. From her detached curiosity and her readiness to cool off any attempt to touch her (v. 26), this desire reveals itself as quite different from sensuality. It is rather a radical desire for domination: Narcissus imagines the other to be enslaved by his beauty.

Whatever narcissistic fantasies Pernette's nudity may express, she seems well aware of the consequences for Scève. Remember that Scève is the source of the doctrine of *honneste amour* (v. 10), and that he is presented as being so trustworthy that Pernette can risk being alone with him (vv. 6–8). In consequence, her act of temptation avoids any trace of lewdness. She seems to remain at least partly covered by the clear water that both conceals and reveals—or, rather, that allows for idealistic transformation by the spectator. Her nudity and her song appeal only to the two higher or spiritual senses of sight and hearing. Scève's reactions, delicately presented as hypothetical (vv. 22, 24), nonetheless are separated from the scene of pure seeing and hearing by the abrupt "Mais si. . . " (v. 22). The lover's yielding to the movement of desire is expressed by his direct motion toward his object (v. 22) and by the manner in which he approaches ("boldly," v. 23). All this is permitted, however, unless the lover *wishes* to touch: "s'il vouloit, tant soit peu, me toucher" (v. 24). Of course, the touch is the most material of the senses. But Pernette could easily, had she wanted, have written "s'il . . . me touchait." It does not seem oversensitive to stress that the lover's symbolic purification in the *pure* water of the *clear* fountain or, alternatively, his transformation into Acteon devoured by his hungry passions, is required not so much by actual touching or possession as by the desire to touch.[13] But if the lover does not *desire* to touch the beloved, then the beautiful vision and the song would prolong themselves in an ecstasy of controlled desire that would henceforth be indistinguishable from *affection.* Under such conditions, should the lovers come to perform the act of "touching," but accidentally or without pursuit, then the mysterious state of grace described by Antoine Héroët would apply:

> Que la main touche, ou que la bouche baise,
> Cela n'est pas pour deshonneur compté;
> C'est ung instinct de naifve bonté,
> Si, ce pendant que les maistres jouyssent,
> Les corps qui sont serviteurs s'esjouyssent;
> Et quand des deux la jouyssance advient,
> Prins le plaisir, plus ne leur en souvient.[14]

> If the hand touches or the mouth kisses,
> It is not held a dishonor;
> It is an instinct of natural goodness
> If, while the masters are in joy,
> The bodies—their servants—find enjoyment.
> And when the two have had their enjoyment
> And pleasure is past, gone is the memory of it as well.

Another interpretation of Pernette's motive to be "contente à mon desir" (v. 39) is possible—though less likely—by emphasizing her *contentement,* in the sense already indicated, rather than her narcissistic desire for domination. In this case her transformation into the chaste goddess Diana would signify her attainment of a high level of chastity, again in the sense of mastery of desire rather than of mere sensuality. In a poem that has received little critical attention, Scève takes up the theme of Délie's "nudity":

> Amour des siens trop durement piteux
> Cacha son arc, abandonnant la Terre.
> Delie voit le cas si despiteux,
> Qu'avec Venus le cherche, et le deterre.
>   Garde, luy dist Cypris, qu'il ne t'enferre,
> Comme aultresfois mon coeur l'a bien prouvé.
>   Je ne crains point si petit arc trouvé,
> Respond me Dame haultaine devenue.
> Car contre moy l'Archier s'est esprouvé:
> Mais tout armé l'ay vaincu toute nue. [*Délie* 67]

Love, taking too harsh pity on his followers,
Hid his bow as he was leaving the earth.
Délie judges the case so deserving of pity
That with Venus she seeks and uncovers it.
   "Take care," says Cypris to her, "that he doesn't wound you:
My heart has known such assaults."
   "I don't fear such a tiny bow,"
Answers my Lady, grown haughty.
"For the bowman has tried his skill on me before:
But, fully armed though he was, I conquered totally naked."

If *Amour* means sensuality alone, this is indeed a strange poem. If that were the case, then the chaste Délie would be delighted that *Amour* had abandoned the earth and would consider the situation anything but depressing. The fact is, however, that Délie and *Amour* are not opposites; rather, *Amour* is her servant (*Délie* 63, v. 8). Her conquest of Cupid, therefore, cannot mean his destruction. I suspect that Scève is again playing on words (as in the probable pun in verse 5 on *enferre/enfer*) when he describes Délie's finding of Cupid by the word "deterre": her conquest of *Amour* signifies that the latter is dematerialized. The final verse is then much more than a clever paradox. Délie's nakedness against a fully armed Cupid indicates her mocking lordship over her desires.

Such a doctrine of sensuous chastity, symbolized by the contemplation of nude female beauty, is full of dangers. As far as Pernette is concerned, if our first interpretation of her motives is correct, her narcissistic fantasies create a master/slave relationship that can become destructive of true love, as she recognizes in another poem:

Si je ne suis telle que soulois estre,
Prenez vous en au temps, qui m'a appris
Qu'en me traictant rudement, comme maistre,
Jamais sur moy ne gaignerez le prys. [Epig. 28]

If I am not like I used to be,
You have only time to blame, which has taught me
That by treating me rudely, in a domineering way,
You will never win me over.

The dangers for Scève are of a different order. Even supposing he remains true to his high doctrines and surmounts temptation, such pastimes would prove destructive. Pernette asks:

Vouldrois je bien faire un tel deplaisir
A Apollo, et aussi à ses Muses,
De les laisser privées, et confuses
D'un, qui les peult toutes servir à gré,
Et faire honneur à leur hault choeur sacré? [*Elégie* 2, vv. 40–44]

Would I wish to displease
Apollo and his Muses,
By leaving them upset and deprived
Of one who can serve them all to their liking
And do honor to their high, sacred choir?

Pernette intuited that she was important to Scève more as a source of inspiration than as an object of desire, and that Scève would find his path of spiritual perfection as a poet rather than as a chaste lover.[15] In so judging she also remembered that desire is self-love and thus the opposite of true affection when it is harmful to the other person (not only by inflicting positive harm, of course, but also by impeding his true interests).

I shall now review and extend the distinction between desire and true love. With regards to physical love, it should be clear from the analysis of epigram 12 and *chanson* 6 that the love experience in question is quite removed from the usual notion based on the old antithesis of physical versus Platonic or spiritual love, of sensuality versus chastity. It is misleading to refer to Pernette's idea of love as "incorporeal" or "abstract."[16] Pernette seemed not only to know physical love but also to enjoy it and find it beneficial to the self; just as Leone Ebreo, in somewhat the same vein, observes that physical desires and their fulfillment are "bonds that strengthen love rather than means to dissolve it."[17] Again, the issue is not physical desire but rather desire itself, a more comprehensive concept since it includes, for example, the desire for domination. A further proof of this is the fact that Pernette never denigrates sensual *actions*. Rather, she focuses on the weak heart, seat of the desires; her calls to chastity refer to the chastity of desires, since "he who looks upon a woman with desire (be it even his wife) has already committed adultery with her in his heart, for all desire is adultery."[18]

In true Platonic fashion, the concept of will is unimportant in Pernette. Instead of talk about controlling the passions, there is a steady interest in understanding them. Perhaps the most frequent verbs are "voir et sçavoir" (*chanson* 8, v. 44), verbs of seeing and cognition. What then does one understand? First and foremost, desire and love are distinct, and the first depends on the second. Once this is clearly grasped, then desire is not reprehensible unless it forgets its dependency. Such a condition would manifest itself as a kind of excess:

L'on peult assés en servant requerir,
Sans toutesfois par souffrir acquerir
    Ce que l'on pourchasse
    Par trop desirer . . . [*Chanson* 8, vv. 5–8]

One can very much solicit (by service)
Without, however, acquiring (by suffering)
  What one pursues
  With excessive desire...

Here the rhymed words all describe the nature of desire, which is the pursuit of a remedy:

Pour contenter celuy qui me tourmente,
Chercher ne veulx remede à mon tourment:
Car, en mon mal voyant qu'il se contente,
Contente suis de son contentement. [Epig. 15]

So as to content him who torments me,
I shall seek no remedy to my torment:
For, despite my pain, when I see him content
I am contented with his contentment.

Saulnier comes close to the meaning of this central term *contentement:* "It does not have the modern implication of compromise; rather, it means satisfaction in the fullest sense of the term, as in Leone Ebreo: 'contentment or satisfaction with what is necessary.'"[19] However, in the passage cited, Leone is advocating the peripatetic virtue of moderation, and this also involves a pursuit. The more exact meaning of the term occurs in Leone's following sentence: "And the sages say that the truly rich man is he who is contented with what he has." Perfect contentment has no feeling of lack (the basis of desire) and no impulsion to pursue or dominate or change the beloved:

Je suis tant bien que je ne le puis dire,
Ayant sondé son amytié profonde
Par sa vertu, qui à l'aymer m'attire... [*Epig.* 17, vv. 1–3]

I am happy beyond speech,
Having plumbed his deep friendship by testing
His virtue, which draws me to love him...

Here the only essential activity is knowing, *sondage.* In opposition to excessive desires there arises another kind of "desire":

Mais l'attente mienne
Est le desir sien
D'estre toute sienne,
Comme il sera mien.
Car quand Amour à Vertu est uny
Le cueur conçoit un desir infiny....

Car il luy engendre
Une ardeur de veoir,
Et tousjours apprendre
Quelque hault sçavoir . . . [*Chanson* 8, vv. 21–26, 31–34]

But my goal
Is his desire
That I be all his
As he will be mine.
For when Love is united with Virtue,
The heart conceives an infinite desire. . . .
For it [Love] engenders in it [the heart]
An ardent desire for seeing
And always learning
Some high kind of knowledge.

True understanding of love involves not only abstract doctrine but also
correct application of principle, the ability to distinguish love from desire in
the complex practice of living. The difficulties arise from the fact that love
and desire seem to have the same characteristics. Corresponding to *trop
désirer* there is the excess of *trop espérer:*

Estant ainsi mon espoir asseuré,
Je ne crains point qu'il soit demesuré. [*Chanson* 8, vv. 45–46]

Since my hope is grounded so securely,
I have no fear of its being immoderate.

Also, no less than desire, affection brings suffering, being experienced as a
"sweet martyrdom" (*chanson* 8, v. 29), an "immortal care" (v. 54), and a
"torment" (epig. 15). However, this love brings the conviction that it is
immortal, and, more characteristically, it is always recognizable by its quality
of sweetness, *douceur:*

Je n'oserois le penser veritable
Si ce n'estoit pour un contentement,
Qui faict sentir, et veoir ce bien durable
Par la doulceur, qui en sort seulement.
    De tous les heurs c'est le commencement. [*Epig.* 43, vv. 1–5]

I wouldn't dare think it real,
Were it not for a contentment
That lets me feel and see this lasting good
By the simple sweetness that comes from it.
    It is the starting point of all joys.

Car le tourment, que tu souffres pour elle,
Estre te doit joye continuelle
A ton esprit, et doulx contentement. [*Elégie* 5, vv. 111–13]

   For the torment that you suffer for her
   Must be a continuous joy
   To your spirit, a sweet contentment.

The suffering of love is thus, paradoxically, joyous. Such a state of affairs has one condition, which is both the guarantee of love and its reward: "A fin qu'apparoisse / Mon cueur ferme et fort" (*chanson* 8, vv. 49–50). More than a passing emotion, love is a manifestation of one's inner self: it reveals a faithful and strong heart.

   In the final analysis Pernette's message is so subtle as nearly to escape conceptualization. In this area we as critics guarantee our failure by over-reliance on realistic standards and positivistic information. Pernette's own experience should afford sufficient warning: "As the body doesn't allow us to see / A spirit or know its power... " (epig. 11). Our vulgar inquiries—did she or didn't she, and how often?—tell us nothing, since an act performed out of weakness and pleasure-seeking may also be performed out of abundant strength and virtue. In the perennial idealistic tradition that was Pernette's—whether we call it Neoplatonic or courtly or even humanistic[20]—terms like *savoir*, *vertu*, and *amour* are not conclusions but focal points demanding precise thinking and leading to personal insight through interpretation. Within the perspective of this tradition, Pernette offers us the ideal of an *amour complet*,[21] a love which grants to both body and spirit their full rights and which aims at self-perfection through recognition of the perfection and autonomy of the beloved.

Chapter 6
Erotic Experiment and Androgynous Integration: Héroët's Poetry

Pernette du Guillet's elaborate temptation scene in the second elegy, culminating in her transfiguration into the sensuously chaste Diana, was both a contrived test of Scève's Platonic philosophy and an important instance of a new attitude in France in the 1540s. When, for example, the saintly Marguerite de Navarre boasted that she would not at all be shocked to look upon a naked man,[1] she thereby expressed her sympathy for the same philosophy. The most open advocate for the new eroticism was the future Bishop of Digne, the poet Antoine Héroët, whose influence on his generation was accurately captured by two puns on his name: heroic and erotic.[2] His best-known work, the *Parfaicte Amye* (1542), marked his entry into the *Querelle des Amies* (the famous debate on love and ladies) by a call to arms: "Dames . . . , Veillez, vivez, incessamment aymez" (*Amye*, v. 1116)! Ladies must live and love, and not only ardently but provocatively.

Héroët's critical popularity has lagged so far behind his literary merit that it is hardly an exaggeration to call him the most neglected of important French Renaissance poets. A flurry of interest occurred at the turn of the century with Gohin's edition of the *Oeuvres poétiques*, but even this and Larbaud's sensitive essay could not overcome three centuries of oblivion.[3] One reason for this critical neglect was already sensed by the seventeenth-century critic Guillaume Colletet, when he detected in Héroët's works "a mood contrary to ours, a courtly, old-fashioned atmosphere."[4] This quality is not primarily a matter of diction, although Héroët is resolutely plain in his poetic manner—anti-Petrarchan, he called it; rather, it may be explained by a vibrant narrative personality that perfectly embodies the poet's peculiar Platonism and that seems strange only because its type has passed from our literary environment. Larbaud's portrait of the *parfaite amie* is as suggestive as one could wish:

> Composed, refined, stubborn in her fidelity, and in a better structured society the best of wives and the "angel of the house" . . . . Sensible, not at all a "grande amoureuse" in the romantic manner but as a dutiful woman. . . . Her love is

reliable, attentive, delicate as much as and more than a man's friendship; and this is more than her lover had hoped, who thought only of his own pleasures.[5]

Recalling the sturdy virtues of Clément Marot's good old days, the *amie* evokes that "fine flower of old-fashioned modesty" that George Sand was able to render in her best writing[6] and that would have delighted mystical sentimentalists such as Nerval and Alain-Fournier.

It is clear, however, that the *Parfaicte Amye* had quite another appeal to gentlemen and especially ladies in the 1540s, and this factor is apt to make the work uninteresting for just the opposite reason: its familiarity, which may be attributed both to its reasonable tone and to its peculiarly modern, common-sense insistence on the importance of experience.[7] We tend to be unimpressed by the *amie*'s good sense until we reflect that common sense is the least common of virtues, at least among lovers and their poets. In short, what is distinctive in Héröet's writing is a peculiar blending of old-fashioned chastity and good sense with a third and revolutionary note (and it is here that the filiation with Leone Ebreo may be seen): a reasoned but ardent call to erotic experience.

Love's Exercises

As a path to sexual integration, erotic experimentation—flirtation with sex rather than, primarily, with a person—is extremely rare in the literature of the period, and it is all the more surprising that the following instance, recorded by Marguerite de Navarre in her *Heptaméron*, has not received more comment. As the story goes, ecclasiastical authorities in Milan were informed of a certain community of monks who

> claim that man must train himself in the virtue of chastity, and, to try out their strength, they speak with the loveliest ladies that can be found and that they love the best; and, with kisses and touching of hands, they experiment to see whether their flesh is completely mortified. And if they find themselves moved by such pleasures, they separate, fast and undertake very great penances. And when they have subdued their flesh to this degree and are no longer moved to speak with their ladies or kiss them, they then undergo the strong temptation of sleeping together and embracing without any concupiscence.[8]

Coitus interruptus was hardly a new phenomenon, but it appears not to have been an important ascetic exercise since the Albigensians. The comparison seems appropriate, since in both instances a stoical control of sexual desires was intended. However, the necessary condition—and, secretly, the desired result[9]—of such mastery was the tortured exacerbation of the desire itself, thus revealing the deep metaphysical and psychological motivations of an artificially intensified witholding of vital fluids: on the one hand, a pervasive pessimism concerning love, marriage, and the creation itself; on the other, the desire to cultivate states of ecstasy. Recent apologists of Tantra, the Indian counterpart to Albigensian sexual asceticism, have tried to vulgarize the notion of "ecstasy" by making it synonymous with sexual delight itself, extended through prolonged erection and other such techniques.[10] It seems likely, however, that "ecstasy" is to be taken in its etymological sense as a separation or detachment of the self from the realm of suffering, with the result that the psychological motivation corresponds faithfully to the metaphysical pessimism that supports it.

Héroët stands in sharp contrast to such Albigensian doctrines. He approves the sensual pleasures that induce us to propagate the human race, his attitude toward Nature is optimistic, and he even praises blind Cupid for giving us wings to fly to heaven.[11] Other important differences are that the cultural groups just mentioned seem to have functioned as communities with prescribed techniques, whereas Héroët's *amie* speaks only for herself and with deliberate ambiguity about specifics. She does indeed belong to the elite and secret society of "friends," but the term designates a human type rather than an organized group. We are struck, however, by Héroët's peculiar doctrine of exercises. The following passage captures the essential point:

> Si nous craignons que Volupté destruyse
> Le bon de nous et le plus precieux,
> Vaincre nous fault Cupido l'ocieux
> Par ung louable et plaisant exercice,
> Suyvant plus tost nature que malice....
> Affin q'un cueur en soit vainqueur et maistre,
> Il fault sa fin et ses moiens congnoistre. [*Douleur* 140–44, 147–48]

> If we fear that sensuality may destroy
> What is best and most precious in us,
> Then we must conquer lazy Cupid
> By a praiseworthy and pleasurable exercise,
> Following nature rather than malice....
> To conquer and rule over him,
> A heart must know his aim and methods.

Even though the *amie* rejects the moderation of the ancients as something exceeding her strength (*Amye* 643 ff.), there are traces here of stoical pride in a conquering heart. This is compensated, however, by an extraordinary sense of ease and serenity,[12] the view that our battles or exercises with pleasure are like a game:

> Pour acquerir le repoz que je loue,
> Fault q'un chacun de Volupté se joue. [*Douleur* 199–200]

> To acquire the peace that I praise,
> One must take sensuality as a game.

Similarly, when misfortunes strike, "you shouldn't avoid them / But rather take them as a game and exercise yourselves on them" (*Douleur* 121–22). Specifically referring to the pleasures of love, Héroët observes that with the first arrows of love

> Viennent soulas, envyes et desirs,
> S'offrent baisers, approches et plaisirs,
> Que ne devez à l'amy reffuser,
> Mais prendre en jeu. [*Douleur* 153–56]

> [From Cupid's first arrow] come relief, yearnings and desires;
> The *ami* offers kisses, embraces and pleasures
> That you must not refuse him
> But rather take as games.

The ambiguity of such exercises and of their pleasures presupposes circumstances of unusual delicacy and freedom. For example, the lady is advised to seek out

> ... lieux secretz où l'on se peult jouer
> Loing du danger d'estrange compaignye.
> Fault qu'à l'amy de son ame se fye,
> Ayant espoir, *s'elle s'advanturoit*,
> Que la fortune et le feu dureroit. [*L'Honneur des femmes* 32–36, p. 146]

> ... secret places where one can play around,
> Far from the danger of strangers.
> She must have trust in the friend of her soul,
> With the hope that, *should she decide to take a risk*,
> Good fortune and desire would last.

To arrive at such a state of perfection the apprentice is told to imitate the lady's virtues one by one, beginning with the use of caresses (v. 61), and this will somehow be a show of chastity:

> Ainsi faisant preuve de chasteté,
> Cherchant honneur par labeur et fortune,
> A qui plus près du bout aura esté
> Vous donnerez louenge moins commune. [*L'Honneur des femmes* 63–66]

> Having thus given proof of chastity
> And sought honor through toil and fortune,
> To that person who has come nearest the goal
> You will give uncommon praise.

One may translate "près du bout" as "reaching the goal" of chastity or perfection, but the phrase is an instance of Héroët's ambiguity: she deserves uncommon praise who walks nearest the edge, the brink, without falling in.

Héroët's notion of exercises may best be rendered as experimentation, directed experience. Those studied thus far are to be performed in the presence of the *ami;* they involve both loving attention to his person and, in an erotic context, unspecified kinds of flirtation. There are, in addition, exercises to be carried out in the beloved's absence, and their importance to the success of *amitié* is such that the *Parfaicte Amye* could have been subtitled "les méditations d'amitié" (*Amye*, v. 1500). Their importance is derived from the fact that, while love originates in the stars, its preservation depends on human art and effort, and, in the absence of the beloved, the effort is entirely self-directed and internal. Specifically, if the food of love is *pensée*, the proper sustenance of a noble love is a pure thought, one which is selfless in that it is directed intensely and entirely toward the beloved (*Amye* 116–17). The effect of such deep meditation is "the transformation of the lover into the beloved" (Leone, *Dialoghi*, p. 222):

> . . . noz cueurs à mourir incités
> Se soient l'ung l'aultre entreressuscités,
> Comme le mien aymant au sien aymé
> Ayt, sans changer, sa forme transformé. [*Amye* 127–30]

> [I meditated upon] how our hearts, bent on "death,"
> Revived one another;
> How mine, loving his,
> Transformed itself into his without changing.

For Héroët as well as for Scève, *amitié* is the highest philosophy because it is the exercise of dying that death of selfhood that is well known to readers of Leone and the *Phaedo*. The initiate does not suffer these deaths as passions, however, but through them prepares his total psychic and human integration.

The *Androgyne*

The concept of erotic experiment leading to reintegration is elucidated in the *Androgyne*, a free translation and adaptation of Aristophanes' fable in the *Symposium*. In the springtime of creation, Héroët tells us, there were three kinds of humans: simple men and women such as still exist, and a composite creature having an integrated male and female nature. The first two still people the earth; they are the normal run of mankind,

> Qui simplement de touts temps simples furent,
> Qui oncq amour ny aultre scavoir n'eurent
> Que consommer les biens qui sont sus terre.
> Ils sont grand nombre et nays à faire guerre. [*Androgyne*, vv. 279–82]

Who simply were simple from the beginning of time;
Who never had any love or skill to do anything
Except consume the earth's riches.
They are great in number and born to wage war.

"Simple" is contrasted with the double nature of the androgyne, but it carries the disdainful overtone of "simpleminded"; these are the "consumers" who waste the earth's treasures and who, because of their ignorance and desires, pose a constant threat of aggression. The third race was made up of rational and self-sufficient beings, each having a double portion of heads, arms, feet, and other members "better thought than said" (v. 151), but this androgynous human type took such pride in its divine perfection that Jupiter caused it to be split into two halves, thus resembling the other two kinds of men. The high form of love that motivates the reunion of the androgyne is called *amitié*, defined simply as the "recovery of one's lost half" (v. 228).

The danger of confusing *amitié* with lesser forms of love is ever present and arises from not knowing how to choose (*Androgyne* v. 230). Thus, since our natural desire is for beauty and since mistakes are attributed to ignorance rather than malice, it is permissible to change partners because, again, it is natural to do so (vv. 257–62). The remedy for our natural weaknesses is to put them to proper advantage by plunging into experience and, through trial and error, arriving at one's proper mate:

Après aussi que les recouvrements
Nous avons faicts *par divers changements*
Et chascun vient à la recongnoissance
De sa moytié *par longue experience,*
Soubdain toute aultre alliance s'oublie
Et le vray neud deslié se relie. [Vv. 263–68]

Also, after we have made recovery,
Through various exchanges,
And each succeeds in recognizing
His other half, *through long experiment:*
Suddenly all other attachments are forgotten,
And the true knot—now loosened—is retied.

Such a recovery justifies not only errors of judgment but even "fickleness of will in the past" (v. 270).

In this level of interpretation, which we may call amorous, erotic acquaintance was justified either by the intrinsic value of "experience" or by the fact that two persons were "meant for each other," as we say, since all descendants of the androgyne share the same fate (vv. 211–12). To further his apology for *amitié* Héröet attaches what he calls a more "philosophical" exegesis of the myth. By way of transition the poet says that love is so subtle a flame that it seems to have been sent from heaven "to awaken dormant spirits" (v. 298). Indeed, the androgyne myth itself seems intended to reveal "the soul in this unclean world / And divine love through the love of this world" (vv. 305–6). The two parts of the androgyne are now interpreted as the two "lights" of the human soul, one natural and the other infused by the Creator. The poor little soul ("la povrette") found itself so overwhelmed by such wealth that it became proud and was divided. In the life of the individual this shock occurs at birth and the restoration can begin at adolescence (v. 321), when the absence of the upper half begins to be felt. God Himself is said to favor such self-recovery or discovery, and this process of reintegration is also termed as *amitié*, analogous to that between man and woman:

> ... O heureuse amytié!
> O grand malheur d'estre au corps trebuchée!
> O quel soulas de s'estre tant cherchée
> Que, pour demye, entiere se rencontre! [*Androgyne* 336–39]

> O happy friendship!
> What a misfortune to have stumbled into a body!
> What solace, to have so sought one's self
> That, though half, one finds one's self whole!

Paradoxically, whereas the reunion of man and woman was motivated primarily by a search for beauty, our personal reintegration is to be achieved "in goodness alone" (v. 357). The discrepancy seems lightened when we recall that for Héroët, as well as for Leone Ebreo, beauty is an aspect of goodness.[13] However, when Héroët complains that it is the action of "giving so much pleasure to one's natural being" (v. 349) that causes us to abandon infused grace and leads us away from God (v. 366), he seems to advocate not only a return to God but a denial of natural pleasures as well.

These apparent ascetic tendencies can be clarified by reference to Leone Ebreo's rich exploration of the androgyne myth, with which Héroët's own exegesis has much in common.[14] Like Héroët, Leone does not direct his interest to the dualism of body and soul; rather, he speaks of the soul's tendencies toward spirit and matter. Further, in spite of Leone's clear intellectualistic bias, the thrust of his thought is integrative rather than dualistic: intellectual contemplation is probably beyond our powers and, at any rate, distracts us from our human duties in this world. This allows Leone to develop a positive theology of human action in which normal sensual pleasures, sexual love, and such lower faculties as fantasy have a legitimate and necessary place in the universe. The error consists not of using and enjoying such things but rather of their disproportionate use and enjoyment.

Returning to Héroët, I do not think it possible to view him as a contemplative advocate of a Platonic return to heaven while still in this life. His use of the androgyne myth is entirely integrative, on both intra- and inter-personal levels, and a return to God would have to include—if not to stress—an interest in His creation, "this precious world" (*Amye* 1158). In the same way, to say that it is a mistake "to give so much pleasure to one's natural being / As to dare to relinquish infused grace" (*Androgyne* 349–50) is rather a condemnation of excess and improper integration than a denial of natural pleasures. Indeed, within the perspective of a wider integration—where the androgynous reunion seems to offer a glimpse of "divine love through the love of this world"—it even becomes possible to assert that "the soul in the body is contented" (*Amye*, v. 950).

Héroët's Personalism

Notwithstanding these analogical extensions, which were to become commonplace for all of Leone Ebreo's followers, Héroët's work remains a hothouse experiment in which a single dimension of the androgyne—the primary, amorous sense—is explored in depth. There is no better sign of this than the *amie*'s reduction of the cosmos to the dimensions of her companion: her "all the world," as she calls him (*Amye* 1277, 1296). Thus, the workings of the heavens become worthy of interest only after the *ami* has died and assumed the body of a star (*Amye* 997 ff.). Even the crucial process of self-knowledge has no intrinsic worth; it is derived mediately, through reflection of the self in the beloved, and its value lies in preserving the androgynous relationship intact (*Amye* 1316 ff.). As a result of such intensified isolation, the reunited androgyne moves in a closed system with its own laws, to such a degree that even the gods are excluded from its intimacies.[15] As opposed to the terrifying depth and height of Scève's poetic universe, his need both to plumb the "heavens and the center" and to describe these experiences—not, of course, to the vulgar crowd but to his mistress and himself—Héroët's *amie* remains closed and secretive, deliberately witholding part of what she knows. Such *pudeur* is of course only secondarily motivated by social realities; its real force is derived from the nature of love itself, a reality *sui generis* whose only law is to love "lovingly," detached from any extraneous cause.

The requirement of *pudeur*, or reserve, is taken up in an interesting way with reference to the public disclosure of love through poetry (this suggests that for Héroët there is an aesthetics as well as an ethics of *pudeur*). This is how the *amie* justifies her reluctance to say too much about her love or her lover:

> Ce que j'en sçay, je ne le veulx redire;
> Car le disant, je pourrois trop induire
> A vouloir suyvre amour, qui ne permect
> Qu'on le retienne en lieu, s'il ne s'y mect;
> Et qui l'y tient, son feu luy cuict et deult. [*Amye* 557–61]

What I know I do not wish to repeat;
For in saying it I could give too much encouragement
To follow Love, who permits no one
To hold him down unless he [Love] wishes.
And whoever does hold him down suffers hot, painful desire.

This shows a strong awareness that love is free and that any violence, any attempt to hold it down—by words, for example—would produce a counter-reaction. Such is the technique of Petrarchists, those "heavy persuaders" who fancy that suffering (whether real or contrived poetically) can be used to persuade the beloved, whereas its only real value is as experience leading to a fuller knowledge of the other and of one's self. Stated differently, the error common to Petrarchists and bad lovers is their wish to "reckon as service / What they should have performed as exercises" (*Amye* 1559-60). Héroët's rejection of such a conception of service is to be viewed as an opposition to the courtly love relation of mistress to slave; in fact, the equality of lovers is in Héroët's view a central lesson of the androgyne myth (*Amye* 1228-33).

By way of contrast, Scève's lady does avoid this courtly attribute, only to fall into a no less hierarchical scheme: instead of the tyrannical lady, she is the incarnation of a higher power and as such is not so much to be worshipped as admired and feared: "O fear of pleasurable terrors" (*Délie* 1). For if *Délie* has escaped the religion of love, it is only at the cost of a love that has lost some of its human feeling. Délie cannot be described as without pity since this would imply merely cruel behavior, the usual attribute of ladies who appear in poems addressed to them. Rather, she is *by nature* merciless, an unmoved mistress of her passions, possessing the coldness of a perfected being and, by that very attribute, lacking human warmth. How much closer to us is Héroët's *amie*, the angel of the house.

Héroët's strikingly modern apology of experience, as well as his feminism, represent an historically new kind of humanism that has led one critic to prefer a more recent term:

> I refer to neither their eclectic humanism, nor their encyclopedic knowledge, nor their so-called Platonism. . . . On the contrary, for the first time in France the Lyonese poets deliberately set out to create not so much a subjective literature as a *personal literature*.[16]

The major importance of this development for literature was the discovery of the beloved as an autonomous personality that cannot be subdued or dis-solved away by elevation to the highest heavens (e.g., the Petrarchists) or consignment to the blackest hell (e.g., Etienne Jodelle) through the various metaphoric transmutations known to poets.[17] Héroët helped restore the courtly idea of love but with an entirely positive valuation. Predestined to the Isle of the Blessed (*Amye* 1044 ff.), where bliss depends on the quality of one's inner life rather than on the goodness of one's actions, his reintegrated androgyne already basks in a paradise of innocence, for, the *amie* asks with surprising candor, "can a good man ever do evil?" (*Amye* 787). To the degree that the Lyonese poets project a sense both of human intersubjectivity and of love's sovereign innocence, Héroët is their theoretician and, on both counts, the real French forerunner of John Donne's lyrics on mutual love.

Chapter 7
Ideal Love and Human Reality: Montemayor's Pastoral Philosophy

The Pastoral

The cardinal sin of positivistic criticism was to forget that art is a function of intention, that if Romanesque sculpture or Indian icons are "unrealistic," this shows not ignorance or inability but simply a desire to do something else. These attitudes were especially inappropriate when applied to those great medieval works of mythology and contemplation, of which Jorge de Montemayor's *Los siete libros de la Diana* (1559) is a worthy descendant.[1] Only recently has it been possible to reconsider such charges against the pastoral as "artificial," "extravagant," and "confused." It is now time to suggest the noble profundities of the first and best Spanish pastoral romance.

It has been observed that the pastoral "device" is particularly useful in the study of the complex emotion of love. Mia Gerhardt writes that Montemayor "used the pastoral only insofar as it allowed him to expose the condition of love in its pure state, so to speak."[2] The otiose shepherds of *La Diana* have no social or economic cares that might complicate the free expression of their sentiments. Such abstraction from "real" or material existence and the concomitant idealization of scene and character permit another kind of concentration as well: full aesthetic immersion into the emotions depicted. From this perspective the novel is a sustained contemplation of the mournful pains of love and yields a direct knowledge of, as well as about, love. The characters and situations convey a feeling about existence, a persistence and expansion of emotion. As Sylvano says of his love: "relating my love causes it to increase" (*La Diana*, p. 31). Especially the first half of the novel (books 1–3) may be viewed as an extended complaint over the sorrows of unrequited love. In Montemayor's language of love, it is often music that carries and extends emotion: "music can increase both the affliction of an unhappy person and the joy of a happy person" (*La Diana*, p. 229). The novel alternates between slow, spacious, rhythmical prose and verse experiments that, far from introducing new materials or advancing the action, simply repeat and elaborate what has occurred, but as emotion. The shepherds' song has an ambivalent effect, however: "there is no pain that music cannot dispel, nor sadness that it does not cause to increase" (*La Diana*, p. 30). The singer is removed from the action-world of the prose, where love is suffered as a *mal*, and introduced into a realm of noble sadness that heightens the sorrow of love and transmutes it into something to be contemplated, as a thing detached.

Myth and History

The poetic quality wherein daily suffering subsists as painless contemplation suggests a substratum of consciousness that may appropriately be termed mythical. Flowing beneath and unifying the various concrete episodes and particulars, the pastoral setting sponsors the myth of timeless, universal, idyllic nature. In this respect J. B. Avalle-Arce sees Montemayor's novel as a "desire to harmonize Poetry and History, the two thematical and antithetical poles of Neoaristotelian poetics."[3] The poetic pastoral setting, he continues (Avalle-Arce, pp. 78–80), is from time to time interrupted by interpolated narratives: Selvagia's tale more or less abandons the idyllic world of shepherds and takes place in a Portuguese village; Arsileo's courtship of Belisa is carried out in a Spanish town; and, finally, the author revisits Coimbra and even presents bits of dialogue in Portuguese. Such insertions of nonpoetic (in terms of Neoaristotelian criticism) materials expanded the pastoral form and must be regarded as an advance in narrative art (Avalle-Arce, p. 81). Nevertheless, the experiment, at least in *La Diana*, was only a partial success. History and myth remain antithetical, with the result that "the different vital spheres remain to a large degree self-enclosed. The shepherds are no more than passive spectators watching the bustling spectacle of these vital forces from the isolated and ideal watchtower of their pastoral condition. The tide of life passes by without touching them" (Avalle-Arce, p. 81).

The fault with such a view—beyond its prejudice for the historical—is based on its failure to observe the pervasiveness of historical materials in *La Diana* and the way they are fused, not merely juxtaposed, with pastoral elements. The very opening sentence ("Baxaba de las montañas de León el olvidado Sireno... "), which places a pastoral character into a real locality, is symptomatic. Similarly, the city of Coimbra has a legendary counterpart in Montemôr-o-Velho (*La Diana*, p. 287). The reader is forewarned of such blending of the real and the poetic: in his synopsis of book 1 Montemayor announces "many different stories of cases that really happened, although they are masked behind pastoral names and style." A curious example of the fusion of myth and reality—expressed in an ironic mode—may be seen in the very title of the novel. One eventually wonders to which Diana the title refers, the goddess or Sireno's beloved. The goddess herself never appears in person, yet the entire novel is doctrinally and structurally centered on her temple (book 4). The other Diana is the more logical choice, yet she doesn't appear in person until the second half of book 5. Moreover, she represents a fallen ideal; through her infidelity to Sireno she is conspicuously absent from those admitted to the temple of her chaste patroness. The name "Diana" thus represents the two poles of virtue, the ideal and the unrealized particular. If it is difficult to deny the title to the earthly Diana, each mention of the name is a disturbing reminder of the tension between mythical perfection and reality.[4]

Another example of this tendency is the description of the Temple of Diana, with its column commemorating famous warriors of old. Legendary and mythological figures mingle freely with national and historic heroes: Mars, Scipio, Bernardo del Carpio, El Gran Capitán. A lengthy song follows in praise of contemporary Spanish women noted for their beauty and virtue. The eulogy is performed by the legendary Orpheus, who says he will omit the tale of his own loves in order to sing of "those that confer noble valor upon Spain" (La Diana, p. 180). The sentimental is easily transmuted into the epic-national.[5] Even more noteworthy is the description of the fabulous palace of Felicia, Diana's priestess. Its sumptuous artificiality is reminiscent of medieval visions of the supernatural, and yet "it seemed more a work of Nature than of art or human industry" (La Diana, p. 165). It is impossible to say where human effort ends and nature's gifts begin. This, then, is the basic paradigm: art and nature, history and myth, where both have equal (or indeterminate) value and become, in fact, indistinguishable. It is thus one-sided to view the pastoral as a "pastorilización" of reality, much less as a "desrealización."[6] A constant feature of the novel, the intimate fusion of real and mythical elements is also the necessary clue to Montemayor's anthropology and doctrine of love.

Superhuman Love: The Influence of Leone Ebreo

Much has been said, in moralistic tones worthy of Gil Polo's continuation Diana Enamorada, of the pessimistic doctrine of love in La Diana.[7] It is therefore paradoxical that the central episode of the book is a pilgrimage to the temple of Diana, goddess of chastity who grants happiness to her faithful. If love is irrational and fatalistic, how can it lead to happiness? And how is it possible to speak of virtue, based, in any meaningful sense of the term, on free will and personal merit?

Though its effects are obvious to all, love, in Montemayor's view, is a profound mystery. All love except the nymphs, yet only Felicia is able to pronounce the doctrine, the true understanding. This is why Felicia's explanation is taken almost word for word from Leone Ebreo: truth is not a matter of opinion but of authority; since it is the property of none, it may become available to all initiates, according to the ability and merit of each. Felicia's monologue is followed by no discussion and allows only acquiescence in the mystery. Sireno says simply: "Wise Lady, I am satisfied in what I wished to know and believe that I shall again in the future be satisfied—given your clear understanding—in whatever I could wish you to explain, although it would require a mind more extensive than mine to grasp the abundant wealth that your words contain" (*La Diana*, pp. 198–99).

Following Leone Ebreo, Montemayor argues that true love is born of reason, but lovers soon "leave off loving themselves—which is contrary to reason and natural justice" (*La Diana*, p. 196). To be born of reason means two things: (1) the "razón del conocimiento" (*La Diana*, p. 195) that perceives the beloved's *mérite;* (2) man's natural instinct of self-preservation, according to which it is reasonable "that life may lawfully be preserved" (*La Diana*, p. 198). That is to say, in its origins love seeks the well-being of the lover as well as that of the beloved.

Critics tend to judge the evolution of love from its effects rather than its fruits: extreme pain and hatred of self approaching despair. This is perhaps due to the author's own insistence, as we shall see. It is clear, however, that such danger to the self is to be seen not as a misfortune but as a blessing. Felicia emphasizes the reasonableness of such love:

> If the love which a lover feels for his Lady, even if burning with excessive affection, is born of reason and true knowledge and judgment—I mean that he judges her worthy of being loved solely for her virtues [i.e., the first sense of reason]—then that love (in my view, and I am not mistaken) is not unlawful or dishonest. For every love of this type aims only at *loving that person for herself alone,* with no hope of further gain or reward for his love. [*La Diana*, p. 198]

Such love, which breaks beyond the self and leads to self-sacrifice, is no different from the generous love of virtue or love for God (*La Diana*, p. 197).[8] Such is the love of those many who "solely out of love for their friends lost their lives and all that goes with it" (*La Diana*, p. 198). The so-called irrationality of love, when understood as defined, can hardly be construed as a fault.[9]

The Temple of Diana is a school of perfection from which the bestial (the three *salvajes*) and the unfaithful (Diana) are excluded. The "good love" that all initiates are required to observe is inscribed over the entrance, in words that resound with superhuman virtue:

> Quien entra, mire bien cómo a bivido
> y el don de castidad, si le a guardado
> y la que quiere bien o lo a querido
> mire si a causa de otro se a mudado.
>
> Y si la fe primera no a perdido
> y aquel primer amor a conservado
> entrar puede en el templo de Diana
> cuya virtud y gracia es sobrehumana. [P. 165, vv. 20–27]

Whoever enters here, let her consider her past conduct
And the gift of chastity—whether she has kept it.
And she who loves well or did love well,
Let her consider if she changed her love because of someone else.

And if she has not lost her first faith
And has preserved that first love of hers,
Then she may enter the temple of Diana,
Whose virtuous grace is superhuman.

There are, it seems, two categories of chastity.[10] In the first are the nymphs, those mythical beings who have been touched by neither selfish desire nor experience. They are the permanent servants of the goddess of chastity and are permitted to live within her sanctuary. Their naive inexperience is criticized by those whom love has wounded (e.g., Sylvano, *La Diana*, p. 200), but their exquisite purity and discretion place them on a totally different plane of existence. Their absolute chastity signifies total selflessness and total noninvolvement in love (physical and emotional). In the second category of the virtuous are those who desire and love and yet have remained chaste in their emotions—that is to say, they have remained faithful to the object of their love even when fulfillment and happiness are impossible.

It is small wonder that such love is felt to confer an extraordinary nobility on the lover. Two factors define the lover's virtue: what he is and what he does. The latter is the domain of acquired virtue, due to the free exercise of effort. What a person is may be defined by his inheritance. For Montemayor both acquired and innate—but especially the latter—are virtues. Felicia declares that good lovers must have "a generous spirit and a delicate understanding, a lively judgment, high-minded thoughts, and other virtues *that are born with them*" (*La Diana*, p. 170). Like love itself, chastity is a gift. Man does not become chaste simply because he wills it, nor, by the same token, is this virtue entirely beyond his grasp. Rather, once the gift has been received, his own doing consists in preserving it intact: "y el don de castidat, *si le a guardado.*" These gifts of birth are provided by Nature herself and are felt to be superior even to those that fortune can bestow. Sylvano ascribes Diana's unhappiness to the fact that "Delio, her husband, though well supplied with fortune's favors, is not with Nature's" (*La Diana*, p. 30).

Several ideological patterns emerge. Just as the pastoral is the flowing center from which all particular events arise, or just as Felicia's doctrine is, as it were, the *noumenon* that explains and elevates all manifestations of love, in the same way virtue presupposes an innate capacity which may or may not be actualized by circumstance and human effort. The temple of Diana is a mirror of the noble soul; the fusion of nature and art reflects, on the human level, the mysterious blending of innate and "artificial" or acquired virtues. But such an aristocratic conception of man (whether racial or, as here, sentimental aristocracy) depends on the richness of the "given." The aristocrat is integrally noble from the start; his duty is not to become good but simply to remain true to himself, his gifts. This demands no renouncement of his passions (since, being his, they are good), but rather a complete fidelity to them. It is as unthinkable for Belisa or Felismena to stop loving as for Corneille's Don Rodrigue, for example, to refuse to bear arms against the Moors. Indeed, to the exalted lovers of *La Diana* the existence and expression of their love seem more important than its fulfillment. Arsenio begs his mistress "not to cure my pain but rather to see how I feel it" (*La Diana*, p. 139), while Arsileo complains not of love but of fortune, which prevents him from "showing off my pain" (*La Diana*, p. 153). Montemayor's lovers instinctively display themselves to others, their pride in their natural emotions is inseparable from a social context. [11]

The Socialization of Love

Ideals are seldom realities. Felicia's high doctrine is exemplified to varying degrees of perfection because "cada uno habla según su estado," every man speaks and acts according to his nature. Although both bestiality and infidelity may mark the fall from chastity to selfishness, in *La Diana* this occurs more usually in the form of a socialization of the love ethic. Man, the social animal, works for the approval of his fellows, socialization occurring when this, rather than the intrinsic goodness of any particular action, becomes the goal of behavior. In such a case, virtuous acts are viewed as titles of superiority; man takes pride in rising above his fellows and in being admired for it.

The evolution in literary taste in the second half of the sixteenth century from the romances of chivalry to the pastoral suggests an upgrading of love in social mores. In *La Diana* this change is reflected in the elevation of love to heroic dimensions, equal and perhaps even superior to arms. The gallery of famous men and ladies in the temple of Diana serves as a house of fame for chaste lovers as well as valiant knights. The frequent comparison of Venus with Mars has the same meaning: Belisa, for example, is favored by skill in arms as a sort of consolation prize because of her predicted misfortunes with love.

The intent of this high valuation of love is obvious. If noble manners are necessary to love, the converse is also true: love is a proof of nobility. On the one hand, virtue is said to depend on family ancestry: "persons of high birth will be the best lovers."[12] Montemayor's feelings are more truly stated, however, in Sylvano's reluctance to seek the source of valor and virtue "from a source other than the person himself," since "he who goes looking for nature's gifts among his ancestors must be considerably deprived of these from the start" (*La Diana*, p. 171). Innate nobility is disassociated from race and family and depends only on the person himself. [13]

If the noble's virtue is given, he must nonetheless uphold and prove it. The compulsion is especially strong in the case of aristocracy of the feelings, since these are not obvious nor do they entail automatic acceptance as such by the community, as is the case with racial or family aristocracy. Proof occurs in the form of a trial. Now, in appearance, the plots of the various love episodes are of the banal sort worthy of the *roman d'aventure:* the lovers desire union and happiness but are thwarted by external circumstances (absence, fate). Under the sign of the socialization of love, however, the very difficulties the lovers undergo are, paradoxically, necessary to love's existence as a virtue. The unspeakable pains of love, its irrationality, its alliance with fate and time—all these, when surmounted, confer the glory of heroic virtue: "the best are they who suffer most" (*La Diana,* p. 167).[14] They suffer most who not only experience present loss of the beloved but especially permanent loss. It is hardly by chance that all the major lovers introduced in the first half of the novel face the impossibility of happiness. Belisa believes Arsileo to be dead and still remains faithful to her love for him. Similarly, though Felismena is deserted by her lover Felis, she follows him and, in disguise, even helps him to win the hand of another lady. Note that the chastity which proves the disinterest of the lovers does not reduce the pains of love but rather requires them as continued proof of its existence.

Whenever in doubt the knight could always reassert his valor in a good joust or battle. For the hero of love the availability of a worthy trial was more subject to circumstance. An author can imagine any number of ways to keep lovers apart. The Byzantine novel might have suggested such extranarrative tricks as robbers or storms at sea, just as Montemayor's solution to the problem of love, the sleep potion, is also said to be a *deus ex machina.* It is to Montemayor's credit, however, that the love problems (and their solutions) are not extraneous but arise from the depths of the characters themselves. In other words, insofar as the trial of love is motivated by the proud desire for fame, its difficulty appears in the form of a *willed* impossibility. Felismena's pursuit of Felis is a clear example of this. It is more than plausible that Felismena subconsciously desires the unfaithfulness of Felis (thus making her love impossible of fulfillment, and thus testing or proving her worth). If not, why then did she disguise herself as a page and actually work toward the destruction of Felis's love for her? To assume that this is pure selflessness is to strain credibility, or rather to state a half-truth. Felismena truly desires Felis's happiness, even if it be with another woman, but it is also only under these very conditions that Felismena can prove her heroic fidelity.

The paradoxical nature of Felismena's love is obvious; her pursuit of her lover to her own detriment arouses our instinctive distrust. More subtle is Belisa's love for Arsileo, where Montemayor presents a parallel and more fully documented case but conceals it beneath a veil of dream and magic. Belisa's behavior is best explained as symbolic projections of desires she dares not admit publicly (willed impossibility). Before studying her case in detail, however, it is necessary to reexamine the role of the supernatural in the novel.

The one thing about *La Diana* that has upset nearly everyone is the sleep potion that Felicia administers as a cure for lovesickness. Cervantes' priest (*Quijote*, part 1, chapter 6) simply censures this section of the novel, while the critic J. B. Avalle-Arce sees it as a *deus ex machina* (*La novela pastoril española*, p. 64), a sign of Montemayor's failure in dealing with reality.[15] Others have seen the potion as a kind of allegorical allusion to purely natural processes. Thus, Otis Green (*Spain and the Western Tradition*, vol. 2, p. 328) takes the potion to mean that the pain of love is temporary. A more satisfactory interpretation is hinted at by Gustavo Correa when he reminds us of the depth of the shepherds' sleep. In my view the potion is a cluster of universal symbols that the mind, in a dreamlike haze of poetic knowing, spontaneously revives to illuminate and cope with a particular situation. The liquid potion signifies a desire to purge and renew; water washes away, liquefies the hardened configurations of our destinies, restores the feeling of possibility. As Heraclitus would have it, all things begin in water. The sleep is that of oblivion; it signifies the indeterminacy of the infinite, a contact with the real Self.[16] In this sleep Sireno tries to become what he thinks he really is: Sereno, the serene one. In short, the liquid potion and the sleep it brings on are symbolic solutions of the problems facing the shepherds. They are not expected to solve problems "in reality"—at least not by direct causation. As far as Sireno's real cure is concerned, it is naive to believe that Montemayor was taken in by Felicia's wizardry. Sireno's so-called serenity toward the woman who betrayed him is a shaky resentment, and it was Racine who reminded us that hatred is closer to love than to indifference. The other "cure" effected by the potion, the love between Sylvano and Selvagia, is merely the natural result of their prolonged association.

It is a curious fact that Felicia's potion should arouse so much critical attention, while less attention has been given to the other and stronger undercurrents of black magic and the supernatural. One such is the tale of Belisa, filled with wild dreams and sorcery, and entirely invented, the critics tell us, by Montemayor himself. Belisa is wooed by the elderly Arsenio and in secret by his son Arsileo. One night the father surprises a man in Belisa's garden and kills him out of jealousy. Then, recognizing too late that he has killed his son, Arsenio takes his own life. Belisa withdraws to a lonely island, and it is there that she tells her tale of woe. She later learns that the entire affair in the garden was a dream concocted by the sorcerer Alfeo, out of revenge for unrequited love. Her lover Arsileo lives and is soon reunited with her.

Belisa is convinced, and succeeds in convincing the other shepherds, of the uniqueness of her tragedy. Since only superlatives can be used to describe her grief, her fame is secure. It is Belisa herself who supplies the reasoning behind this: her suffering is not "of those that time can cure," because "a pain that can be cured can be suffered with little difficulty" (*La Diana*, pp. 159–60). Her grief and fidelity will conquer time and death itself. Like Felismena, Belisa desires the impossibility of her happiness, as well as the happiness itself. Arsileo is true happiness, but Belisa can prove her fidelity, paradoxically, only by his being inaccessible. What better way to represent the doubling that the lover has come to take on in Belisa's mind than the "dream" that he is dead (i.e., dead and not dead)? Alfeo's black magic is a profound psychological mechanism signifying Belisa's symbolic murder of her beloved.

Belisa's psychological density must surely disconcert those critics who have been pleased to see nothing but stock characters in the novel. She first appears in a sleeping posture. Her disordered hair shows suffering and despair: "but never was beauty so embellished by order as by the disorder of her hair" (*La Diana*, p. 132). Whatever restrained sensuality or baroque "order within disorder" this may evoke, it also suggests a despair that, far from being pure, observes and presents itself to best advantage. Belisa's boasting that her tears have watered and nourished the green grass of the island on which she is stranded is hyperbolic in the extreme, and yet such a conviction is very much in character. Like the island on which she has exiled herself, it is another sign of her egocentrism and detachment from reality.

Curiously, before Belisa begins to tell her story, Montemayor pauses to observe: "All were astonished to see the spirit which, with facial expressions and bodily movements, she gave to her words, for, *certainly*, her words *appeared* to come from the soul . . . ; for the unhappy course of her love *removed the suspicion* that her behavior could be contrived" (*La Diana*, p. 134). Why is it necessary to assert this at all, unless the suspicion to the contrary is somehow suggested in Belisa's manner? Her inexperience in love is revealed in her adolescent taste for flattery: "I loved the father as a repayment for the love he felt for me" (*La Diana*, p. 146). Yet this simple avowal is felt to be a dangerous indiscretion when she later acknowledges: "There is no woman who, understanding that she is truly loved, does not return the love to some degree, although she may try to conceal the fact. But be silent, my tongue, for you have spoken more than you should" (*La Diana*, p. 160). Her discomfiture indicates that there are secrets below the surface. But she has already spoken: she loved the old man, "among the first in wealth and lineage in that entire province" (*La Diana*, p. 136), because of the glory it implied. This perhaps explains why the father murders (symbolically) the son, and not vice versa: Belisa values glory more than love.

The most telling point in Belisa's story is her explanation of how the tragedy came about. She recalls that inviting Arsileo was not only dangerous but pointless, since the lovers could see one another whenever they wished:

> I can't understand why I placed him in such danger, since every day, whether in the fields or next to the river, . . . he could speak with me whenever he wished and in fact did speak with me on most days. [Pp. 157–58]

She claims to have acted without knowing why:

> Poor Arsenio, his father, most evenings strolled the street in front of my house. If only I had remembered this—but misfortune blotted it from my mind!—I would never have allowed him to place himself in such danger. But it escaped my mind as if I had never known it. [P. 158]

The necromancy that murders Arsileo is not an extraneous invention of the author; it is the workings of Belisa's own psyche. Having brought herself to believe that Arsileo is really dead, she can withdraw to her island of despair, which henceforth becomes the sign of her heroic solitude. Arsileo accepts her story about the magic: "This was told to me by the shepherdess Armida, and I truly believe it" (p. 235). In this way Montemayor bridges the gap between psychotic fantasy and reality by the testimony of a "shepherdess" without credentials who never appears in person. When Arsileo turns up again, it is in the dual role of lover and audience. In confirming public belief in the authenticity of Belisa's trial of fidelity, he thereby implies her victory in the greater trial as well, the ultimate *raison d'être* of her existence: the test of public opinion.

Belisa's symptoms are not unique, however, but merely represent, drawn to their extremes, the same exalted sentimentalism seen to be rampant throughout the novel. Belisa may well have reached the depths of enjoying despair for its own sake, but even here it is impossible to separate despair from the exalted pride of the privileged sufferer. What better proof of this than her claim that she would kill herself not out of love and its pains but only if these pains were to stop (*La Diana* p. 133)? Mia Gerhardt is struck by the contrast between such an attitude and Tasso's Aminta who "wants to kill herself to put an end to her suffering" (*La Pastorale*, p. 183). The critic comments: "the gesture or at least the intention of suicide comes naturally to Italian shepherds; the Spanish pastoral replaces this with the idea of *desengaño:* to die to his affections, his illusions, his folly, this is the Spanish shepherd's suicide." Belisa's very being has become identified, in her own eyes, with her heroic, extravagant despair.

The Universal Pilgrimage to Felicia

Arsileo's reappearance causes no surprise, since he was not really dead. His rebirth for Belisa, however, is, like his death, a symbolic achievement. Belisa reluctantly joins the other unfortunates in their journey to Felicia. Felicia is an allegory and means the desire for happiness, either as positive fulfillment in marriage (Belisa, Felismena, Selvagia), or a firm turning away when impossibility is absolute (Sireno). The universal pilgrimage to her castle is a simple and profound reminder that fidelity may be damaging as well as ennobling when the goal is only the morbid enjoyment of despair and the heroic duty to sustain it. Love necessarily implies the hope for success. Granted that nothing worthwhile can be achieved without effort (*La Diana*, p. 163), still the primary goal of suffering is not the glorification of the sufferer but happiness.[17]

No one to my knowledge has offered an interpretation of Felicia. Avalle-Arce considers the problem of locating her castle and observes cautiously: "Felicia's castle is not in the pastoral world, but it is not in the natural world either" (*La novela pastoril*, p. 79, n. 57). The contrary is also true: Felicia's castle is the highest point of synthesis of both worlds, the inner one of sentiment and the outer one of reality. For the aristocrat, success begins as the will to happiness, but this urge requires a simultaneous pursuit in the world. Montemayor's answer, the ideal of marriage, contrasts sharply with the barren purity of certain kinds of troubadour love.[18] Like the other binary movements of thought studied above (nature and art, pastoral and history), inner and outer happiness are, fate willing, not opposed but rather complementary. Felicia's castle is first in the psyche as the desire for happiness, and then in the world wherever the ideal conditions of virtue and grace may be found. On the narrative level, it is no accident that the problems presented in the pastoral beginning (books 1–3) are resolved by a dissolution into the more purely historical (books 5–7). the two held in perfect balance and joined by the pivotal book 4, Felicia's temple of Diana.

It would be silly to claim that this reading of *La Diana* is the only one possible. It is sufficient that it be suggestive and consistent both with the spirit of the novel and with the erotic tradition it interprets. Montemayor has probed some of the paradoxes of love's mystery: how love implies and requires a search for happiness; how natural pride can destroy as well as reinforce virtue; how love is, in the very renunciation of the self, its highest exultation. The novel's ending is an affirmation that passionate love, selflessness, and happiness—a strange mixture in any world—can coexist in the noble life.

Chapter 8
John Donne's Philosophy of Love in "The Ecstasy"

Donne's Platonism

As an approach to Donne's Platonism I shall offer two propositions that, while not limited to Platonists, were strongly endorsed by such authors as Plotinus and Ficino. According to the first, the human soul, due to its mixed nature, acts as an intermediary between spirit and matter or body and may turn in either direction. To turn toward the former is to contemplate, to turn toward the body is to do—a distinction that Donne affirms in such poems as "Love's Growth" and "Air and Angels." A second proposition has to do with the object of contemplation. A lady can be perceived through three aspects: her physical beauty, her interior beauty or virtue, and her mind. Contemplation—as opposed to doing but as necessarily engaging the emotions as well as the intellect—can be focused on any level, but Neoplatonic preference weighed heavily on mental and moral aspects and viewed the aesthetic level as but a first step toward a purely inner contemplation of the image of the beloved. At these levels of the psyche and once the beloved's physical and even imagined presence has been abstracted, the lover can focus on characteristics deeper than aesthetic ones, can conceive the beloved's virtue and even her mind, can glimpse, finally, his own ideal, integrated image, what Scève calls "his highest potentiality" (*Délie* 144).

On the evidence of the poems, "The Undertaking" sets the tone but not the limits of Donne's Platonizing:[1]

But he who loveliness within
Hath found, all outward loathes. [Vv. 13–14]

If, as I have, you also do
Virtue attired in woman see... [Vv. 17–18]

It is noteworthy that Donne undercuts his Platonic love by the even nobler imperative, dictated by a sense of the supreme value of love's doctrine, to "keep that hid" (v. 28). Of course, silence is only one way of keeping that hidden. Leone Ebreo alternated between fable and abstruse philosophy; Scève tried the *trobar clus*, and Héroet, simple reticence. Donne seems to have preferred wit.

Despite such reserve, Donne certainly does evoke Platonic leanings in texts other than "The Undertaking":

> I never stooped so low, as they
> Which on an eye, cheek, lip, can prey,
>   Seldom to them, which soar no higher
>   Than virtue or the mind to admire,
> For sense, and understanding may
>   Know, what gives fuel to their fire. ["Negative Love," vv. 1–6]

Again, Platonic experience is downgraded, this time in favor of love's mystery, but the "seldom" carries the admission that the poet does turn that way occasionally. For example, it is an aspect of his love in "A Valediction: of the Book":

> Here Love's divines (since all divinity
>   Is love or wonder) may find all they seek,
>   Whether abstract spiritual love they like,
> Their souls exhaled with what they do not see,
>   Or, loth so to amuse
>   Faith's infirmity . . . [Vv. 28–33]

"The Primrose" takes up the Platonic/physical antithesis of "Negative Love" and again expresses a preference for the Platonic over the other form of "monstrosity" (v. 18), if that indeed is the correct reading of "I could more abide, / She were by art, than nature falsified" (vv. 19–20). Finally, the text of "Air and Angels" is unique in its delicate suggestion of the angelic quality of a love that arises from deep psychic reminiscences and desires previous to its descent into a particular body.

Summarizing the evidence of these texts we should be forced to conclude that Donne's Platonism is real but secondary. However, the base of discussion is considerably enlarged when we turn to "The Ecstasy," and to Helen Gardner's authoritative study of this aspect of the poem.[2] The importance of this essay lies not only in showing Leone Ebreo to be the likely source of "The Ecstasy" but even more in directing our research to an entire tradition that can make the poem intelligible in its own terms. I shall therefore take this essay as a starting point and acknowledge the correctness of Gardner's findings, especially her explanation of the central notion of ecstasy; although, in my reexamination of the "argument" of the poem I shall be led to expand and even modify certain of her views.

Eye-pictures

The two essential notions connected with ecstasy to readers of Leone Ebreo are the following: (1) ecstasy describes a separation of soul from body—not of body from soul, for that would be permanent death;[3] (2) the experience of ecstasy is primarily one of cognition, although intense emotion and enjoyment are also involved. To support her special reading of the poem, Helen Gardner introduces yet another notion:

> The discussion does not arise out of the experience of an ecstatic union of the lovers, but from the lover's experience of an ecstatic union *with the idea* of the beauty of his beloved.[4]

The reference is to the beginning of Leone's Dialogue Three, where Filone is so absorbed with the inner image of Sofia that he, rather ludicrously, fails to notice her physical presence. But surely Donne's situation is quite different, for whereas Filone is oblivious to all bodies—his mistress' as well as his own—and is united with Sofia's image, Donne's lover is aware of both a participation of bodies ("our hands") and especially an interpenetration of consciousnesses ("our eye-beams"). "The Ecstasy" is thus as distant from Filone's solitary contemplations of his beloved's image as from the Platonic descent of the soul from angelic intuitions to bodily form as presented in "Air and Angels." Rather, the situation is one of *mutual love* ("one another's best"—another divergence from the *Dialoghi*, where the amorous context is one of courtship) projected as an intensely physical and passionate *presence* of the lovers to one another. In such an instance one may understandably prefer A. J. Smith's antiplatonic bias: "But the disembodied colloquy of souls yields no vision of supernatural truths or universal forms. It simply shows the lovers to themselves."[5]

What the lovers see when they look at one another is anything but simple, however, and we might begin our analysis of their ecstatic vision by noticing a progression in their awareness of "we": "We like sepulcral statues lay" (v. 18). From this perception of "we" as bodies, the lovers advance to: "We then, who are this new soul... " (v. 45). And, finally: "we are / The intelligences... " (vv. 51–52).

Such an expansion of their identity is characterized both by a progressive dematerialization and by a reduction of difference. Thus, the martial image of the souls as two armies—suggesting Cupid's lust for victory rather than mutual love—is neutralized by a more reasonable give and take ("negotiation") of the parties. This suggests that ethical knowledge is an aspect of their findings:

> We then, who are this new soul, know,
>   Of what we are composed, and made,

For, th' atomies of which we grow,
    Are souls, whom no change can invade. [Vv. 45–48]

If the revealed changelessness of the soul means that their love "will continue forever" (Gardner, p. 299), then the burden of the poem is love's
faithfulness, and this would allow symbolic use of the violet imagery.[6] Such a
reading finds support in the closing verse—though Gardner chose not to use
it as such—in its assertion that the lovers' fidelity will remain unaltered after
their sexual union. Whether such kind of "knowledge" is one of supernatural
truth may be open to debate, but it is clear that Donne's contemporaries so
regarded it. In fact, faithfulness was considered as love's supreme *truth*, and
the meaningful ambivalence of the term prevents us from separating its
cognitive and ethical components.[7]

    We may wish, however, to inquire further into the content of the ecstatic
vision in order to understand more precisely what kind of knowledge supports faithfulness. Concretely, what do the lovers see when they look at one
another? Donne takes special pains to stress the lovers' postures and their
remarkable duration: "*All day*, the same our postures were, / And we said
nothing, *all the day*" (vv. 19–20). Curiously, the postures do *not* remain the
same, for at some point the lovers pass from a sitting position (v. 4) to a prone
one (v. 18), suggestive of dead bodies rather than more intimate erotic
coupling. What the lovers see is not a particular posture, however, since this
only supports or permits the important thing:

Our eye-beams twisted, and did thread
    Our eyes, upon one double string... [Vv. 7–8]

"And pictures in our eyes to get
    Was all our propagation. [Vv. 11–12]

It is essential to note that the propagated pictures are not of the beloved as
such but only of the beloved's eyes, so that the content of the picture is a
reflection of a reflection. The situation can be imagined by placing two
mirrors one opposite the other so that, if perfectly focused ("on the same
string") and executed, the image would reflect or propagate itself infinitely
and be its own content. The fascination of such a speechless, daylong, intensely passionate gazing into one another's eyes—as difficult for the critic to
imagine as it would be for the lovers to sustain—suggests important but
forgotten rituals. To find adequate parallels we would have to look to Tantric
sources;[8] or, in Western literature, to the myth of Narcissus[9] or to the lover's
gaze into the pool in Guillaume de Lorris's *Roman de la Rose;* or to Shakespeare's remarkably similar intuitions in such texts as Achilles' speech in
Troilus and Cressida, where the eye both reflects the other's "form" and
finds both that form and its own form reflected in the eye of the other:

> ... nor doth the eye itself,
> That most pure spirit of sense, behold itself,
> Not going from itself; but eye to eye opposed,
> Salutes each other with each other's form;
> For speculation turns not to itself,
> Till it hath travell'd and is mirror'd there
> Where it may see itself. [III,3,105-11]

Taken as mere conceits, such a multiplication of reflections can at best be followed to the third or fourth degree before exhausting our interest. It is certain, however, that Shakespeare did not view them as mere clever inventions, nor the reflections as mere reports of physical appearance. This is why he speaks of the other's "form" or, in a poem even closer to "The Ecstasy," of one's "true image":

> Mine eyes have drawn thy shape, and thine for me
> Are windows to my breast, wherethrough the sun
> Delights to peep, to gaze therein on thee. [Sonnet 24]

The reverberations of such rapidly repeated eye-images, the content of which now appears as light rather than as mere physical image, provoke an expansion of consciousness wherein the medium of perception is transformed into the light of the sun. The perceiver, moreover, who looks "through these windows, *your* eyes, into *my* breasts, where it sees you,"[10] becomes momentarily identified with the Sun himself, that is to say, with "some greater consciousness enjoying and using human experience."[11]

The eyes' reproductive power is deeply related to eye-beams and eye-threads, and Donne's use of these complex symbols is remarkably coherent. According to both Eastern and Western sources, writes A. K. Coomaraswamy,

> vision is traditionally thought of as effected by means of a ray projected from the eye, rather than by means of a reflected light that strikes the eye. The reason is that these sense powers are not "our own," but are the Sun's, Prajapati's, who sees in us, looks out through every creature and "Other than whom there is no seer."[12]

In other words, "Whoever sees, it is by His ray that he sees"; for "the Gods ... caused the pure fire within us, which is akin to that of day, to flow through the eyes in a smooth and dense stream ... of vision" (*Timaeus* 45c).[13] Further, it is explained that "prima substantiarum est lux," the "spiritus qui vivificat," which "as the sun, connects all things to himself by means of a thread or thread-spirit."[14] Such symbolisms help us understand the paradox of a love that both grows and yet remains unchanged. Its dynamism is related to that of the sun, which begets and vivifies all things and yet remains the same, precisely because love can "of the sun his working vigor borrow" (Donne, "Love's Growth"). When perfect lovers gaze upon one another they are thus able to sense a great Prince, that numinous presence that will forever "dwell in lovers' eyes" (Shakespeare, Sonnet 55).

As the most spiritual of the senses, the eyes were thus regarded as the best means of portraying that feeling of transparency and permanence that is the burden of the argument of "The Ecstasy." Already at an early stage of the poem and before the "two equal armies" have abandoned their desire for victory, the image of the "one double string" of light, in its dual reference to sense perception and eternal beauty, forecasts the reconciliation of Donne's two antinomies: the subject-object relation of two personalities in love, and the tension—exacerbated by ecstatic separation—between body and soul. In order to understand these reconciliations more clearly we must examine yet other elements of the poem's introduction.

"A pregnant bank": Body-thoughts

Structurally, "The Ecstasy" is a studied composition of three groups of five quatrains each: strophes 1–5, 8–12, and 13–17. Strophes 6–7 are merely transitional and also introduce the hypothetical listener; strophes 18–19 return to a listener and offer the poet's conclusion. The sensual atmosphere of the introductory section ("pillow on a bed," "pregnant bank," "our hands were firmly cemented") is governed by two principles. On the one hand there is a parallelism—not quite an opposition—between physical and spiritual entities, notably between hands and eyes (the most spiritual of the senses), and this notion is reinforced by a strict parallelism of content in strophes 2 and 3. On the other hand, the passage from the sensuous opening to verse 18 must be viewed as a gradual abstraction of physicalism[15] resulting in the "death" of the bodies. The balance between physical and spiritual components is thus upset, but only momentarily, for it will return as a structural principle: part two (str. 8–12) will relate the disembodied ecstatic experience and part three will return to the body—precisely and interestingly to the hands (v. 63). Part three, in fact, proposes the resurrection of the body, no longer located at the periphery of sensation (the hands and eyes of part one) or at the tips of nerve endings (as sensualists and empiricists would have it) but rather at its proper locus: the human heart.

The opening section is more than a picturesque prelude, although it certainly does provide a setting of repose wherein the lovers' transports can rise above their enchanted bodies. A. J. Smith has provided the correct method of reading these lines:

> There is no question of evocation of atmosphere, or indirect motivation through sensuous description of nature. The point is the enunciation of theme

by wittily introduced emblem... in which a figurative account is treated as though it were literally intended.[16]

With reference to lines 5–6 ("Our hands were firmly cemented / With a fast balm, which thence did spring... "), while noticing the realism and dense sensuality of the sweating hands, we would agree that the slightly repugnant impression is neutralized by the reference to "balm," which points to its emblematic usage: "a moisture that preserves them [the lovers] steadfast. In Paracelsan medicine balm was the 'natural inborn preservative'... which while our bodies retain it keeps us from decay."[17] In short, the figure echoes one of the poem's main arguments: the lovers' fidelity and the changeless nature of their love. It is in fact characteristic of the emblem to force the natural or credible limits of the physical image, for in the present instance the metaphoric transmutation of sweat into balm does seem, at least in Shakespeare's "Venus and Adonis," a ludicrous pretense:

> With this she seizeth on his sweating palm,
> The precedent of pith and livelihood,
> And trembling in her passion, calls it balm. [Vv. 25–27]

In both passages the presence of sweat implies sensuality,[18] but Donne makes a crucial distinction: whereas in Shakespeare the palm is already dripping, in "The Ecstasy" the balm "springs" from the joined hands. It is therefore not a question of sensuous dispositions that are brought *to* the situation—and indeed that cause such a situation to arise—but rather an awareness of sensuality that emerges from a larger and as yet unspecified condition. Such a subtle emblematic distinction strengthens Donne's contention that the lovers' awareness of their bodies occurs only after both their mutual love and their ecstatic discoveries have fully developed.

The opening strophe presents an emblematic exaggeration of perhaps even more striking proportions:

> Where, like a pillow on a bed,
> A pregnant bank swelled up, to rest
> The violet's reclining head,
> Sat we two, one another's best.

It hardly suffices to view the bank as pregnant because it swells up;[19] rather, the bank swells up *for the purpose of* resting the violet's head. Donne thus ascribes intentionality to the lower element, the ground (in both senses) of the violet that will later multiply (v. 40), one feels, because of the strength it derives from the pregnant bank. To have overstressed the point would have involved Donne in absurd teleological arguments; as presented, it suggests an attitude of gracious fullness and active receptivity. It thus emblematically anticipates Donne's notion that, concomitant with the spirit's influence from above, there arises an analogous activity from below:

As our blood labours to beget
  Spirits, as like souls as it can,
Because such fingers need to knit
  That subtle knot, which makes us man:

So must pure lovers' souls descend
  T' affections, and to faculties,
Which sense may reach and apprehend,
  Else a great prince in prison lies. [Vv. 61–68]

Helen Gardner noticed the "purposeful action of the blood" in these lines and described the blood's labors as a striving to become spiritual.[20] Similarly, after alluding to the mind's love for the body, Leone Ebreo speculates as follows:

> The body, in its love for the intellect (just as a woman loves her male or husband) rises above itself in its desire for the latter's perfections: with its senses, eyes, ears, common sense, fantasy and memory it seeks to acquire whatever is necessary for true knowledge and eternal habits of intellect, through which human intellect attains to felicity. [Leone, *Dialoghi*, p. 307]

Again, it is the movement from below that prepares its union with the higher element.

The notion of consciousness as arising from the body has become fashionable of late, to sectarians of Wilhelm Reich, for example. The modern attempt has been not merely to supply a sane counterbalance to dehumanizing idealisms, for Rabelais already did that. Philosophically it is much closer to Epicurus' atomistic theory of consciousness, though recent authors could hardly take pride in such a mechanistic and demystified ancestor. For D. H. Lawrence, for example, the body is a repository of primeval myths; for Henry Miller it signifies a dithyrambic genesis of the imagination; for Carlos Castaneda it is the locus of powerful but forgotten centers of cosmic awareness.

From such hyperbolic perspectives Donne is tame indeed:

> . . . her pure and eloquent blood
> Spoke in her cheeks, and so distinctly wrought,
> That one might almost say, her body thought.
> ["The Second Anniversary," vv. 244–46]

The very possibility of a thinking body is presented as hypothetical ("might") and paradoxical ("almost"), possible only in a being so exceptional as to prove the received antithesis between bodily matter and thought or spirit. Yet, for his time Donne does suggest a new orientation that has clear parallels in Leone Ebreo and in the important kabbalistic idea of a solicitation or a "support from below."[21] In verses 61–68 of "The Ecstasy" Donne makes the daring insinuation that pure lovers' souls must descend *because of* the prior activity of the blood spirits. However, in "Air and Angels" he presents the complementary view that the impetus *descends*, that consciousness of the beloved originates in angelic premonitions and *then* seeks incarnation in concrete faculties and affections.

"That subtle knot"

It would thus seem that for Donne the question of "priority of impetus" remains a mute one, that both mind and body can lay claim to love's origins. Upon further study it seems best to ascribe Donne's ambivalence not to indecision but rather to an attempt to "ballast love" ("Air and Angels"), to find the proper place where love can "inhere" (v. 22). At this crucial point in his thinking Donne does not quite abandon Leone's model of the soul as a mediating link between spirit and body; rather, he gives this link more ontological density. For Leone the soul was defined both by its ability to turn from spirit to body to spirit and by its proportion of light to darkness; at death, darkness and light return to their former conditions and the link, having lost its function, presumably ceases to exist. Donne, by contrast, focuses on the link's permanence, to such an extent that "That subtle knot *that makes us man*" heralds a new creation, a fresh link in the great chain of being. The final section of "The Ecstasy" is thus not adequately described as a return to the body. It rather extends one of Donne's main preoccupations—finding a ballast for his love—by delineating an area of consciousness and experience, situated between idealisms and bestiality, where *human* beings may dwell and love. The summons to return to the body is, more than a call to physical delight, an affirmation of the unity of upper and lower through the efficacy of that subtle knot that defines and guarantees our humanity.

We know that such a creation is tenuous and that it is located between mind and body. From Leone Ebreo and his followers we also know that this knot is the heart-soul, which is the bond both of life and of love. Such a perspective suggests limitations of Donne's Platonism better based than those usually advanced from sensualist or materialistic points of view. The matter is well put by Charles Mitchell when he summarizes the function of the Platonic observer in "The Ecstasy":

> The lover observing the ecstasy is said to be a purely Platonic one, "growen all minde" and hence capable of understanding the "dialogue of one." He is said to be "by love refin'd" before he became an observer of the ecstasy, and yet departing after it he will be "farre purer than he came." The Platonic lover is not so pure as he thinks, for as long as he believes that he has "growne all

minde," he looks upon his body as "drosse." As a whole man, then, the
Platonic lover is in need of further refinement. When he is able to accept the
definition of man as a fusion of body and soul into one substance, then the dross
will be transformed into an element which combines with the soul to form an
alloy.[22]

Platonists may indeed claim a more sensitive understanding of love than the
sensualists, but their next step is dialectically to engage—rather than
avoid—the opposing claim.

Finally, it is noteworthy that, while Donne later repudiated his erotic
writings, he retained the basic preoccupations of "The Ecstasy" but came to
justify them by theological argument rather than simple "metaphysical" con-
ceit. Consider the following texts.

> As thou didst so make Heaven, as thou didst not neglect Earth, and madest
> them answerable and agreeable to one another, so let my Soul's Creatures have
> that temper and Harmony, that they be not by a misdevout consideration of
> the next life, stupidly and trecherously negligent of the offices and duties
> which thou enjoynest amongst us in this life . . . [23]

Or, again:

> But for me, if I were able to husband all my time so thriftily, as not onely not to
> wound my soul in any minute by actuall sinne, but not to rob and cousen her
> by giving any part to pleasure or businesse, but bestow it all upon her in
> meditation, yet even in that I should wound her more, and contract another
> guiltinesse: As the Eagle were very unnaturall if because she is able to do it,
> she should pearch a whole day upon a tree, staring in contemplation of the
> majestic and glory of the Sun, and let her young Eglets starve in the nest.[24]

Here Donne is advancing concerns similar to those in "The Ecstasy," but he
now argues from theological perspectives and the pleasure principle has
yielded to the ideal of "service." Or, rather, the two are perhaps integrated
into a wider view, as suggested by Donne's notion of a "meteoric" human
nature where "earthly pleasure" and "some errand to do" seem combined in
their opposition to the joys of heaven and the spirit, and yet both are theologically sanctioned. Leone Ebreo argued no differently; nor does Shakespeare
in *King Lear*, where the subtle knot becomes the emblematic essence of one
of his most beloved characters: Cordelia.

Chapter 9
Withdrawal or Service:
The Paradox of *King Lear*

From thinking us all soul, neglecting thus
Our mutual duties, Lord deliver us.
                    JOHN DONNE, "A Litany"

It will be useful at this point to review briefly the reinterpretation that the idea of detachment underwent during the sixteenth century. As we have seen, Leone Ebreo took the ascetic sense of the term from Plato's *Phaedo* and added the contemplative sense: it was the philosopher who could unbind (*délie*) his soul from the body and turn to eternal delights. Scève extended this notion of death when, following Leone, he recognized the aesthetic death of separation from the body and union with the soul, or at least the inner image, of the beloved. But a competing sense of *délie* may be traced back to Leone as well, and it is competing rather than antagonistic because it engages a dialectical relation with its opposite. In this motion of the soul, which Scève calls love motivated by faithfulness (*Délie* 247), the soul dies, is unbound or *déliée*, not to allow it a more perfect withdrawal from the body and this world—rather, detachment becomes the quality of soul that best enables it to reattach itself to the body and its earthly duties.

In this chapter I shall propose that Shakespeare's Cordelia may be regarded as the measure of this development in the sense that she carries the notion of reattachment or service to its most perfect expression. I mean that, beyond but including the body's union with the soul (Scève), the androgynous integration of man and woman in marriage (Héroët), and the reconciliation of heaven and earth, Cordelia points both emblematically and dramatically to a fourth dimension, one that hardly interested the love poets: the integration of the body politic, of man in his communal being, through the proper understanding and enforcement of bonds. In so doing, Cordelia represents—in her opposition to Lear—that tension between the active and contemplative ideals that was Leone Ebreo's central theme.

Cor-Delia

Of all of Shakespeare's characters only Iago and perhaps Cleopatra are as marvelously mysterious as Cordelia—not that Cordelia has the evasive complexity of Iago; the mystery flows rather from her paradoxical aura of heavenly distance and practical concern, of patience and passion, of walking on the earth without being touched by it. She shares Desdemona's innocence but not her helplessness. She has, rather, something of Cleopatra's sufficiency, and when the Egyptian queen's infinitely scattered multiplicity deepens to include heavenly longings she suggests a reconciliation of opposites that approaches Cordelia. But Cleopatra is a centrifugal force, an escape from selfhood in the opposite directions of sensuality and divinity; Cordelia is always present, reliably so, even when she is absent, and it surprises us to be reminded that she speaks barely one hundred lines in the play.

Shakespeare alluded to her paradoxical nature by a variation on the well-known medieval *topos* of the *puer-senex:*

Lear. "So young and so untender?"
Cordelia. "So *young*, my Lord, and *true*."[1] [I,1,105-6]

The phrase has been narrowly read as Cordelia's telling the truth[2] as against her sisters' hypocrisy, but here she is referring to a quality of heart rather than of mind. She is of course also telling the truth, but her emphasis is on *being true*, "true of heart" (*Twelfth Night* II,4,106, as opposed to "false of heart," *Lear* III,4,90) as against her sisters' infidelities. And like plainness, its extension into outward behavior,[3] being true is associated with age. In *Twelfth Night* (II,4,43) the Duke finds the innocence of love best expressed by a song that is "old and plain" (cf. also *King John* IV,2,22: "plain old form"). In *Lear* itself it is only Cordelia (I,1,128 and 147) and the old and faithful Kent (II,2,89ff.) that merit the epithet. Nor is there any doubt as to the locus and origin of such virtue:

" . . . I cannot heave
My heart into my mouth." [I,1,90-91]

Lear. "But goes *thy heart* with this?" [I,1,104]

In such utterances "heart" is synonymous with "self," but in Cordelia's case a more emblematic essence is also intended. Moreover, as in Shakespeare's "The Phoenix and Turtle," the terms "love," "constancy," and "true" are virtually synonymous and refer to the heart's highest and most mysterious virtue, its faithfulness ("according to my bond"). It may indeed be proposed that the moral elevation in *Lear* is best explained by the faithfulness of its three best characters: Kent to the king, Edgar to his father, and Cordelia to Lear and her husband but also to an ancient covenant that defines faithfulness in its most inclusive and precise sense.[4]

Cordelia by any other name would seem as sweet, but her mystery would be even more impenetrable. Seen from the vantage point of the tradition studied above, the name has poetic and philosophical dimensions that admirably reflect Cordelia's dramatic functions; it is, in fact, the best hint that could be devised to picture, in both the small world of man and the larger universe, those entities that, by a reconciliation of opposites, defines what is properly human: the *Cor* or heart, viewed by Leone Ebreo as the mediator between man's mind and body, and *Delia* the moon, the sign of reconciliation between heaven and nature, spirit and matter. Moreover—and here we properly return to Scève's etymology—the Delian person, whose center is the human heart, is expert both in binding that "subtle knot that makes us man" and, when need be, in unbinding man from all nonhuman attachments, be they "false Fortune's frown," alienating affections, and even contemplative withdrawal.

Shakespeare's onomastic interests are beyond doubt, as his creation of Malvolio (*Twelfth Night*) and Benvolio (*Romeo and Juliet*) suggests. In the romances, Van Doren noted that Marina, Perdita, and Miranda are all "named for their qualities."[5] In *Timon of Athens* Kermode suspects that Timon may be "exploring the etymology of his own name."[6] The form *Cordelion* (Coeur-de-lion) in *King John* has no emblematic force but could have suggested the analysis of Cordelia's name into its component parts. The precise form of Cordelia's name may have been taken from Spenser, as Muir suggests, but we should still want to explain why, in this instance, Spenser was preferred over more influential sources and especially why, of the seven forms of the name proposed by the sources,[7] Shakespeare chose the most Latin one for a family having most un-Latin names: Lear, Regan, Goneril.

It is John Danby, I think, who makes the best case for seeing in Cordelia emblematic "meanings that transcend psychology," either as the "apex of the pyramid," the image of a "fully human integration," or as a "beneficent Goddess of Nature," or, again, as a conciliator of opposites.[8] In her creative role the Delian person, through a constant and faithful administration, assures the preservation of the world and in particular of man's world—his person but also his society. Cordelia of course plays a crucial role both in restoring the throne and in healing her father, but it is the quality of her aid that is peculiar. There is a numinous aspect to her, a secret contact with the great forces of nature that she invokes: "O you kind Gods, / Cure this great breach in his abused nature!" [IV,7,15]. This is followed by a musical background that in *Winter's Tale* (V,3,98) and *Pericles* (III,2,91 and V,1,222) is a mark of restorative forces and, as in *Cymbeline* (V,4,30ff.) and *Antony and Cleopatra* (IV,4,15), of divine presences:

"O my dear father! Restoration hang
Thy medicine on my lips, and let this kiss
Repair those violent harms. . . ." [IV,7,26-28]

We are made to feel that the healing is brought about through Cordelia's
mediation, not through any trick or even knowledge she may possess but
rather through her merciful tears, which are in mysterious contact with
nature's forces:

"All bless'd secrets,
All you unpublish'd virtues of the earth,
Spring with my tears! be aidant and remediate
In the good man's distress!" [IV,4,15-18]

The surest proof of Cordelia's elevation, in fact, is her ability to weep:

And now and then an ample tear trill'd down
Her delicate cheek. . . . You have seen
Sunshine and rain at once; her smiles and tears
Were like a better way; those happy smilets
That play'd on her ripe lip seem'd not to know
What guests were in her eyes; which parted thence,
As pearls from diamonds dropp'd. [IV,3,12-22]

Physiologically, tears were thought to originate in the heart,[9] but through
metaphorical extension they evoke and even become identified with the rain
from above, which, as the "gentle rain from heaven" in the *Merchant of
Venice* (IV,1,185), are waters of blessing and mercy: " . . . she shook / The
holy water from her heavenly eyes" (IV,3,30). Through her merciful tears
Cordelia both symbolizes and dramatizes the heart that helps "the heavens
to rain" (*Lear* III,7,60).

On the basis of such impressions, a dominant trend in *Lear* criticism has
argued the angelic status of Cordelia, and we are inclined to receive this
view uncritically, I suspect, because this indeed is the effect she has on Lear:
"Thou art a soul in bliss" (IV,7,46). To get the more accurate view that
Shakespeare intended, however, we must seek to determine whether Lear's
judgment of his youngest daughter is correct or rather, as I shall propose,
whether it is conditioned by his own unresolved tragic flaws.

Lear as a Tragic Hero

To argue this point we must first review the nature of tragedy in *Lear* and
especially that influential critical view that rather surprisingly questions its
very existence in the play, or at least that judges Lear's tragic flaws to be

transcended through his repentance. I refer to Bradley's theory of what may be called the transparency of tragedy in *Lear*, the artistic achievement whereby the illusion of our lives' sweetness is so skillfully contrived that we are supremely aware of both its grandeur and its falsity. Somewhat like a Mallarmé poem, which achieves completeness only to dissolve into nothingness, the tragedy—while still maintaining the illusion, let us not forget—intimates its own limits and dissolution:

> This, if we like to use the word, is Shakespeare's "pessimism" in *King Lear*. As we have seen, it is not by any means the whole spirit of the tragedy, which presents the world as a place where heavenly good grows side by side with evil, where extreme evil cannot long endure, and where all that survives the storm is good, if not great. But still this strain of thought, to which the world appears as the kingdom of evil and therefore worthless, is in the tragedy, and may well be the record of many hours of exasperated feeling and troubled brooding. Pursued further and allowed to dominate, it would destroy the tragedy; for it is necessary to tragedy that we should feel that suffering and death do matter greatly, and that happiness and life are not to be renounced as worthless. Pursued further, again, it leads to the idea that the world, in that obvious appearance of it which tragedy cannot dissolve without dissolving itself, is illusive.[10]

There is a strong suspicion that in Bradley's mind the tragedy is in fact dissolved, for from the third act onward he sees Shakespeare as intent on developing the following imperative:

> Let us renounce the world, hate it, and lose it gladly. The only real thing in it is the soul, with its courage, patience, devotion. [P. 260]

> ... the outward is nothing and the inward is all. [Ibid.]

Whatever tragic faults Lear may have had are now transcended in his final renunciation of the world,[11] and Lear is therefore ultimately not a tragic hero. Again, it is tragic art rather than religious conviction that requires the illusion that death and suffering are important, for, in reality, as Bradley would have Shakespeare say, "the world appears as the kingdom of evil and therefore worthless" (p. 261).

It was perhaps to save humanity from Bradley's sublime Manicheism that some recent critics have stressed the irreducible nature of Lear's suffering, to such an extent that Frank Kermode is willing to call human suffering the theme of the play.[12] By itself, the argument does not carry much weight; otherwise the victims of, say, the Lisbon earthquake would all have been good candidates for tragic heroes, and yet Voltaire wrote no tragedy on that event. Furthermore, Shakespeare seems to make a crucial distinction in *Lear* between suffering and the more active and human quality of patience, and he seems to stress the latter at the expense of the former. Along lines similar to Kermode's, Barbara Everett has urged the contrast between Lear's strong love of life and self as against an empty, cruel universe that gives nothing in return.[13] Such a critical vision calls to mind recent existentialist definitions of the human condition: that of Camus, for example, for whom the absurd is neither consciousness nor extended matter but rather their coexistence in the same universe. What perhaps saves Everett from a Manicheism even more radical than Bradley's is what she describes as Lear's "one heroic quality": "a habit of totality of experience"—which, of course, things being what they are, is rewarded by "an apprehension of the one absolute that the tragic world can offer: the absolute of silence and cessation" (Everett, p. 336). Curiously, and by a line of argument quite different from Bradley's, Everett nevertheless arrives at her own version of Bradley's view that in *Lear* Shakespeare reached the limit beyond which tragedy cannot go without dissolving: "The hero is only a hero insofar as he is able to envisage the limits of the heroic world" (Everett, p. 336). While not being a hero in Bradley's sense, then (because he cannot see beyond his human condition), Everett's Lear remains tragic nevertheless, but in the metaphysical sense suggested by Pascal: Lear is tragic not so much because of his sufferings as because of his awareness of them. Perhaps the most serious objection to this view was Danby's trenchant complaint about the failure to distinguish psychology from the "much more searching and radical concern" of conduct.[14] It may be added that Everett is being every bit as metaphysical as Danby is accused of being. At any rate, while Pascal's thoughts about man the "thinking reed" may indeed explain why foxes and tulips have never filled the role of tragic heroes, they hardly account for the specificity of Lear's misfortunes.

Lear's Tragic Flaws

Else a great Prince in prison lies.
                              JOHN DONNE, "The Ecstasy"
I could live and die in the eyes of Troilus.
                    SHAKESPEARE, *Troilus and Cressida* I,2,242

I would like to begin my assessment of Bradley's analysis of *King Lear* by accepting the criterion of repentance as an antitragic form of conduct and by arguing the opposite conclusion: that Lear is a tragic hero because he in fact does *not* repent. In so doing we certainly should not neglect the clear evidence of Lear's moral awakening in acts three and four, the confession of the shortcomings of his rule and of his inattention to the poor, his sharp need for forgiveness, and his acknowledgement of rash misjudgment. But neither should such psychological and circumstantial elements (rashness, old age) be stressed unduly without diminishing the king's tragic dignity; nor should we fail to distinguish a properly tragic flaw from various instances of misconduct, though the one may clearly generate the others. Moreover, in the prison scene, regarded by the Bradley-Muir position as the culmination of Lear's spiritual development, it can be shown that Lear does not repent. I would now like to describe Lear's tragic flaws as Shakespeare appears to me to have presented them.

Coleridge's lengthy analysis of the first scene of *King Lear* is probably the best demonstration we have of the importance of Shakespeare's "seminal" opening scenes.[15] With several brief touches the dramatist evokes an entire social and moral context that gives rise to the individuals and situations that follow. In *Winter's Tale*, for example, Leontes' jealousy is made plausible—but surely not justified—by what Mark Van Doren, with a slight exaggeration, has called the "animal leisureliness" of the court.[16] The function of the preparatory scene in *Lear* has been suggestively glossed by William Frost:

> By this means the gap between ritual and more naturalistic drama is bridged at the same time that ritual itself is thrown into high relief.[17]

The focus here is on the rim around the picture, the thirty-two lines that precede the tremendous court scene. In addition to highlighting the latter, this preparatory sketch introduces both a moral ambiance and crucial themes that later become shaded behind the megalithic formality of Lear's court.

In Shakespearean usage Kent's opening words strike a note of warning: "I thought the King had more affected the Duke of Albany than Cornwall." Rather than denoting reasoned judgment, "affection" was usually seen as a *passion* that, as the etymology tells us, one undergoes and suffers.[18] In *Julius Caesar* (II,1,20) affection is opposed to reason; in *Othello* (I,1,36) it explains for Iago his master's irrational choice of a lieutenant. In *Winter's Tale* it is at the origin of Leontes' raging jealousy: "Affection! thy intention stabs the centre" (I,2,138). A precise account of its evil effects may be found in Hector's famous speech in *Troilus and Cressida*, a passage most apposite to the situation in *Lear:*

> ... Nature craves
> All dues be rendered to their owners: now,
> What nearer debt to all humanity
> Than wife is to the husband? *If this law*
> *Of nature be corrupted through affection* ... [II,2,177]

From the start, then, we learn that the king inclines to his affections, and we recall that such passions can stab the very heart and corrupt the natural order.

The three characters who open the play represent the entire range of *Lear's* moral universe. The prime mover of the scene is Gloucester, morally tainted but redeemable. He is flanked, on the one hand, by Kent, "the nearest to perfect goodness of all of Shakespeare's characters" (Coleridge) and, on the other, by the brooding villain Edmund. We learn that the bastard Edmund "hath been out nine years, and away he shall again" (I,1,32), and this comes to be viewed as a sign of his exile from his father's affections. For what is most striking in this scene is Gloucester's attitude toward Edmund's illegitimacy, which ranges from shame ("I have so often blushed") to an indecent bragging over the "good sport at his making."[19] Kittredge's wish to save the appearances by placing Edmund out of hearing range of such humiliating remarks is a mere quibble, for Edmund's subsequent rancor is clearly fired by a deep awareness of parental disfavor. The theme recurs in the case of those other two children, Goneril and Regan, better examples of pure villainy, but who also show that their motive, like Edmund's, was not solely greed for land and gold: "He [Lear] always lov'd our sister [Cordelia] most" (I,1,289), an echo of Lear's own public admission that "I lov'd her most, and thought to set my rest / On her kind nursery" (I,1,122–23). The mixture and perhaps confusion of motives is well expressed in Edmund's monologue:

> Legitimate Edgar, I must have *your land:*
> *Our father's love* is to the bastard Edmund
> As to th' legitimate. [I,2,16–18]

This "intense desire to be intensely loved" (Coleridge), linked from the beginning to a lack of paternal affection, receives its culminating disclosure at the very end of Edmund's career. As he lies dying, the corpses of Goneril and Regan are brought out:

> *Yet Edmund was beloved:*
> The one the other poison'd *for my sake,*
> And after slew herself. [V, 3, 238–40]

In a fine comment, Muir (Shakespeare, *King Lear,* p. 201) does not hesitate to suggest that "Edmund's career of crime was caused by his feeling that he was not loved." Certainly one cannot exaggerate the pathos of such a hunger for affection, wherein violent crimes come to be pictured simply as proofs of love.[20]

These hints prepare us for the Lear of the court scene, who must be imagined as unhappy, tense, and strangely perplexed. He shakily insists on his unwavering decision ("fast intent," "constant will"), alludes mysteriously to a "darker purpose," and, with a touch of pathos and seeming renunciation, announces his plan to "unburthened crawl toward death." If the darker purpose is merely a "gloomy" one (Empson), then our attention is fixed upon the announced purpose of the whole scene, the division of the kingdom: an event indeed so fraught with disaster that whatever small sense of satisfaction to be felt at the conclusion of *Lear* may be attributed, I think, to the

kingdom's reunification. We may reflect, however, that the division could
have been effected in the form of a last will and testament, as in all the major
sources (Geoffrey of Monmouth, Holinshed, Higgins) except *King Leir,* and
that it becomes a matter of impending tragedy only with the king's concomitant but totally unnecessary decision to abdicate. We may wish to recall
Shakespeare's disapproval of the early retirement of two other princes:
Ferdinand's ridiculed retreat to academe in *Love's Labour Lost,* and the
Duke's false abdication in *Measure for Measure.* The modern idea of retirement is of no help here, and we would do better to ask whether it is ever
possible to retire from being a parent to one's children, or a king to one's
subjects. It has been well observed that "both Kent and Cordelia continue to
regard it [the master-servant bond and the parent-child bond] as binding
even after Lear has cut it."[21]

Lear's manner of dividing the kingdom does indeed point to a mysterious
purpose, for, as has often been noted since Coleridge, it is known be-
forehand that each daughter will get a third of the kingdom and their required protestations of love are thus empty formalities. Again, it is a question
of Lear's affections, in the passive sense of being shown that he is loved.
Such a preoccupation appears unclear, if not altogether foolish, however,
and one of the play's sources, *King Leir,* at least offered a motive for the
king's sudden craving. In that text Cordeila is presented as one of that breed
of daughter who, like Juliet or Desdemona, would marry for love even at the
risk of paternal displeasure. In Shakespeare's version, however, Cordelia *is*
disposed to accept her father's choice of husband, and France's willingness to
give her up to Burgundy is clear proof that no romantic love exists between
him and Cordelia. Clearly, what Lear is demanding is not obedience but
affection.

To the two major announcements of the day—the division of the kingdom
and Lear's withdrawal—there is added a third, often neglected by critics,
and that is Cordelia's marriage. The wifeless king has already married off his
two eldest daughters, and now comes the turn of his best beloved:

> ... The Princes, France and Burgundy,
> Great rivals in our youngest daughter's love,
> *Long in our court* have made their amorous sojourn,
> And here are to be answered. [I,1,45–47]

Is the long delay to be explained by the difficulty of choosing the better
suitor, or has Lear temporized for other reasons? Whatever the reasons,
Lear never intends the marriage to separate him from Cordelia, and this may
indeed be the secret motive—made public under the pressure of his wrath-
ful disappointment—for his withdrawal from the kingship: "I lov'd her most,
and thought to set my rest / On *her* kind nursery" (I,1,122–23).

At this point we become lost in a psychological nexus that blurs act and
motivation, but we may be guided by textual responses that are clear in their

implications: the reactions of Lear's daughters themselves, who are not for a moment mistaken about the king's weaknesses.

With acute insight Goneril and Regan attune their flattery to the two values that Lear has still not renounced: life and affection. Goneril, as in the sources, declares that she values her father as much as life itself and is rewarded with life-giving possessions: "champains rich, plenteous rivers" (later Lear returns to the theme when, in his rage, he curses her with sterility, in I,4,276). Regan plays a different tune, significantly. Whereas in Holinshed she vaunts a love "farre above all other creatures of the world," in Shakespeare's version she is more explicit, claiming to be

> . . . an enemy to all other joys
> Which the most precious square of sense possesses,
> And find *I am alone felicitate*
> In your dear highness' love. [I,1,72–75]

Such words have a touch of the incestuous[22] and, spoken before a full assembly that includes Regan's husband, are outrageously indecent as well as hypocritical. But they are strategically correct, for Regan has sensed Lear's deep need for affection—the extreme form of which is Pandarism: "I could live and die in the eyes of Troilus"—just as she later fathoms and exploits the same need in Edmund (V,1; V,3,77) and Oswald (IV,5,21).

Lear or Cordelia

In Cordelia's response to the love-trial Shakespeare dramatizes the basic conflict between father and daughter. Cordelia pays little heed to the sisters' hypocrisy or greed for gain; rather, she focuses on the distinction between fathers and husbands and on the fact that each has his due: "Sure I shall never marry like my sisters, / To love my father all" (I,1,102–03). Her concern is, first of all, with her own imminent commitments: how could she declare herself insensitive to the marriage bond at the very moment that her suitors are standing in the wings? But, beyond this, she senses in Lear's strange need for affection a far deeper threat, a denial of the marriage bond itself: "Why have my sisters husbands, if they say / They love you all?" (I,1,98–99). The danger posed by Lear thus resembles that of other Shakespearean heroes in the grips of passion. Othello and Leontes become possessed by their jealousy, Macbeth by his lust for power, until all competing affections have become swallowed up. Lear also loses the requisite sense of balance and his greed for affection becomes dragonlike by being denied.

By contrast, Cordelia's faithfulness is a multiple task involving distinct but interrelated bonds of loyalty: between body and soul, wives and husbands, parents and children, kings and subjects. Such an attachment to bonds is termed "service"[23] and implies both self-mastery (IV,3,13) and a firm attachment to the precondition of all bonds, whether her devotion to her father or Kent's to his master:

> This devotion presupposes an even more fundamental
> devotion to the truth, and it therefore serves
> only the truth in Lear—in "Royal Lear"—and
> not the caprices of vanity or senility.[24]

Here is yet another dimension of Cordelia's "truthfulness": beyond sincerity and faithfulness, it refers to the true doctrine as to how bonds both constitute and preserve humanity. In Lear's case it is the interdependent nature of bonds that are stressed, the doctrine that the neglect of one endangers them all, as Sydney pointed out in a passage remarkably apposite to the situation in *King Lear:*

> ... that whoever breaks the marriage bond
> "dissolues al humanitie," and that the laws fold
> us within assured bounds, "which once broken,
> man's nature infinitely rangeth."[25]

To get the accurate view of Cordelia that Shakespeare intended, it seems proper to place her, as the psalmist suggests, a little lower than the angels and closer to earth. And here we may return to Bradley's lesson of *Lear:* "Let us renounce the world, hate it and lose it gladly. The only real thing in it is the soul, with its courage, patience, devotion" (p. 260). Such a belief could be ascribed to Lear, especially to his desire for renouncement, less so to his willingness to lose the world gladly. But there is little to be gained in viewing Cordelia in this light, not that she does not show the soul's greatness, or courage, patience, and devotion. But she simply never projects a sense that the world is to be hated and renounced—nor, for that matter, do the other righteous characters in the play, Kent and Edgar. We have already noted that such a view comes, significantly, from Lear himself:

> Thou art a soul in bliss. . . . [IV,7,46]

> Upon such sacrifices, my Cordelia,
> The Gods themselves throw incense. [V,3,20–21]

This is because bliss and renouncement are part of Lear's vision of things. But they are not Cordelia's, and to argue her angelic status at this juncture would require us to overlook the simple fact that her only speech in the entire departure scene concludes with a proposal that is resolutely concrete and practical: "Shall we not see these daughters and these sisters?" (V,3,7). Further, and without denying the king's tremendous suffering and moral progress, we should view his final renouncement as but a heightened form of the very withdrawal and sentimental dependency that characterize his entire career: from the staged love-trial, through the reconciliation ("I know that you do not love me"), to the final love song and withdrawal from the world of "We two alone." It is clear that Lear continues to refuse the simple reality that Cordelia is married and that the bond with her husband is as valid as the bond with her father.[26] We are still confronted, then, with the same tension between father and daughter that existed at the outset: a father who renounces the world so as to delight in his daugher, and a daughter who retains a fuller ideal of duty and doing. It would have been cruel of Cordelia to press her point, in view of the old man's suffering and mental instability. But we, for whom the question of Lear's fault is crucial for grasping the depths of the tragedy, when we hear the king's desperate "Have I caught thee?" do we not hear echoes of the daughter's reproach: "What, shall I love my father *all?*"

Few critics have elaborated the tragic nature of Lear's escapism, the fact that his final abdication "spells out the repudiation of all worldly service."[27] Even Danby has generously judged that in this instance the "king's goodness is convalescent."[28] Robert Heilman correctly views Lear's abdication as a "refusal of responsibility, a withdrawal from the necessary involvement in the world of action,"[29] but I dissent from his view that this flaw "is echoed in Cordelia."[30] To describe Cordelia's patient tirade of scene 1 (or Kent's, similar in intent) as narrow self-protection is adventurous. To speak of her nonparticipation is to disregard her forgiving reception and care of her father, her military invasion, and her plea with Lear to see the sisters rather than be dragged off to prison. As an alternative explanation, Roy Battenhouse has imagined Cordelia's conversion, and Kent's as well, from a calculating kind of love (the bond) to an open, unlimited charity.[31] What all such views overlook is both Cordelia's *legitimate* self-love—in this case her interest in the integrity of her imminent marriage—and especially the organic relation between Cordelia's moral activism and her doctrine of natural bonds. In brief, is it adequate to speak of "mere bonds," or are these not in fact coextensive with true love and service?

Justice and Death in "King Lear"

If Bradley seems wrong in his discovery of renouncement and world-hatred in *King Lear*, then, it is not because such feelings are not to be found in the play, but because he extends them beyond the king, to whom they are appropriate, to Cordelia and to Shakespeare himself. It is likewise difficult to find proof in *Lear* that power and prosperity are evil by nature or that adversity is necessarily blessed. "Throughout that stupendous Third Act the good are seen as growing better through suffering, and the bad worse through success" (Bradley, p. 260). Again, neither Cordelia nor Kent grow better through suffering, and the fact that villains such as Goneril or sinners such as Lear do suffer may perhaps better be viewed, given the play's idea of strict retributive justice, as wrong being set right, as the restoration of a good natural order.

The point must be pursued a bit further because of a confusion traceable to Johnson's shock upon finding *Lear* "contrary to the natural ideas of justice":

> A play in which the wicked prosper and the virtuous miscarry may doubtless be good because it is a just representation of the common events of human life; but since all reasonable beings naturally love justice, I cannot easily be persuaded that the observation of justice makes a play worse.[32]

While Cordelia's innocence and suffering may be granted, the play offers no proof whatever for the second and quite distinct proposition that the wicked prosper. To be sure, *if* the world lacked an agent of retribution, then man's outrage and revolt would lead him to despair in the very possibility of doing good: "I'll never care what wickedness I do / If this man come to good" (III,7,97–98), says the servant after Cornwall has put out Gloucester's eyes; and in the course of the play it is true that the wicked do enjoy their moment of triumph. But would Johnson's criterion of reasonableness be more satisfied if punishment always followed immediately upon misconduct and before the wheel of retribution could come full circle? Cornwall's rapid death is exceptional in this regard and is doubtless due to the atrocious nature of his crime:

> Albany. "This shows you are above,
> You justicers, that these our nether crimes
> So speedily can venge!" [IV,2,78–80]

But, in the end, all of the play's villains perish: Goneril, Regan, Cornwall, Edmund, Oswald, and the knave who murders Cordelia, and their deaths are not constitutive of tragedy: "This judgment of the heavens, that makes us tremble, / Touches us not with pity" (V,3,230–31). It is rather visible proof that "The gods are just, and of our pleasant vices / Make instruments to plague us" (V,3,169–70). In *King Lear* there is not a single infringement of this iron rule of justice.

But in *King Lear* the good also die. And what about Lear himself? It seems to have escaped notice that in this play death is governed by strict patterns. At the lowest level are the characters of complete wickedness, and these die by external and violent means: Goneril, Oswald, Edmund, and Cornwall by the blade, Regan by poison, the murderer of Cordelia by strangulation. The second and most important group of characters to die in *Lear*—Gloucester, Kent, and Lear himself—are not villains but are nevertheless subject to the wheel of justice. They perish from no external violence but rather from within, specifically from *broken hearts,* in a wide range of meaning that includes the literal as well as the pathetic. The extreme coherence of these images of dying is highlighted when, in the final scene, Albany utters the grave oath: "*Let sorrow split my heart,* if ever I / Did hate thee or thy father" (V,3,176–77). Gloucester's manner of dying is a paradigm for those to follow. In a paroxysm of reconciliation,

> ... *his flaw'd heart,*
> Alack, too weak the conflict to support,
> 'Twixt two extremes of passion, joy and grief,
> *Burst* smilingly. [V,3,195–98]

In the telling, the characters drop hints as to how the audience is to react:

> Edgar. "List a brief tale;
> And when 'tis told, O! *that my heart would burst.*" [V,3,180–81]

Similarly, Albany:

> " ... I am almost ready *to dissolve,*[33]
> Hearing of this." [V,3,202–03]

Edgar then proceeds to tell of Kent's arrival and of the onset of his death:

> Edgar. "[Kent] fastened on my neck, and bellow'd out
> As he'd burst heaven; threw him on my father;
> Told the most piteous tale of Lear and him
> That ever ear receiv'd; which in recounting
> His grief grew puissant, and *the strings of life*
> Began to crack."[34] [V,3,211–16]

The image is sustained to the very end when, at the climax of his despair, Kent implores: "Break, heart; I prithee, break!" (V,3,311). The Quarto text ascribes these words to Lear himself—an unlikely suggestion if Lear is "already beyond speech" (Muir), but consonant with the symbolic resolution of Lear's destiny and with the play's coherent metaphorical structures.

For the heart, as traditionally understood and as studied above, is the center of the self or ego ("my heart and me," *Lear* I,1,114), the counterpart, in the phenomenal world, of the soul, with which it forms that substantial unity that defines the nature of man for the extent of his earthly life. In this view death is defined as the unbinding of the soul from the heart-body,[35] with the resultant dissolution of Donne's "subtle knot that makes us man." Going back at least to the *Phaedo,* this metaphorical tradition receives magnificent poetic expression in Cleopatra's farewell:

> " ... Come, thou mortal wretch,
> [*To an asp, which she applies to her breast.*]
> With thy sharp teeth this knot intrinsicate
> Of life at once untie." [*Antony and Cleopatra,* V,2,303–05, italics in text]

"Intrinsicate" is synonymous with Donne's "subtle" and the "knots" are the same.[36]

It is to be noted that in Shakespeare the wicked don't die of broken hearts, either because they have none—who could imagine Iago to show an emotion, even under torture, someone has asked—or because their hearts, as Othello's under the passion of jealousy, have turned to stone (IV,1,182). In such cases violence is the only possible (dis-)solution: the heart-body, as it were, has become too attached to the world and must be forcibly dispatched. It is rather to a partially reconciled humanity that the privilege[37] of a broken heart is reserved, to such an extent that, in *Lear* at least, to die of a broken heart is virtually a tautology. One always dies of a broken heart, and the best are those who acknowledge and even solicit the final breaking. Gloucester's heart, it is true, burst because of a failure of strength. But the more protean Kent and especially Lear call it down upon themselves: "Break heart; I prithee, break!" (V,3,311).[38] If, as the Quarto says, it is Lear who utters these words, then Bradley's now popular hint that Lear dies in a fit of ecstasy because he thinks Cordelia has revived must be rejected. For, just as Kent can die only when the source of his affection (Lear) has been extinguished, Lear cannot conceivably have a broken heart, in the pathetic sense, if his beloved Cordelia still lives. For it is one of the play's deepest intuitions that the bonds of our life and our affections (and, Cordelia would add, the bonds of our duties) are synonymous.

At the third and highest level is the death of the innocent, he whose heart-soul is already in this life so *délié*, detached or dead in the Platonic sense, that actual death is received with equanimity. Such is the death of Cordelia, which raised Johnson's very legitimate and anguished question as to why the innocent suffer, but strikes us with sadness rather than either outrage or a feeling of senselessness. There is rather a proud feeling that this is the best that mankind can offer, that if the gods accept anything it will be this fragile strength: "Upon such sacrifices, my Cordelia, / The Gods themselves throw incense" (V,3,20–21).

I would propose that Cordelia's death does not appear as tragic to the degree that she can be viewed in her own terms, that such an event is a measure of our own degree of reconciliation with things. If this feeling is correct, it but reflects the source of our Delian metaphors, Socrates' death in the *Phaedo*. Thoroughly practiced in Delian detachment, the philosopher goes to his death with serenity, but his disciples weep nevertheless.

Conclusion

To return to the issue of tragedy in *Lear,* Bradley, as we have seen, situates the tragic element *in* the world and in man's *failure* to withdraw from it and value inwardness, whereas for Everett the tragedy arises from the metaphysical divorce between man and his cosmic environment. Against both I have argued that Lear's flaw, on the level of conduct, lies in his *voluntary withdrawal* from the world from first to last, that his renouncement is, far from a redemption from tragedy, its very source. Perhaps it is beside the point to speak of *Lear* in terms either of hatred of the world or love of the world, or, if the latter, only in the sense of Montaigne's final wisdom: "As for me then, I love my life and cherish it, such as it hath pleased God to grant it us" (*Essais*, bk. 3, chap. 13, trans. J. Florio). Patience and ripeness would then mean simply taking life on its own terms and not trying to restyle its rules to please us; it would mean, in other words, neither hating nor loving life but rather accepting it.

And preserving it, the play adds, by teaching an activism that is the opposite of renunciation and that is adequately summarized by Edgar's astonishingly simple:

> Albany. "How have you known the miseries of your father?"
> Edgar. "*By nursing them*, my Lord." [V,3,179–80]

Too much has been written about the gods in *Lear*, without noticing that quoted speeches commit only their speakers and that there is a general and positive evolution of such notions as the play progresses.[39] But the stress is on conduct:

> Lear. "O! I have ta'en
> Too little care of this. Take physic, Pomp;
> Expose thyself to feel what wretches feel,
> That thou mayst shake the superflux to them,
> *And show the Heavens more just.*" [III,4,32–36]

Perhaps, as the *Leir* source had suggested, the heavens are already just, but in Shakespeare they will be made more so by man's actions. Moreover, man's service is mightily independent, not only of the gods but also of the affection and acceptance of the recipients:

> Kent. "Now, banish'd Kent,
> If thou canst serve where thou dost stand condemn'd." [I,4,5]

It would be a critical failing to assume that a recognition of Lear's second fault—the motive or "affection" that gives rise to his tragic abdication—must involve moral condemnation. If this fault is no different from Edmund's—a craving need for affection—its attachment to an especially beloved child and under conditions of world-weariness strikes us as humanly justifiable. Abraham apparently saw beyond this point in the binding of his son Isaac; we cannot.[40] This is perhaps why it has been mentioned so seldom in critical writing. It is so deeply rooted as to be constitutive of our condition and, as such, tragic rather than reprehensible; so deeply rooted, in fact, that poets have ascribed the need for man's love to the very Being that is self-sufficient: "Was willst Du tun, Gott, wenn ich sterbe?" (Rilke). For, according to one theological tradition that was disappearing in Shakespeare's world but that still left its echoes, God delights in contemplative man's attachment to Him, in the union with His beloved in the Garden of Spices. From this perspective, Lear's prison must be seen not only as a vehement withdrawal from the world but also as his paradise: "No, no, no, no! Come, let's away to prison; / We two alone will sing like birds" (V,3,8–9), and this call to Cordelia may be viewed as the contemplative's reply to Donne's "Else a great Prince in prison lies" ("The Ecstasy"). The princely soul, like the God it worships, lies in prison because that is where it wishes to be.[41]

But if I love my father *all*, asks Cordelia, who will take care of his world? The question was asked on a theological level by Leone Ebreo and his followers, and their answer is Cordelia's. And if the answer has mainly a dramatic interest for us, its implications are important, nevertheless, in terms of the debate over the contemplative versus the active life. Freud touched upon a deep truth when he identified Cordelia as the death-wish, to which Harbage reacted by claiming for her a life-wish as well.[42] Both are helpful insights if we specify that it is for the withdrawn and contemplative father that Cordelia is the death-wish, but for the inhabitants of the kingdom she is very much the opposite. She is both death and life, like the moon by which she is symbolized and whose name—Delia—she carries.

From the sources we could expect Cordelia to have committed suicide, but this would have negated her emblematic essence as an ideal link between heaven and earth and as humanity's bond both with nature and with one another. Her death, brutal and incomprehensible, symbolizes a break in the link, a weakening of social bonds and a separation from natural forces. It in fact seems to signify the end of an era (and this may account for its being "too large for the stage"),[43] the impossibility, under the present historical dispensation, of "speaking what we ought to say," as Cordelia did in the court scene. Rather, in these sad times we must be content with speaking "what we feel." Stated differently, modern man has lost his contact with the objective order of natural duties and is reduced to relying on the revelations of his own heart. We recall that Montaigne also insisted on the importance of sincerity, but he had no illusions as to the purely relative value of its disclosures.

Perhaps, finally, *King Lear* hints at yet another and earlier revolution in the history of human consciousness, and this involves the withdrawal and death of the Father, the end of the contemplative tradition. Cordelia's "nothing" is perfectly motivated in terms both of her sisters' hypocrisy and of what she "ought" to have said. But in the purity of ancient traditions, when kings could be brought to serve the community only under compulsion and when ritual and praise had a rationale that superseded even natural duties, Cordelia's answer would have seemed a profanation, a refusal of the soul to acknowledge its true source.

Notes

Introduction

1. Helen Gardner, "The Argument about 'The Ecstasy,'" in *Elizabethan and Jacobean Studies Presented to F. P. Wilson*, eds. Herbert Davis and Helen Gardner (Oxford, 1959), pp. 279–306.

2. A. J. Smith, "Donne in His Time: A Reading of 'The Extasie,'" *Review of English Studies* 36 (1958): 261.

3. Edmund Gosse, *The Life and Letters of John Donne* (New York, 1899), vol. 1, p. 291.

4. Michel de Montaigne, *Essais* (trans. John Florio), bk. 3, chap. 5.

5. A "scholastic Don Juan" is Pierre Legouis's well-known epithet for Donne in such poems as "The Ecstasy," in *Donne the Craftsman* (Paris, 1928), p. 70.

6. C. S. Lewis, "Donne and Love Poetry in the Seventeenth Century," in *John Donne: A Collection of Critical Essays*, ed. H. Gardner (Englewood Cliffs, 1962), p. 92. The need for a synthetic approach may be seen J. B. Leishman's observation that "the intense personal drama of Donne's love-poetry has seemed incomprehensible to two kinds of critic: to those whom we may call the idealists, because the experience described does not seem to be leading anywhere or pointing to anything beyond itself; and to those whom we may call the materialists, because it all seems to be much ado about nothing"; in *The Monarch of Wit: An Analytical and Comparative Study of the Poetry of John Donne* (London, 1962), p. 217.

7. From Grierson's introductory essay to his edition, *The Poems of John Donne*, 2 vols. (London, 1912), 2: p. xxxiv.

8. Héroët likens sexual pleasures to servants (bodies) having fun while their masters (souls) are out; see his *La Parfaicte Amye*, vv. 598–604, in *Oeuvres poétiques*, ed. Ferdinand Gohin (Paris, 1909). Robert Ellrodt sees the similarity with the situation in Donne's "The Ecstasy" and tries—unsuccessfully in my opinion—to distinguish them on the basis of Héroët's relative bad faith (*Les Poètes métaphysiques anglais* vol. 3 [Paris, 1960], pp. 89–90). The connection between Héroët and Donne had been made previously by Merritt Hughes, in "The Lineage of 'The Extasie,'" *The Modern Language Review* 27 (1932): 2–3.

9. Héroët, *Parfaicte Amye*, vv. 1595–1606.

10. Héroët, "Epitaphe de Louise de Savoie," vv. 101–6, in *Oeuvres*, ed. Gohin, p. 118.

11. Pernette du Guillet, epigram 49, in *Rymes*, ed. Victor Graham (Geneva, 1968).

12. Speron Speroni, *Dialoghi* (Venice, 1606), p. 19; quoted in Merritt Hughes, "Some of Donne's 'Ecstasies,'" *PMLA* 75 (1960): 516, n. 73.

13. Peter Dronke, *Medieval Latin and the Rise of European Love-Lyric*, 2 vols. (Oxford, 1965–66); Richard Cody, *The Landscape of the Mind* (Oxford, 1969).

14. Ananda K. Coomaraswamy, "Love and Art," *The Modern Review* (Calcutta), May 1915, p. 574. In his *Four Quartets* T. S. Eliot noted that both attachment and detachment—as opposed to indifference—are forms of love.

15. Montaigne, *Essais* (trans. John Florio), bk. 3, chap. 13; quoted in Cody, *Landscape*, p. 172.

16. See, for example, Agrippa d'Aubigné's early poetic synthesis of Leone's eroticism, *Le Printemps, stance* xvii, ed. Henri Weber (Paris and Montpellier, 1960), pp. 250–64.

Chapter 1

1. Marcelino Menéndez y Pelayo, *Historia de las ideas estéticas en España*, vol. 1 (Madrid, 1974), p. 488.

2. The *Dialoghi d'amore* were first published in Rome in 1535. Throughout this book I refer to the standard critical edition by Santino Caramella (Bari, 1929; cited hereafter as Leone, *Dialoghi*). In my translations of Leone, I rely heavily on Pontus de Tyard's excellent French translation, *Dialogues d'amour* (Lyon, 1551; cited hereafter as Léon, *Dialogues*), which I have published in the University of North Carolina Studies in Comparative Literature (Chapel Hill, 1974).

3. Aristotle, *Nicomachean Ethics* 8.2.1155b. Leone is indebted to this passage throughout much of the present discussion.

4. On the active versus the contemplative life, see Aristotle, *Nicomachean Ethics* 10.7ff. This same work (10.8) may have prompted Leone's observation that the virtue of liberality requires money, as well as the assertion that moral virtue depends as much on actual performance of virtuous acts as on right intention.

5. For a concise discussion of these terms see Jacques Maritain, *Art and Scholasticism*, trans. J. W. Evans (New York, 1962), pp. 5–6.

6. Moses Maimonides insists that study is necessary to human perfection and gives the curriculum in the following order: logic, the various branches of mathematics, physics, metaphysics. He goes on to observe that little advance is possible, however, without moral goodness; in *The Guide for the Perplexed*, trans. M. Friedländer, rev. ed. in 1 vol. (1904, reprint ed., New York: Dover Publications, 1956), pt. 1, chap. 34.

7. See the important discussion of final beatitude in Leone in Heinz Pflaum, *Die Idee der Liebe: Leone Ebreo* (Tübingen, 1926), pp. 90–94.

8. In addition to the authors studied below, a more liberal attitude toward sexuality was held by the Italian theoreticians Benedetto Varchi and Flamineo de Nobili; on the first see Robert Ellrodt, *Neoplatonism in the Poetry of Spenser* (Geneva, 1960), p. 145; on the second see idem, *Les Poètes métaphysiques anglais*, vol. 3, p. 403.

9. The most successful literary use of Leone's theory of extraordinary reason occurs in Jorge de Montemayor's *Los siete libros de la Diana*, ed. Francisco López Estrada (Madrid, 1962). See below, ch. 7.

10. See Pflaum, *Die Idee der Liebe*, p. 98. Leone himself summarizes the *Dialoghi* by observing that "love is a *vivifying* spirit that penetrates the entire world" (*Dialoghi*, p. 165).

11. The view that sperm is produced by the entire body is found in *The Zohar* (vol. 2, p. 82), the major work of the Kabbalah (trans. H. Sperling, M. Simon, and P. Levertoff, 5 vols. [London, 1933–34]).

12. See below, n. 17.

13. See also Maimonides, *Guide for the Perplexed*, pt. 1, chap. 72: "You must therefore consider the entire globe as one individual being which is endowed with life, motion, and a soul. This mode of considering the universe is ... very useful for demonstrating the unity of God; it also helps to elucidate the principle that He who is One has created only *one* being" (trans. Friedländer, p. 115, italics in text).

14. Ananda K. Coomaraswamy, *Spiritual Authority and Temporal Power in the Indian Theory of Government* (New Haven, 1942), p. 75, n. 56. This work gives some interesting Indian parallels to Leone's view that "generation is common to all things in the universe" (*Dialoghi*, p. 107) and that this generation always depends on two principles: "one formal or giving, the other material or receiving; therefore the poets call the formal principle 'giving Father' and the material principle 'receiving Mother'" (*Dialoghi*, p. 108).

15. Similarly, according to Plotinus, "light is separate from air and air from light, and they do not mingle," *Enneades* IV,14,4, in Arthur H. Armstrong, *Plotinus* (New York, 1962), p. 97.

16. In view of Leone's polarization of the entire universe in terms of sexual components, it comes as no surprise to learn that the soul, the great intermediary between spiritual and material reality, is "female" or receptive with respect to the former, and "male" with regard to matter (*Dialoghi*, p. 195). Similarly, the moon is the female of the sun and the male of the earth (*Dialoghi*, p. 197). The general principle involved here and implicit throughout Leone's work is that all beings in the supramundane world have a "double relationship" (*Zohar*, vol. 3, p. 9), receptive or feminine toward their superiors and masculine or active toward their inferiors.

17. Notwithstanding, Leone frequently returns to the view that God Himself depends on man's righteousness (*Dialoghi*, pp. 157, 223), a notion common to many Kabbalistic writers and often based on the saying that the Just Man is the foundation of the universe (Proverbs 10:25); see Gershom Scholem, *Les Origines de la kabbale*, trans. Jean Loewenson (Paris, 1966), p. 165.

18. Alexander Altmann ascribes this doctrine to the Islamic Aristotelians and credits Maimonides (*Guide*, pt. 1, chap. 68) with its currency among Jewish philosophers; see his "Moses Narboni's Epistle on *Shi'ur Qoma*" in *Jewish Medieval and Renaissance Studies*, vol. 4, ed. A. Altmann (Cambridge, Mass., 1967), p. 265, n. 1.

19. The doctrine that even the angels or pure spirits are composed of form and matter or chaos is probably due to the Neoplatonic Jewish philosopher Solomon Ibn Gabirol, who was known to Leone only as "Albenzubron" but still recognized as a Jew by Leone, who refers to him as "il *nostro* Albenzubron." For his doctrine on form and matter see Ibn Gabirol's *Fons Vitae*, bk. 4, chaps. 8–9, ed. Clemens Bäumker (Munster, 1895), p. 230. For his influence on Leone Ebreo see Pflaum, *Die Idee der Liebe*, pp. 124–27.

20. See Pflaum, *Die Idee der Liebe*, p. 128.

21. The first doctrine, the view that the agent intellect is the lowest of the angels, was maintained by Jewish Neoaristotelian philosophers in Italy such as Jehudah Romano (born 1292), while the identification of the agent intellect with God, which Leone favors, was defended especially by Christians such as Thomas Aquinas. On

this complicated question see Josef B. Sermoneta, *La dottrina dell'intelletto e la "fede filosofica" di Jehudah e Immanuel Romano* (Spoleto, 1965). On the central problem of intellection in Leone, see Suzanne Damiens, *Amour et intellect chez Léon l'Hébreu* (Toulouse, 1971), reviewed by T. A. Perry in *Modern Language Notes* 88 (1973):421–25.

22. A detailed analysis of this complex aesthetic is not possible here. The most extensive study is that of Marcelino Menéndez y Pelayo, *Historia de las ideas estéticas*, vol. 1, pp. 488–520.

23. See Robert Ellrodt's study of "Spenser's Sapience and Leone Ebreo" in his *Neoplatonism in Spenser*, pp. 183–93.

Chapter 2

1. Leone, *Dialoghi*, p. 200; page references throughout the text of chapter 2 are from this edition (Caramella's) unless otherwise noted.

2. Cervantes' beautiful shepherdess Marcella (*Quijote*, pt. 1, chap. 14) exemplifies such a close connection between amorous detachment and a more philosophical and general disregard for all earthly things whatever. Her refusal to show mercy to her suitors is justified, in Platonic language, as a desire to "contemplate the beauty of heaven, steps with which the soul approaches its original dwelling."

3. Scant attention has been paid to the literary dimensions of the *Dialoghi*. See, for example, *Dialoghi*, pp. 427–28, and Pflaum, *Die Idee der Liebe*, p. 96.

4. Jacques Schlanger, "Le Maître et le disciple du *Fons Vitae*," *Revue des Etudes Juives* 127 (1968):393.

5. See Pflaum, *Die Idee der Liebe*, pp. 124–27.

6. The opposing Augustinian view, according to which love is both epistemologically and ontologically prior to knowledge, is brilliantly treated by Max Scheler, *Liebe und Erkenntnis* (Bern, 1955), pp. 5–28.

7. Later, Filone reviews the conclusions of the first dialogue and, while agreeing with Sofia that "love, being the more excellent word, is applicable first of all to persons that exist and to things excellent either for their perfection or because they are possessed," he again somewhat paradoxically adds that "in substance" the meaning of the terms love and desire is identical (Leone, *Dialoghi*, p. 213). Sofia recognizes the perspective of such a view: "I concede that *among mortals* all love is desire and all desire is love."

8. This is the opinion of Josef Klausner, "Don Yehudah Abrabanel ufilosofiat ha-ahavah shelo," *Tarbiz* 3 (1932):89. See above, chap. 1, n. 17.

9. Schlanger, "Le Maître et le disciple," pp. 393–97, reaches similar conclusions regarding the function of dialogue in Ibn Gabirol's *Fons Vitae*.

10. For example, Menéndez y Pelayo, *Historia de las ideas estéticas*, vol. 2, p. 491: "Filone and his beloved Sofia, purely abstract characters which symbolize, as their names suggest, love or appetite and knowledge or wisdom."

11. Caramella's assertion that Sofia's beauty is only spiritual (Leone, *Dialoghi*, p. 428) is not supported in the text, and Filone's judgments are naturally to the contrary (pp. 52, 172, 174).

12. On the use of the term *Chokhmah* (the traditional rendering of Greek *sophia*)

in Jewish philosophy in the sense of philosophical rather than revealed knowledge, see Josef B. Sermoneta, *Un glossario filosofico ebraico-italico del xiii secolo* (Rome, 1969), pp. 354–55, and p. 349 n.

13. A better understanding of this kind of temperament has been made possible by recent changes in critical attitudes. See, for example, Dronke's *Medieval Latin*, vol. 1, which stresses the similarities and continuity between earthly and divine love, in contrast to the theological terminology of a sinful "this world" versus a higher world, characteristic of previous studies.

14. Merritt Hughes notes a similar concept in Donne, in "Some of Donne's 'Ecstasies,'" *PMLA*, 75 (1960), p. 515.

15. The most popular section of the *Mishnah*, the collection of ethical maxims known as "Chapters of the Fathers" (*Pirkei Avoth*) which Leone undoubtedly knew by heart, abounds in such sayings as the following: "The chief thing is not study but action" (chap. 1, par. 17); "all Torah without work ends in failure and leads to sin" (chap. 2, par. 2); "do not sever yourself from other people" (chap. 2, par. 5); "if there is no Torah there is no worldly occupation, and if there is no worldly occupation there is no Torah" (chap. 3, par. 21); in *The Mishnah*, trans. Philip Blackman, 7 vols. (New York, 1964). While not in the habit of citing his Judaic sources, Leone Ebreo nevertheless relies on the *Pirkei Avoth* (chap. 4, par. 1) in two instances: "Who is strong? He who conquers his passions. . . . Who is rich? He who is satisfied with his portion." Leone Ebreo: "dicono che 'l vero forte è quello che se medesimo vince" (*Dialoghi*, p. 17); "e li savi dicono che 'l vero ricco è quello che si contenta di quel che possiede" (*Dialoghi*, p. 14).

16. Deut. 6:4–5 is part of the *Shema'*, which Jews recite twice daily. The passage "Et con esso Dio vi coppularete" may be the rendering of Hos. 2:22: "And you shall know the Lord," which Jews recite daily upon laying on the phylacteries.

Chapter 3

1. Jean-Pierre Attal, *L'Image métaphysique et autre essais* (Paris, 1969), p. 34. Porphyry, *Sententiae*, ed. B. Mommert (Leipzig, 1907), ix; quoted in A. Altmann and S. M. Stern, *Isaac Israeli* (London, 1958), p. 30.

2. The translation of *Phaedo* used in this paragraph is David Gallop's (Oxford, 1975); cited hereafter as *Phaedo*, ed. Gallop. It is quite likely that Scève was directly familiar with the *Phaedo*, since Ficino's Latin translation appeared at the time that Scève was writing the *Délie* (Lyon: Jean Petit, 1536). In addition, Abel Lefranc alludes to Jean de Luxembourg's French translation of the *Phaedo*, which was dedicated to the duc d'Orléans, son of François I. Lefranc thinks that the translation was done before 1540 and that it circulated in courtly circles in manuscript form (*Grands Écrivains français de la Renaissance* [Paris, 1914], pp. 134–35). A further indication of the popularity of the *Phaedo* in Platonic circles in the 1540s is Marguerite de Navarre's allusion to Socrates' death in her *Prisons*, in *Les Dernières Poésies de Marguerite de Navarre*, ed. Abel Lefranc (Paris, 1896), p. 209.

3. Léon Robin's translation of 64e–65a (Paris, 1967) is suggestive of the thesis I wish to develop: "lorsque le plus possible, il *délie* l'âme du commerce du corps."

4. All references to *Délie* are to Maurice Scève, *La Délie*, ed. I. D. McFarlane

(Cambridge, 1966); cited hereafter as Scève, *Délie*. Individual strophes or *dizains* (e.g. *dizain* no. 22) are cited as *Délie* 22 or simply *D*22.

5. Verdun Saulnier, *Maurice Scève*, vol. 1 (Paris, 1948), p. 151; see pp. 146–51 for a convenient summary of current theories. Dorothy Coleman enriches the discussion but offers no radically new theories in her "Scève's Choice of the Name 'Délie,'" *French Studies* 18 (1964):1–15.

6. Cited in Héroët, *Oeuvres poétiques*, ed. F. Gohin (Paris, 1909), p. xvi. All references to Héroët are to this edition.

7. François Rabelais, *Le Tiers Livre*, ed. M. A. Screech (Geneva, 1964), p. 2.

8. Marguerite de Navarre, *Les Marguerites de la Marguerite des Princesses*, ed. Felix Frank (Paris, 1873), vol. 1, p. 12 and vol. 3, p. 166.

9. Saulnier, *Maurice Scève*, pp. 209, 249.

10. All references to this rare and important text are to my edition, Léon Hébreu, *Dialogues d'amour* (Chapel Hill, 1974; cited hereafter as Léon, *Dialogues*). For convenience I also give references to Caramella's Italian edition (Leone, *Dialoghi*).

11. See above, chap. 2.

12. Marsile Ficin, *Théologie platonicienne de l'immortalité des âmes*, 2 vols., ed. Raymond Marcel (Paris, 1964), 1:138: "Between those beings which are only eternal and those which are only temporal, the soul is a kind of link (*vinculum*)." See also Emile Bréhier, *La Philosophie de Plotin* (Paris, 1961), pp. 47ff.

13. Héroët, *L'Androgyne de Platon*, vv. 129–30, in *Oeuvres*.

14. Héroët, *Parfaicte Amye*, vv. 1431–32. The body's "obligation" to the soul will figure prominently in Donne's "The Ecstasy."

15. Héroët, *Parfaicte Amye*, vv. 939–40. Similarly, Leone, *Dialoghi*, p. 46: "In this life our intellect is tied down in some way to the matter of this frail body of ours."

16. *Phaedo*, ed. Gallop, 82d–e. It is interesting that a similar usage occurs in a letter to Marguerite dated 1524 from Guillaume Briçonnet: "[the soul] awaiting the last awakening [i.e., death], when its attachments and bonds [*laz et liens*] will be broken," cited in Marguerite de Navarre, *Théâtre profane*, ed. Verdun Saulnier (Geneva, 1963), pp. 246, 260. This important theme of the *lien* has not received the attention it deserves. Marcel Tetel gives a brief summary in his *Marguerite de Navarre's "Hemptaméron": Themes, Language, and Structure* (Durham, N.C., 1973), pp. 79–80.

17. *Phaedo*, ed. Gallop, 82e–83e. Marguerite refers to the *liens* of her hope in her "Epître à Henri II" (*Les Dernières Poésies*, p. 3). In his *Anotaciones* the Spanish poet Fernando de Herrera gives a concise statement of this stoic notion: "Hope is one of the four affections or passions of the soul to which all of its disturbances may be reduced, these being pleasure and pain, fear and hope"; cited in *Garcilaso de la Vega y sus comentaristas*, ed. Antonio Gallego Morell, 2nd ed. (Madrid, 1972), p. 323.

18. Léon, *Dialogues*, p. 68; Marguerite de Navarre, "Comédie sur le trépas du Roy," vv. 339–40, in *Théâtre profane*, p. 230.

19. In Marguerite de Navarre, *Les Dernières Poésies*, p. 248. All references to the *Prisons* are to this edition. Scève speaks of his passion as "this mortal knot [*noeud*] that ties up my heart" *Délie* 163; see also Héroët, *Parfaicte Amye*, vv. 1410–11. Hugues Salel's couplet is extremely relevant to the thesis I am advancing: "I break the knot, I unlink the chain that tightly holds my heart in pain" ("Je romps le noeud, je deslye la chaine, / Qui tient mon coeur estroictement en peine"), in *Oeuvres poétiques*, ed. L.-A. Bergounioux (Paris, 1930), p. 264.

20. Léon, *Dialogues*, p. 73; Leone, *Dialoghi*, p. 56. For the distinction between love and desire, see chapter 5.

21. Leone, *Dialoghi*, p. 135; Tyard translates (in Léon, *Dialogues*), p. 129: "les desirs excessifs se trouvent *liez*, sans liberté ny puissance."

22. Pierre Jourda, *Marguerite d'Angoulême, duchesse d'Alençon, reine de Navarre*, vol. 1 (Paris, 1930), p. 628.

23. Marguerite de Navarre, *Nouvelles* [*L'Heptaméron*], ed. Yves Le Hir (Paris, 1967), p. 168: "ceus qui par maryage nous lient aus femmes, et qui essayent par leur méchanceté à nous en délier"; again: "le lyen de maryage ne peut durer, si non autant que la vie. Et puis après on est délyé" (p. 359).

24. "Ode à Nicolas Denizot du Mans," in *Oeuvres de Pierre de Ronsard (Texte de 1587)*, ed. Isidore Silver, vol. 5 (Chicago, 1968), p. 248.

25. "Trop, prou, peu, moins," vv. 865–66, in *Théâtre profane*, p. 197.

26. The view that love is a kind of death was commonplace. The early Lyonese Platonist Symphorien Champier, recalling Ficino's commentary on Plato's *Symposium*, observed that "as Orpheus declared, he who loves dies," in *Le Livre de vraye amour*, ed. James Wadsworth (The Hague, 1962), p. 63.

27. See Coleman, "Scève's Choice of the Name 'Délie,'" p. 7.

28. See Eugène Parturier's notes to *Délie* 12, 14, 296, in his edition of *Délie, object de plus haulte vertu* (Paris, 1916).

29. See the glossary appended to the Seigneur du Parc Champenois's translation of Léon Hébreu's *Dialogues d'amour* (Lyon, 1551): "Soudre et dissoudre en propre signification valent délier." See also the examples given in Edmond Huguet's *Dictionnaire de la langue française du seizième siècle*, art. "dissoudre." The usage is traceable to the Vulgate version of Philippians 1:23. In English it goes back at least to Chaucer and is common in Donne's prose writings.

30. See Henri Weber's excellent commentary in *La Création poétique au 16e siècle en France*, vol. 1 (Paris, 1955), p. 182.

Chapter 4

1. This tradition was ultimately rejected by Montaigne in bk. 1, chap. 20, "Que philosopher c'est apprendre à mourir," *Essais*, ed. Pierre Villey (Paris, 1965), p. 81. See also Hugo Friedrich's remarks in his *Montaigne*, trans. Robert Rovini (Paris, 1968), p. 279.

2. Pierre de Ronsard, *Odes*, bk. 5, ode 7; in *Oeuvres*, ed. Silver (Chicago, 1967), vol. 3, p. 342.

3. Coleman, "Scève's Choice of the Name 'Délie,'" p. 1.

4. All references to Scève, *Délie* (see n. 4, chap. 3).

5. Leone, *Dialoghi*, p. 214.

6. For an instance of a strict assimilation of beauty to the body and goodness to the soul see Gohin's note in Héroët, *Oeuvres*, p. 43.

7. As Enzo Giudici seems to suggest in his *Maurice Scève, poeta della "Délie"* (Naples, 1969), p. 408, n. 121.

8. Jean Lemaire de Belges, *Les Epîtres de l'amant vert*, ed. Jean Frappier (Lille and Geneva, 1948), p. 7, vv. 65–66. The passage that inspired Scève's poem begins on v. 221.

9. Lemaire de Belges, *Les Epîtres*, p. 47, n. 30. By stark contrast, Giudici feels that *D247* is "of an absolute clarity" (*Maurice Scève*, p. 316).

10. In *D74* Scève seems to joke about his lack of physical appeal by a pun: "Alas! I have neither the bow nor the arrows [*traictz*, which also means 'physical features'] needed / To move my Lady to pity" (vv. 9–10).

11. For the sexual meaning see Léon, *Dialogues*, p. 79: "among the animals there are some which have sexual union [*s'accointent et apparient*] with a single female...." For a wider and more ambivalent sense see Héroët's *Androgyne*, vv. 234–35: "At times we take *accointance* / With a mate we think to be ours...."

12. Hans Staub, *Le Curieux Désir: Scève et J. Peletier du Mans, poètes de la connaissance* (Geneva, 1967), p. 40.

13. Coomaraswamy, "Love and Art," p. 580. See also Weber, *La Création poétique*, vol. 1, p. 197.

14. While inferring from Scève's poem that "hyperbole is not the monopoly of *précieux* poetry," Odette de Mourgues is comforted by its relevance to the serious metaphysical problem of absence treated in the poem; in *Metaphysical, Baroque and Précieux Poetry* (Oxford, 1953), p. 128.

15. Leone, *Dialoghi*, pp. 245–50.

16. Ibid., p. 195; Scève himself composed a poem entitled *Le Microcosme*.

17. See Giudici, *Maurice Scève*, p. 373, n. 2.

18. It is most important to note that in this poem the full moon's decline, compared to the turning away of the lady's face, is a "presage" of a decline of "foi," faithfulness. Also compare *D295*, where "ronde" refers to the moon; in *D383* the "face" is the lady's but with reference to the moon. Further, in *D376* Délie's movement is described as a *doulx contournement* ("sweet rotating"), an unusual term but one capable of evoking planetary motion (see Huguet's *Dictionnaire*, art. "contourner"). Elsewhere Scève refers to "l'influence et l'aspect" of Délie's eyes (*D416*), but the "influence" of celestial bodies was well known. Moreover, "aspect" means a "look or gaze" (*D373*), but it was a common astrological term as well. In *D319* the usage is again ambivalent.

19. Leone, *Dialoghi*, p. 189.

20. Ibid., pp. 178–79.

21. Ibid., p. 179.

22. Ibid., pp. 189–90.

Chapter 5

1. Du Moulin's brief preface "Aux Dames Lyonnoizes," reprinted in Graham's edition (see note 2 below), is virtually our only source of biographical information on Pernette and has merely been reproduced in subsequent studies. Pernette is thought to have been born around 1520; she died in July 1545.

2. Pernette's poems, left without titles, have been numbered and labeled by V. L. Saulnier in his "Etude sur Pernette du Guillet et ses *Rymes*," *BHR* 4 (1944):9–119. These *Rymes* were republished in 1546, 1547, 1552, 1830, 1856, and 1864. In our own century Albert-Marie Schmidt gave an edition in the accessible Pléiade volume *Poètes du 16e siècle* (Paris, 1953) but neglected to include Saulnier's handy titles and numbering. For convenience of reference, therefore, I use the edition of Victor Graham, *Rymes* (Geneva, 1968).

3. Leone, *Dialoghi,* p. 5.

4. Ibid., p. 51.

5. Sofia: "whatever is loved is first desired; and when the desired object has been acquired, love awakens and the desire ceases" (ibid., p. 5). For Filone's analysis of love and desire as being based on *conoscimento* or knowledge and *mancamento* or lack, see ibid., p. 260 ff.

6. Staub, *Le Curieux Désir,* p. 39ff.

7. Leone, *Dialoghi,* p. 51. In addition to their psychological differences, Filone and Sofia have important philosophical divergencies as well; see above, chap. 3.

8. Pernette's desire for knowledge and precision expresses itself as a need to "satisfy her mind": "Et toutesfois voicy un tresgrand poinct, / Lequel *me rend ma pensée assouvie . . .* " (epig. 24, vv. 8–9). Such formulas are typical of Leone's Sofia: "Solvemi, o Filone, questi dubi, *perché meglio m'acquieti l'animo* in questa materia" (Leone, *Dialoghi,* p. 273).

9. *Consommer* here means "to complete or perfect," as in *Délie* 444, v. 6; it cannot be rendered "to consume or destroy" (as in Graham's glossary to his edition of *Rymes,* p. 169), since a wish to destroy *Amour* would be totally without motivation in this context.

10. We find the same verbal distinction—but within a moralizing context—in Gilles Corrozet's *Compte du rossignol* (Lyon, 1546): " . . . pour *plaisir* si soudain abbattu, / Ne pers l'honneur et l'acquise vertu / Qui te rendra cent fois plus glorieux / Et plus *content* que l'amour furieux . . . " (reissued by F. Gohin, Paris, 1924, p. 46).

11. For *Délie* I use the edition of I. D. McFarlane:

"L'heur de nostre heur enflambant le desir
Vnit double ame en vn mesme povoir:
L'vne mourant vit du doulx desplaisir,
Qui l'autre vive a fait mort recevoir.
    Dieu aveuglé tu nous as fait avoir
Sans aultrement ensemble consentir.
Et posseder, sans nous en repentir,
Le bien du mal en effect desirable:
Fais que puissions aussi long [temps] sentir
Si doulx mourir en vie respirable." [*Délie* 136]

For a lucid interpretation of these two poems, see Weber, *La Création poétique,* vol. 1, pp. 197–98.

12. "Pour un peu veoir quelz gestes il tiendroit" (v. 21). Gaston Bachelard has reminded us that Narcissus desires as much *to be seen* as to see himself, in *L'Eau et les rêves* (Paris, 1942), p. 31.

13. Compare epigram 54: "the spirit, seeking chaste desire, / Has acquired, instead of death, new life" (vv. 7–8). Again, the stress is on chaste desire rather than chaste actions.

14. Héroët, *Parfaicte Amye,* vv. 598–604.

15. According to Pontus de Tyard, poetry and love are two of the four types of *fureur* under the guidance of which man can regain his divine image. See his *Solitaire premier,* ed. Sylvio Baridon (Geneva, 1950), p. 17.

16. Saulnier, "Etude sur Pernette," p. 74, calls Pernette's love "chaste, ethereal, *incorporeal.*" For a balanced discussion of this point see Robert Griffin, "Pernette du Guillet's Response to Scève: A Case for Abstract Love," *Esprit Créateur* 5 (1965): 110–16.

17. Leone, *Dialoghi*, p. 51.

18. This quotation is from Ananda K. Coomaraswamy's beautiful and profound essay on ideal love, "Sahaja," in *The Dance of Shiva* (New York, 1957), p. 129.

19. Saulnier, "Etude sur Pernette," p. 63; Leone, *Dialoghi*, p. 14.

20. "Humanistic" is Saulnier's term, "Etude sur Pernette," pp. 70, 75.

21. Staub, *Le Curieux Désir*, pp. 46–47, writes excellently that Scève tries to maintain, "against the autonomy of desire and the temptation of sublimation, the totality of a love *humanly* experienced."

Chapter 6

1. Marguerite de Navarre, *Les Dernières Poésies*, p. 305.

2. It seems not to have been noticed that Valéry Larbaud's well-known epithet for Héroët, "le digne Evêque de Digne," was probably inspired by Guillaume Colletet's remark: "François premier... jugea celui-ci bien digne d'être évêque, et d'être même évêque de Digne en Dauphiné"; cited in Héroët, pp. 154–55. For the puns *heroic* and *erotic* see ibid., pp. xliv, xxxvii.

3. Valéry Larbaud, *Notes sur Antoine Héroët et Jean de Lingendes* (Paris, 1927).

4. In Héroët, *Oeuvres*, p. 155. For Héroët's works I use the Gohin edition cited in note 8 of my introduction (a second edition appeared in 1943 with a different pagination), giving verse and title with the following abbreviations: *Amye* (La Parfaicte Amye), *Androgyne* (L'Androgyne de Platon), *Douleur* (Douleur et volupté). Jean de Tournes's excellent edition of most of Héroët's works (Lyon, 1547) has been reissued by M. A. Screech, *Opuscules d'amour par Héroët, La Borderie, et autres divins poètes* (New York and The Hague, 1970).

5. Larbaud, *Notes*, pp. 73–74.

6. George Sand, *La Mare au diable*, ed. Léon Cellier (Paris, 1973), p. 183. Interesting parallels exist between Héroët's and Sand's heroines, especially Marie (*Mare au diable*) and Fadette.

7. For the American critic Philip Rahv (*Literature and the Sixth Sense* [Boston, 1970], p. 28), "a positive approach to experience"—that is, the attitude that concrete experience rather than puritanical abstention is the proper medium for the creation of value—"is the touchstone of the modern."

8. Marguerite de Navarre, *L'Heptaméron* (published under the title of *Nouvelles*), ed. Yves Le Hir (Paris, 1967), p. 202.

9. As Denis de Rougemont has shown in *Love in the Western World*, trans. Montgomery Belgion (New York, 1956), p. 100.

10. On this delicate subject see Alan Watts, *Erotic Spirituality: The Vision of Konarak* (New York, 1971), pp. 72–76.

11. See *Amye* v. 1158; on Nature see *Amye* v. 1130 and *Douleur* v. 144; for Cupid see *Amye* v. 915, in Héroët, *Oeuvres*.

12. C. S. Lewis was struck by a similar contrast between Aristotelian ethics and the new state of mind characteristic of both Stoics and Christians; see his *Allegory of Love* (New York, 1958), pp. 58–60.

13. *Amye* 1379–80, in Héroët, *Oeuvres;* Leone, *Dialoghi,* p. 219 ff.

14. Leone, *Dialoghi,* p. 289ff.

15. When the androgyne was reintegrated, Héroët observes—with a touch of humor and a large measure of seriousness: "We have no information on the meetings they had: / They were so embarrassed that all their get-togethers / Since that time have been in secret. And they kept hidden, both from *the Gods* and from men, / That pleasure that abounds in all good things" (*Androgyne* 204–8 in Héroët, *Oeuvres*). The variants in such a heterodoxical work are of great interest. In this instance two early sources carry the variant "à Dieu": they managed to conceal their reunions even from God.

16. Albert-Marie Schmidt, *Etudes sur le 16e siècle* (Paris, 1967), p. 192.

17. The notion of personalism in this extended sense can be applied to Scève as well, since Délie, in addition to being a call to the purification of desires, is also a concrete person. Nevertheless, a generalizing spirit can be detected in such positions, as may be seen in André Festugière's approach, which seems to me an acceptable statement of a Scèvian attitude: "One cannot love a concept, a universal. For the soul to be drawn to an object it must be able to aspire to that object as to a *Principle which,* in itself unique and singular, *would have in some sense the characteristics of a person";* in *Contemplation et vie contemplative selon Platon* (Paris, 1936), p. 254.

Chapter 7

1. Jorge de Montemayor, *Los siete libros de la Diana,* ed. F. López Estrada, 3rd ed. (Madrid, 1962), cited hereafter as *La Diana* (page references in the text of chapter 7 refer to this edition, unless otherwise noted).

2. Mia Gerhardt, *La Pastorale: essai d'analyse littéraire* (Assen, 1950), p. 188. See also Bruce Wardropper, "The *Diana* of Montemayor: Revaluation and Interpretation," *Studies in Philology* 48 (1951):126–44.

3. J. B. Avalle-Arce, *La novela pastoril española* (Madrid, 1959), p. 81.

4. A second and related irony is in the character of Diana herself. Unfaithful to her first love and unhappily married, her natural beauty and manners remain exemplary in their perfection ("exemplary" is one meaning of "poetic" in Neoaristotelian criticism; see Américo Castro, *El pensamiento de Cervantes* [Madrid, 1925], pp. 29–30). It is she who chastizes Sylvano because he has allowed his attention to stray from the one worthy occupation: praise of love and beauty (*La Diana,* p. 272). Diana is Montemayor's cautious experiment in courtly love, in her wanderings from her husband and especially in her role of *belle inconnue,* of beautiful absence that causes suffering.

5. See Gustavo Correa, "El Templo de Diana en la novela de Jorge de Montemayor," *Thesaurus* 16 (1961):69, n. 11.

6. Avalle-Arce (*La novela pastoril,* p. 79, n. 58) rejects Lapesa's concept of a "dematerialization" and prefers to speak of a "pastoral-ization of reality where reality values are transmuted—and gain thereby in universality—upon passing from History to Myth."

7. An extreme example of this is A. Solé-Leris, "The Theory of Love in the Two *Dianas:* A Contrast," *Bulletin of Hispanic Studies* 36 (1959):65–79.

8. Against Solé-Leris's peculiar assertion that "the theory of extraordinary reason never comes into the *Diana* at all" ("Theory of Love," p. 77), one need only read *La Diana*, pp. 195–98. The further and consequent claim that through this putative omission "Montemayor drastically distorts his thought to suit his own point of view" ("Theory of Love," p. 77) is unintelligible. Like Leone Ebreo before him, Montemayor tried to account for both sides of the paradox wherein love can be both irrational *and* reasonable in a higher sense. Far from being a "last minute expedient" that was "shamefacedly conjured up" ("Theory of Love," pp. 77–78), the theory of extraordinary reason was grasped in its higher rationality and made the doctrinal core of *La Diana*.

9. Is Felicia's doctrine any different from the perfect love attributed by Coomaraswamy to the troubadours as the deepest meaning of their courtly love? Consider the love song of Chandidas, which combines wild devotion with perfect selflessness: "I have taken refuge at your feet, my beloved. When I do not see you my mind has no rest. You are to me as a parent to a helpless child. You are the goddess herself—the garland about my neck—my very universe. All is darkness without you, you are the meaning of my prayers. I cannot forget your grace and your charm—*and yet there is no desire in my* heart." In Coomaraswamy, *Dance of Shiva*, p. 127. For desire implies, as the readers of Leone Ebreo knew, consciousness of a lack on the part of the lover. But to love the person entirely for herself ("with no hope of further gain or reward"), this alone is perfect selflessness. Felicia's doctrine is hermetic because it is an absolute ideal, never fully understood because never perfectly experienced. Further parallels may be found in Dronke, *Medieval Latin*, vol. 1. Relevant to our discussion of ideal love are the following topics of Dronke's study: the unity of human and divine love—"you are the goddess herself"—(*Medieval Latin*, vol. 1, pp. 5–7, 66–69); love as a school of perfection ("one must love 'by Love'—lovingly, not calculatingly," ibid., p. 34; cf. also Héroët's *Parfaicte Amye*, vv. 101, 596, 1572); love as a quality of mind rather than a passing emotion (*Medieval Latin*, vol. 1, pp. 37, 85); the paradox of a suffering that is also serene and even joyful (ibid., pp. 36–38; cf. also Scève's famous motto "souffrir non souffrir," in *La Délie*, ed. McFarlane, p. 119).

10. See Correa, "El Templo de Diana," p. 74.

11. Paul Bénichou finds this aristocratic and "feudal" conception of life dominant in the France of Louis XIII: "What is most striking, with these writers as with Corneille, is the exalted tone, the conceited posturing of the heroes that are offered to the public as models. 'Great souls'—as they were then conceived—seem to have been endowed with neither restraint nor tranquil appetites; all of them display the same proud and ostentatious sublimity, the same egotistic energies, the same moral expansiveness of pride and love"; in *Morales du grand siècle* (Paris, 1948), p. 16.

12. "Persons of high birth" is Otis Green's translation of "personas de suerte" (*La Diana*, p. 170). See his *Spain and the Western Tradition*, vol. 2 (Madison, Wis., 1964), p. 327.

13. In view of this I cannot entirely agree with Wardropper's belief that the relationship between generations in *La Diana* is harmonious, that amorous and filial duties are "of equal validity" ("The *Diana* of Montemayor," p. 137). The quality of Diana's love is disturbing. She tries to conceal her bitterness over the fact that no one loves her any more: "although she had loved Sireno more than her own life and had despised Sylvano, yet she was more upset by Sylvano's neglect—for now he belonged

to someone else—than by Sireno's, who no longer thought about her at all" (*La Diana*, pp. 266–67). Such jealousy over another's happiness, such a vanity that prefers the hated lover, simply because he is inaccessible, to the supposedly true beloved, is not very edifying. It seems that Diana's exclusion from the temple of Chastity is due not to filial devotion but rather to her failures as a lover. The case for harmony between generations is hard to document. Arsileo competes with his father Arsenio for Belisa's affections. Belisa's origins are not disclosed. Felismena's parents die in her infancy, but she casts her good name and theirs to the winds as she pursues her lost Felis (*La Diana*, p. 105).

14. Gustavo Correa writes: "The shepherds think that their labors (troubles) are titles of honor in proportion to the degree of difficulty and intensity of suffering. The torments of love are thus viewed as executions of heroic deeds (cf. the labors of Hercules) and by virtue of these take on the dimensions of heroism ("El Templo de Diana," p. 72).

15. In a similar vein Mario Casella (*Il Chisciotte*, vol. 1 [Firenze, 1938], p. 425) speaks of the potion as a "mechanical gimmick." For Castro (*El pensamiento*, p. 151), Cervantes' criticism inveighs against Montemayor's "frivolity" in trying to change the powerful impulse of love with a simple gulp of water.

16. Swami Nikhilananda (*The Upanishads*, vol 3 [New York, 1956], pp. 157–58) explains that the notions of action, agency, and result "which are the results of past action, are not experienced in deep sleep." In such a state the soul "remains in its undifferentiated, natural, absolute self" (p. 158). In *Brihadaranyaka Upanishad*, ibid., vol. 2, some distinctions are drawn between the states of waking and deep sleep.

17. Felicia's lesson to the lovers is an allegorical transposition of Diego de San Pedro's admonitions to Leriano in his *Cárcel de amor* (in *Obras*, ed. Samuel Gili y Gaya [Madrid, 1958], p. 139): "I see you glorying in your suffering. . . . In great trials the strong show greater courage. Remember that in a long life anything can be achieved; along with your faithfulness (*fe*) be of good hope."

18. I am thinking especially of Rudel's *amor de lonh*, where the antithesis between desire and satisfaction is final. Consumation destroys the charm of desire, and it is by desire that man lives. See Leo Spitzer, *L'Amour lointain de Jaufré Rudel et le sens de la poésie des troubadours* (Chapel Hill, N.C., 1944), pp. 8–10. Whereas the beloved, in Montemayor's view, is a real person, for Rudel the Other is beyond existence, by definition unattainable. Dronke discusses this question (*Medieval Latin*, vol. 1, pp. 48–49) and decides that *amor purus* is not essentially related to *amour courtois*. Of interest to Montemayor's ideal of marital felicity is Dronke's further assertion that adultery and *amour courtois* are only casually connected (ibid., pp. 46–48).

Chapter 8

1. For Donne's poetry, I use *John Donne: The Complete English Poems*, ed. A. J. Smith (London, 1971).

2. Gardner, "The Argument," pp. 279–306.

3. See chapter 3.

4. Gardner, "The Argument," p. 290.

5. A. J. Smith, "The Dismissal of Love," in *John Donne: Essays in Celebration,* ed. A. J. Smith (London, 1972), pp. 128–29.

6. See Donne, *Complete English Poems,* p. 368, n. 3.

7. See, for example, the Funeral Song that concludes Shakespeare's "The Phoenix and Turtle"; see also chapter 9.

8. Alan Watts has translated the Tantric view into layman's language as follows: "[In the act of love] there is an extraordinary melting sensation in which 'each is both,' and, seeing their eyes reflected in each other's they realize that there is one Self looking out through both"; in *Erotic Spirituality,* p. 89; see p. 59, n. 1 for further bibliography.

9. Such a parallel suggests a different interpretation of Narcissus' death from the usual one: not that he loved his own features but rather that, gazing into his own eyes (which he *may* have taken to be those of his beloved—the ambivalence is necessary) he became aware that the mirror of his beloved's eyes reflected his own mirror, which only reflected his beloved's, and so on infinitely. From this it follows that Narcissus drowns not as punishment for the moral error of self-love; rather, he dies from overindulgence in the ecstasy of union. There would then be no essential difference between such a "death" and the ecstatic death of lovers, except that the latter discover infinity through the perception of a common soul, whereas Narcissus' union is more properly contemplative and centers on the discovery of his Self.

10. G. Wilson Knight, *The Mutual Flame* (London, 1955), p. 41.

11. Ibid.

12. Ananda K. Coomaraswamy, "The Sun-Kiss," *Journal of the American Oriental Society* 60 (1940):63.

13. These texts are quoted in ibid., p. 50, n. 15.

14. Ibid., p. 46 and n. 2.

15. Charles Mitchell's analysis of the poem's tripartite structure is similar to mine, as is his perception that section one (vv. 1–20) shows "an upward progress from the physical to visual-mental to spiritual"; in "Donne's 'The Extasie': Love's Sublime Knot," *Studies in English Literature* 8 (1968):94–95.

16. Smith, "Donne in His Time," pp. 262–63.

17. Donne, *Complete English Poems,* p. 368, n. 6.

18. See *Shakespeare, The Poems,* ed. F. T. Prince (London, 1969), p. 5, n. to v. 25.

19. Smith, "Donne in His Time," p. 261.

20. Gardner, "The Argument," p. 302, n. 2.

21. See *The Zohar,* trans. Sperling, Simon, and Levertoff, vol. 1, p. 131.

22. Mitchell, "Love's Sublime Knot," p. 100.

23. John Donne, *Complete Poetry and Selected Prose,* ed. John Hayward (London and New York, 1930), p. 429.

24. Ibid., p. 455; see also "Sermon 53," p. 634.

Chapter 9

1. All quotations are from Shakespeare, *King Lear,* ed. Kenneth Muir (London, 1972); cited hereafter as Shakespeare, *King Lear* or simply *Lear.* Quotations from

Shakespeare's other works, unless stated otherwise, are from *The Riverside Shakespeare*, ed. G. Blakemore Evans (Boston, 1974).

2. A. C. Bradley, for example: "Yes, 'heavenly true.' But truth is not the only good in the world, nor is the obligation to tell the truth the only obligation. The matter here was to keep it inviolate but also to preserve a father. And even if truth *were* the one and only obligation, to tell much less than truth is not to tell it"; in *Shakespearean Tragedy* (New York, 1963), p. 256; quoted with approval by Barbara Everett, "The New *King Lear*," *Critical Quarterly* 2 (1960):331.

3. Lear's "Let pride, which she calls *plainness,* marry her" (I,1,128) can only refer to Cordelia's "So young, my Lord, and *true.*" In *Troilus and Cressida* (IV, 4,58ff.) Troilus gives a veritable exegesis on being "true of heart," which means chaste, loyal, *faithful,* but also unaffected or *plain* (vv. 106–08).

4. A broader loyalty—that of all the king's subjects to the king—is hinted, I think, by Cordelia's greeting to Lear: "How does my royal Lord? How fares your Majesty?" (IV, 7, 44); and Kent, replying to Lear's "Am I in France?" responding, "In your own kingdom, Sir" (IV, 7, 76).

5. Mark Van Doren, *Shakespeare* (Garden City, 1953), p. 255.

6. Frank Kermode, in his introduction to *Timon of Athens;* in *The Riverside Shakespeare* (Boston, 1974), p. 1443. Leo Marx explains how "the names of several characters in *The Tempest* have overtones of symbolic significance"; in *The Machine in the Garden* (London and New York, 1964), pp. 55–56.

7. See Muir's introduction in Shakespeare, *King Lear,* p. xxxi. In the sources reproduced by Muir in his appendices (pp. 207–29), the following variants were available: Cordella (*King Leir*); Cordeilla (Holinshed); Cordeill and Cordelia (Spenser); Cordell, Cordilla, and Cordile (John Higgins).

8. John F. Danby, *Shakespeare's Doctrine of Nature* (London, 1961), pp. 117, 137, 134, 133.

9. A common notion among Petrarchan poets; see, for example, Scève, *Délie,* pp. 307, 331, 369.

10. Bradley, *Shakespearean Tragedy,* pp. 260–61.

11. See Shakespeare, *King Lear,* on *Lear* V, 3, 20, where Muir approves Bradley's reading of "such sacrifices" as referring to both Lear's and Cordelia's renunciation of the world.

12. Kermode, in his introduction to *King Lear;* in *The Riverside Shakespeare,* p. 1253.

13. Everett, "The New *King Lear*," pp. 334–39.

14. See Danby's reply to Everett in *Critical Quarterly* 3 (1961):69.

15. The phrase is Kermode's, in his introduction to *Coriolanus;* in *The Riverside Shakespeare,* p. 1393. Coleridge's remarks on *Lear* have been reprinted in Kermode, ed., *"King Lear": A Casebook* (London, 1969), pp. 33–44.

16. Van Doren, *Shakespeare,* p. 272.

17. William Frost, "Shakespeare's Ritual and the Opening of *Lear,*" in *Shakespeare: The Tragedies,* ed. Clifford Leech (Chicago, 1965), p. 198.

18. See Donne's ninth "Devotion": "in our affections, in our passions"; in John Donne, *Devotions,* ed. Anthony Raspa (Montreal and London, 1973), p. 47. For a good listing of contemporary examples see Pafford's edition of *Winter's Tale* (London, 1966), pp. 165–67.

19. "Sport" here means sexual pleasure, as in *Othello* II,1,226: "When the blood

is made dull with the act of sport"; and Emilia's "And have we not affections, / Desires for sport?" (IV,3,100–01). One suspects that Shakespeare's irony was deliberate when Gloucester later perceives the gods in the only terms that his past actions have deserved: "As flies to wanton boys, are we to the Gods; / They kill us for their sport" (IV,1,37). The iron rule of retribution is pushed to extremes of cruelty in *Lear* (V,3,170) when Gloucester's very appearance momentarily takes on the shape of his transgression, when Lear identifies him as "blind Cupid" (IV,6,136).

20. The context of Edmund's exclamation should be closely noted. It comes right after Edmund's recognition that "The wheel is come full circle; I am here" (V,3,173). Beyond the possible meaning that his fortunes have ebbed (the wheel of fortune), the image is but an acknowledgement of Edgar's statement that "The Gods are just"; for Edmund now sees that "Th'hast spoken right, 'tis true. / The [purgatorial] wheel is come full circle; I am here." In recognizing that his own misfortune is but a show of divine justice, Edmund, as it were, regains a state of moral neutrality ("I am here") from which can arise both a supported sense of self-worth ("Yet Edmund was beloved") and—however belated and pathetically inadequate—a desire for doing good: "I pant for life; some good I mean to do" (V,3,242). Instead of two disconnected statements, moreover, this last remark points to the play's moral activism by suggesting a virtual equivalence between goodness and life, much like Cordelia's "how shall I live and work?" (IV, 7, 1).

21. Jonas Barish and Marshall Waingrow, "Service in *King Lear*," *Shakespeare Quarterly* 9 (1958):349.

22. For the theme of incest see below, note 41.

23. Barish and Waingrow, "Service," p. 349. Danby gives a lucid analysis of these multiple bonds in their interrelationships, and of the continuity between proper self-love and selflessness, in *Shakespeare's Doctrine*, pp. 129–33.

24. Barish and Waingrow, "Service," p. 349.

25. Fitzroy Pyle, in *Modern Language Review* 43 (1948):454, quoted in Shakespeare, *King Lear*, p. xxxvi.

26. "Relatedness with a young daughter in a prison cell may suit a man of eighty, but he should not assume it will suit her; if he has become so truly related, he might remember that she has just been married for love" (William Empson, quoted in A. L. French, *Shakespeare and the Critics* [Cambridge, 1972], p. 187). French comments: "This is extreme, no doubt; nevertheless it is a necessary protest against the odd Quietism that some modern critics mistake for Christianity: the notion that spiritual health is in inverse proportion to engagement and commitment and in direct proportion to the degree of one's opting out."

27. Barish and Waingrow, "Service," p. 355.

28. Danby, *Shakespeare's Doctrine*, p. 194.

29. Robert Heilman, *This Great Stage: Image and Structure in "King Lear"* (Seattle, 1967), pp. 35–36.

30. Ibid., p. 35 and n. 33, p. 300, and p. 36: "in both her withdrawal and Lear's there is a rather narrow self-protection, an attempted elusion of the fettering of circumstance . . . ; the immaculateness of nonparticipation must be balanced against action which may bespot the actor but is yet a responsibility."

31. Roy Battenhouse, *Shakespearean Tragedy: Its Art and Its Christian Premises*, (Bloomington, Ind., 1969), pp. 282–88.

32. Quoted in *A Casebook*, ed. Kermode, p. 29.

33. In addition to "melt in tears" (Muir, *King Lear*, p. 199), the parallel with *Lear* (V, 3, 181) suggests a dissolving of the heart or dying, as in the phrase "dissolve the life" (*Lear* IV, 4, 19) and "dissolve the bands of life" (*Richard II* II, 2, 71). See above, p. 41, for the equivalence in sixteenth-century French texts between *dissoudre* and *délier*, which both mean "to die."

34. The heartstrings are the bonds of affection (*Antony and Cleopatra* III, 11, 57: "My heart was to thy rudder tied by the strings") or of life (*King John* V, 7, 55: "My heart hath one poor string"), or both simultaneously, as when Claudius prays that his unreconciled heart, "with strings of steel, / Be soft as sinews of the new-born babe" (*Hamlet* III,3,71). The same polyvalence may be noted in the parallel notion of *bond*: the "bond of life" (*Richard III* IV,4,77); of affection: "But out, affection, / All bond and privilege of nature, break! (*Coriolanus* V, 3, 25); and especially Posthumous's "take this life, / And cancel these cold bonds" (*Cymbeline* V, 4, 28), where the additional sense of conscience and even of Cordelia's bond or obligation may be intended.

35. One must always bear in mind the metaphorical dimension wherein "death" means repentance, reconciliation, and rebirth, as in the previous note, where Claudius cannot "die" and be reborn:

> O limed soul, that struggling to be free
> Art more engag'd! Help angels! Make assay,
> Bow, stubborn knees, and heart, with strings of steel,
> Be soft as sinews of the new-born babe.

36. This enables us to assign a more precise meaning to Kent's description of Oswald:

> Cornwall. "Why art thou angry?"
> Kent. "That such a slave as this should wear *a sword*,
> Who wears no honesty. Such smiling rogues as these,
> Like rats, oft bite *the holy cords* a-twain
> *Which are too intrince t'unloose.*" [II, 2, 68–72]

If, as in Cleopatra's speech, the "intrince" cords are the subtle knot of life, then Kent's words are prophetic of Oswald's cowardly attempt to slaughter a blind and defenseless Gloucester:

> Oswald. "Briefly thyself remember: the sword is out
> That must destroy thee." [IV, 6, 226–27]

This explanation has the merit of integrating the phrase with the detail of the sword: the "rats" who violently dissolve ("bite") the lives ("holy cords") of others are "such smiling rogues as these" who "wear a sword" without honesty.

37. Lear's tears "do scald like molten lead" (IV,7,48), but he has the gift of tears. One should note the high incidence of heart imagery in *Lear:* of hard-heartedness (I,4,257; III,6,76); cracked hearts (II,1,89; II,4,283; III,4,4); and of Lear's heart as being constantly under attack (II,4,54, 118, 132, 158; III,1,17).

38. Through emblematic transposition this statement becomes an invocation to Cordelia: *Cor-délie!*

39. Gloucester, for example, progresses from a sportive view to a perception of the "ever-gentle Gods" (IV,6,214). H. B. Charlton strangely equates Gloucester's earlier view (IV,1,36) with Edgar's discovery that "The Gods are just" (V,3,169), claiming that this latter view also shows signs of hedonism among the gods; in *Shakespearean Tragedy* (Cambridge, 1971), p. 212.

40. Frequent parallels have been made between Lear and Job, but a more likely and unstudied source, with which the Job story itself has much in common, is the binding of Isaac (Genesis 22:1–19). John Holloway approaches the spirit of the two stories when he detects in *Lear* "the quality of a stylized and ritual execution.... We are led, in fact, to envisage a new metaphor for the status of the tragic rôle . . . : the developing line, unabridged, of a human sacrifice"; in *The Story of the Night: Studies in Shakespeare's Major Tragedies* (London, 1961), p. 98.

41. Alex Aronson presents an interesting restatement of the situation in Jungian terms: "It is as if Shakespeare had created her [Cordelia] as a symbol for universal redemption and as if he wanted to portray Cordelia's final encounter with her father as symbolizing the primordial encounter of father and daughter in terms of God, the creator, and the soul that is his own handiwork, and without which no life at all would be possible"; in *Psyche and Symbol in Shakespeare* (Bloomington, Ind., 1972), p. 185. Aronson's allusion to Lear's "need for feminine support, be it that of daughter, wife, or mother" (p. 187) receives some confirmation in the Fool's taunt that Lear "mad'st thy daughters thy mothers" (I,4,169). For the Freudian view of Lear's "repressed incestuous claims on the daughters' love," see Aronson, pp. 327–28; also Helmut Bonheim, ed., *The King Lear Perplex* (San Francisco, 1960). The proper context of these perceptions, I have proposed, is the theological problem of contemplation or abdication versus action and for which Cordelia is the emblematic resolution.

42. Alfred Harbage, "*King Lear:* an Introduction," reprinted in *Shakespeare: The Tragedies*, ed. Harbage (Englewood Cliffs, 1964), p. 113. This essay is an excellent introduction to *Lear* as myth and ritual.

43. Arthur Sewall senses a "veritable change of dispensation" in *Lear*, in "Character and Society in *King Lear*," in ibid., p. 145.

Bibliography

Altmann, Alexander. "Moses Narboni's Epistle on *Shi'ur Qoma*." In *Jewish Medieval and Renaissance Studies*, vol. 4, edited by Alexander Altmann. Cambridge, Mass.: Harvard University Press, 1967.

Altmann, Alexander, and Stern, S. M. *Isaac Israeli*. London: Oxford University Press, 1958.

Aristotle. *Nicomachean Ethics*. Translated by Martin Ostwald. New York: Bobbs-Merrill, 1962.

Armstrong, Arthur H. *Plotinus*. New York: Collier Books, 1962.

Aronson, Alex. *Psyche and Symbol in Shakespeare*. Bloomington: Indiana University Press, 1972.

Attal, Jean-Pierre. *L'Image métaphysique et autres essais*. Paris: Gallimard, 1969.

Aubigné, Agrippa d'. *Le Printemps*. Edited by Henri Weber. Paris and Montpellier: Presses Universitaires de France, 1960.

Avalle-Arce, Juan Bautista. *La novela pastoril española*. Madrid: Revista de Occidente, 1959.

Bachelard, Gaston. *L'Eau et les rêves*. Paris: Jose Corti, 1942.

Barish, Jonas, and Waingrow, Marshall. "Service in *King Lear*." *Shakespeare Quarterly* 9 (1958):347–55.

Battenhouse, Roy W. *Shakespearean Tragedy: Its Art and Its Christian Premises*. Bloomington: Indiana University Press, 1969.

Bénichou, Paul. *Morales du grand siècle*. Paris: Gallimard, 1948.

Bonheim, Helmut, ed. *The King Lear Perplex*. San Francisco: Wadsworth, 1960.

Bradley, Andrew Cecil. *Shakespearean Tragedy*. 1904. Reprint. New York: Meridian, 1963.

Bréhier, Emile. *La Philosophie de Plotin*. Paris: Vrin, 1961.

Casella, Mario. *Il Chisciotte*. 2 vols. Florence: Felice Le Monnier, 1938.

Castro, Américo. *El pensamiento de Cervantes*. Revista de Filologia Española, Anejo 6. Madrid: Casa Editorial Hernando, 1925.

Champier, Symphorien. *Le Livre de vraye amour*. Edited by James B. Wadsworth. The Hague: Mouton, 1962.

Charlton, H. B. *Shakespearean Tragedy*. Cambridge: Cambridge University Press, 1971.

Cody, Richard. *The Landscape of the Mind*. Oxford: Clarendon Press, 1969.

Coleman, Dorothy. "Sceve's Choice of the Name 'Délie.'" *French Studies* 18 (1964):1–15.

Coomaraswamy, Ananda K. *The Dance of Shiva*. Revised edition. New York: The Noonday Press, 1957.

———. "Love and Art." *The Modern Review* (Calcutta), May 1915:574–84.

————. *Spiritual Authority and Temporal Power in the Indian Theory of Government.* New Haven: The American Oriental Society, 1942.

————. "The Sun-Kiss." *Journal of the American Oriental Society* 60 (1940):46–67.

Correa, Gustavo. "El Templo de Diana en la novela de Jorge de Montemayor." *Thesaurus* (Bogotá) 16 (1961):59–76.

Corrozet, Gilles. *Compte du rossignol.* Lyon: Jean de Tournes, 1546. Reissued by Ferdinand Gohin. Paris: Garnier, 1924.

Damiens, Suzanne. *Amour et intellect chez Léon l'Hébreu.* Toulouse: E. Privat, 1971.

Danby, John F. "Correspondence on *King Lear.*" *Critical Quarterly* 3 (1961):67–72.

————. *Shakespeare's Doctrine of Nature.* London: Faber and Faber, 1961.

Donne, John. *Complete Poetry and Selected Prose.* Edited by John Hayward. London: Nonesuch Press and New York: Random House, 1930.

————. *Devotions.* Edited by Anthony Raspa. Montreal and London: McGill-Queen's University Press, 1973.

————. *John Donne: The Complete English Poems.* Edited by A. J. Smith. London: Penguin Books, 1971.

————. *The Poems of John Donne.* Edited by Herbert Grierson. 2 vols. 1912. Reprint. London: Oxford University Press, 1968.

Dronke, Peter. *Medieval Latin and the Rise of European Love-Lyric.* 2 vols. Oxford: Clarendon Press, 1965–66.

Du Guillet, Pernette. *Rymes.* Edited by Victor Graham. Geneva: Droz, 1968.

Ellrodt, Robert. *Les Poètes métaphysiques anglais.* 3 vols. Paris: José Corti, 1960.

————. *Neoplatonism in the Poetry of Spenser.* Geneva: Droz, 1960.

Everett, Barbara. "The New *King Lear.*" *Critical Quarterly* 2 (1960):325–39.

Festugière, André J. *Contemplation et vie contemplative selon Platon.* Paris: Vrin, 1936.

Ficin, Marsile [Marsilio Ficino]. *Théologie platonicienne de l'immortalité des âmes.* 2 vols. Edited and translated by Raymond Marcel. Paris: Les Belles Lettres, 1964.

French, A. L. *Shakespeare and the Critics.* Cambridge: Cambridge University Press, 1972.

Friedrich, Hugo. *Montaigne.* Translated by Robert Rovini. Paris: Gallimard, 1968.

Frost, William "Shakespeare's Ritual and the Opening of *Lear.*" In *Shakespeare: The Tragedies,* edited by Clifford Leech. Chicago: University of Chicago Press, 1965.

Gallego Morell, Antonio, ed. *Garcilaso de la Vega y sus comentaristas.* 2nd ed. Madrid: Gredos, 1972.

Gardner, Helen. "The Argument about 'The Ecstasy.'" In *Elizabethan and Jacobean Studies Presented to Frank Percy Wilson,* edited by Herbert Davis and Helen Gardner, pp. 279–306. Oxford: Clarendon Press, 1959.

Gerhardt, Mia. *La Pastorale: essai d'analyse littéraire.* Assen: Van Gorcum, 1950.

Giudici, Enzo. *Maurice Scève, poeta della "Délie."* Naples: Liguori, 1969.

Gosse, Edmund. *The Life and Letters of John Donne.* 2 vols. New York: Dodd and Mead, 1899.

Green, Otis. *Spain and the Western Tradition.* 4 vols. Madison: The University of Wisconsin Press, 1963–1966.

Griffin, Robert. "Pernette du Guillet's Response to Scève: A Case for Abstract Love." *Esprit Créateur* 5 (1965):110–16.

Harbage, Alfred. "*King Lear:* an Introduction." The Pelican Shakespeare. Penguin

Books, 1958. Reprinted in *Shakespeare: The Tragedies,* edited by Alfred Harbage. Englewood Cliffs, N.J.: Prentice-Hall, Twentieth Century Views, 1964.

Heilman, Robert. *This Great Stage: Image and Structure in "King Lear."* Seattle: University of Washington Press, 1967.

Héroët, Antoine. *Oeuvres poétiques.* Edited by Ferdinand Gohin. Paris: Edouard Cornély, 1909.

Holloway, John. *The Story of the Night: Studies in Shakespeare's Major Tragedies.* London: Routeledge and K. Paul, 1961.

Hughes, Merritt Y. "The Lineage of 'The Extasie.'" *The Modern Language Review* 27 (1932):1-5.

————. "Some of Donne's 'Ecstasies.'" *PMLA* 75 (1960):509-18.

Huguet, Edmond. *Dictionnaire de la langue française du seizième siècle.* 7 vols. Paris: E. Champion, 1925-1967.

Ibn Gabirol, Solomon. *Fons Vitae.* Edited by Clemens Bäumker. Munster, 1895.

Jourda, Pierre. *Marguerite d'Angoulême, duchesse d'Alençon, reine de Navarre.* 2 vols. Paris: Champion, 1930.

Kermode, Frank, ed. *"King Lear": A Casebook.* London: Macmillan Casebook Series, 1969.

Klausner, Josef. "Don Yehudah Abrabanel ufilosofiat ha-ahavah shelo" [Don Y. A. and His Love-Philosophy]. *Tarbiz* (Jerusalem) 3 (1932):67-98.

Knight, G. Wilson. *The Mutual Flame.* London: Methuen, 1955.

Larbaud, Valéry. *Notes sur Antoine Héroët et Jean de Lingendes.* Paris: Editions Lapina, 1927.

Lefranc, Abel. *Grands Écrivains français de la Renaissance.* Paris: Champion, 1914.

Legouis, Pierre. *Donne the Craftsman.* Paris: H. Didier, 1928.

Leishman, J. B. *The Monarch of Wit: An Analytical and Comparative Study of the Poetry of John Donne.* 6th ed. London: Hutchinson University Library, 1962.

Lemaire de Belges, Jean. *Les Epîtres de l'amant vert.* Edited by Jean Frappier. Lille and Geneva, 1948.

Léon Hébreu [Leone Ebreo]. *Dialogues d'amour.* Translated by Pontus de Tyard. Lyon: Jean de Tournes, 1551. Edited by T. Anthony Perry. Studies in Comparative Literature, no. 59. Chapel Hill: University of North Carolina Press, 1974.

————. *Dialogues d'amour.* Translated by Le Seigneur du Parc Champenois [Denys Sauvage]. Lyon: Rouille, 1551.

Leone Ebreo. *Dialoghi d'amore.* Edited by Santino Caramella. Bari: Laterza, 1929.

Lewis, C. S. "Donne and Love Poetry in the Seventeenth Century." In *John Donne: A Collection of Critical Essays,* edited by Helen Gardner. Englewood Cliffs, N.J.: Prentice-Hall, Twentieth Century Views, 1962.

Maimonides, Moses. *The Guide for the Perplexed.* Translated by M. Friedländer. Rev. ed. in 1 vol. 1904. Reprint. New York: Dover Publications, 1956.

Marguerite de Navarre. *Les Dernières Poésies de Marguerite de Navarre.* Edited by Abel Lefranc. Paris: Armand Colin, 1896.

————. *Les Marguerites de la Marguerite des Princesses.* 4 vols. Edited by Felix Frank. Paris: Librairie des Bibliophiles, 1873.

————. *Nouvelles* [*L'Heptaméron*]. Edited by Yves Le Hir. Paris: Presses Universitaires de France, 1967.

————. *Théâtre profane.* Edited by Verdun L. Saulnier. Geneva: Droz, 1963.

Maritain, Jacques. *Art and Scholasticism.* Translated by Joseph W. Evans. New York: Charles Scribner's Sons, 1962.

Marx, Leo. *The Machine in the Garden*. London and New York: Oxford University Press, 1964.

Menéndez y Pelayo, Marcelino. *Historia de las ideas estéticas en España*. 2 vols. 4th ed. Madrid: Consejo de Investigaciones Científicas, 1974.

The Mishnah. Translated by Philip Blackman. 7 vols. New York: Judaica Press, 1964.

Mitchell, Charles. "Donne's 'The Extasie': Love's Sublime Knot." *Studies in English Literature 1500–1900* 8 (1968):91–101.

Montaigne, Michel de. *Essais*. Edited by Pierre Villey. Paris: Presses Universitaires de France, 1965.

———. *The Essayes of Montaigne*. Translated by John Florio. New York: Modern Library, 1933.

Montemayor, Jorge de. *Los siete libros de la Diana*. Edited by Francisco López Estrada. Clásicos Castellaños no. 127. Madrid: Espasa-Calpe, 1962.

Mourgues, Odette de. *Metaphysical, Baroque and Précieux Poetry*. Oxford: Clarendon Press, 1953.

Opuscules d'amour, par Héroët, La Borderie, et autres divins poètes. Lyon: Jean de Tournes, 1547. Reprinted with an Introduction by M. A. Screech. New York and The Hague: Johnson Reprint Corp. and Mouton, 1970.

Perry, Theodore Anthony. Review of *Amour et intellect chez Léon l'Hébreu* by Suzanne Damiens. *Modern Language Notes* 88 (1973):421–25.

Pflaum, Heinz. *Die Idee der Liebe: Leone Ebreo*. Tübingen: Mohr, 1926.

Plato, *Phaedo*. Translated by David Gallop. Oxford: Clarendon Press, 1975.

———. *Phaedo*. Translated by Léon Robin. Paris: Les Belles Lettres, 1967.

Porphyry. *Sententiae*. Edited by B. Mommert. Leipzig: Teubner, 1907.

Pyle, Fitzroy. "'Twelfth Night,' 'King Lear' and 'Arcadia.'" *Modern Language Review* 43 (1948):449–55.

Rabelais, François. *Le Tiers Livre*. Edited by M. A. Screech. Geneva: Droz, 1964.

Rahv, Philip. *Literature and the Sixth Sense*. Boston: Houghton Mifflin, 1970.

Ronsard, Pierre de. *Oeuvres de Pierre de Ronsard (Texte de 1587)*. Edited by Isidore Silver. 8 vols. Chicago: University of Chicago Press, and Paris: Marcel Didier, 1966–70.

Rougemont, Denis de. *Love in the Western World*. Translated by Montgomery Belgion. New York: Pantheon Books, 1956.

Salel, Hugues. *Oeuvres poétiques*. Edited by Louis-Alexandre Bergounioux. Paris: Editions Occitania, 1930.

San Pedro, Diego de. *Obras*. Edited by S. Gili y Gaya. Clásicos Castellaños no. 133. Madrid: Espasa-Calpe, 1958.

Sand, George. *La Mare au diable*. Edited by Léon Cellier. Paris: Gallimard, 1973.

Saulnier, Verdun L. "Etude sur Pernette du Guillet et ses *Rymes*." *Bibliothèque d'Humanisme et Renaissance* 4 (1944):9–119.

———. *Maurice Scève*. 2 vols. Paris: C. Klincksieck, 1948–1949.

Scève, Maurice. *La Délie*. Edited by I. D. McFarlane. Cambridge: Cambridge University Press, 1966.

———. *Delie, object de plus haulte vertu*. Edited by Eugène Parturier. 1916. Reprint. Paris: Droz, 1931.

Scheler, Max. *Liebe und Erkenntnis*. Bern: Francke, 1955.

Schlanger, Jacques. "Le Maître et le disciple du *Fons Vitae*." *Revue des Etudes Juives* 127 (1968):393–97.

Schmidt, Albert-Marie, ed. *Poètes du 16e siècle*. Paris: Gallimard, 1953.

————. *Etudes sur le 16e siècle*. Paris: A. Michel, 1967.

Scholem, Gershom. *Les Origines de la kabbale*. Translated from the German by Jean Loewenson. Paris: Aubier-Montaigne, 1966.

Sermoneta, Josef B. *La dottrina dell'intelletto e la "fede filosofica" di Jehudah e Immanuel Romano*. Spoleto: Centro Italiano di Studi sull'Alto Medioevo, 1965.

————. *Un glossario filosofico ebraico-italico del xiii secolo*. Rome: Edizioni dell' Ateneo, 1969.

Sewall, Arthur. "Character and Society in *King Lear*." In *Shakespeare: The Tragedies*, edited by Alfred Harbage. Englewood Cliffs, N.J.: Prentice-Hall, Twentieth Century Views, 1964.

Shakespeare, William. *King Lear*. Edited by Kenneth Muir. The Arden Shakespeare. London: Methuen, 1972.

————. *The Poems*. Edited by F. T. Prince. The Arden Shakespeare. London: Methuen, 1969.

————. *The Riverside Shakespeare*. Edited by G. Blakemore Evans. Boston: Houghton Mifflin, 1974.

————. *The Winter's Tale*. Edited by J. H. P. Pafford. The Arden Shakespeare. London: Methuen, 1966.

Smith, A. J. "The Dismissal of Love." In *John Donne: Essays in Celebration*, edited by A. J. Smith. London: Methuen, 1972.

————. "Donne in His Time: A Reading of 'The Extasie.'" *Review of English Studies* 36 (1958):260–75.

Solé-Leris, A. "The Theory of Love in the Two *Dianas:* A Contrast." *Bulletin of Hispanic Studies* 36 (1959):65–79.

Spitzer, Leo. *L'Amour lointain de Jaufré Rudel et le sens de la poésie des troubadours*. Studies in the Romance Languages and Literature, no. 5. Chapel Hill: University of North Carolina Press, 1944.

Staub, Hans. *Le Curieux Désir: Scève et J. Peletier du Mans, poètes de la connaissance*. Geneva: Droz, 1967.

Tetel, Marcel. *Marguerite de Navarre's "Heptaméron": Themes, Language, and Structure*. Durham: Duke University Press, 1973.

Tyard, Pontus de. *Solitaire premier*. Edited by Sylvio Baridon. Geneva: Droz, 1950.

The Upanishads. Translated by Swami Nikhilananda. 4 vols. New York: Bonanza Books, 1949–1959.

Van Doren, Mark. *Shakespeare*. Garden City: Doubleday Anchor Books, 1953.

Wardropper, Bruce. "The *Diana* of Montemayor: Revaluation and Interpretation." *Studies in Philology* 48 (1951):126–44.

Watts, Alan. *Erotic Spirituality: The Vision of Konarak*. New York: Macmillan, 1971.

Weber, Henri. *La Création poétique au 16e siècle en France*. 2 vols. Paris: Nizet, 1955.

The Zohar. Translated by Harry Sperling, Maurice Simon, and Paul Levertoff. 5 vols. London: Soncino, 1933–34.

Index